Acclaim for Vanessa Miller

THE LIGHT ON HALSEY STREET

"*The Light on Halsey Street* is an emotional story that takes you on an up close and personal journey across the decades with two friends. The plot is woven with friendship, forgiveness, and faith. An unforgettable read from cover to cover by Vanessa Miller."

—Tia McCollors, bestselling author

"Vanessa Miller delivers a poignant story of friendship and betrayal, bringing Lisa and Dana full circle, with an uplifting ending that proves there is power in prayer."

—Lacey Baker, *USA TODAY* bestselling author

"Vanessa Miller set *The Light on Halsey Street* in Bedford-Stuyvesant, New York, but she takes readers on a decades-long exploration of the heart. In her coming-of-age story, two women learn about the impact of bitterness and resentment and the power of love to heal and restore what was lost. Readers will find it hard to put this novel down, and they'll hold on to these life lessons long after they turn the last page. Well done!"

—Robin W. Pearson, Christy Award-winning author

"Vanessa Miller's *The Light on Halsey Street* is women's fiction at its finest. Riveting and redemptive, *The Light on Halsey Street* vividly transports us back to 1980s Brooklyn with an unforgettable cast of characters and leaves you with the firm belief that light can truly never be extinguished by darkness."

—Joy Callaway, international bestselling author of *All the Pretty Places*

"Vanessa Miller's latest, *The Light on Halsey Street*, reawakened memories of my own growing up in the neighborhood of Bedford Stuyvesant in Brooklyn, which is a testament to her skill as a weaver of words. *The Light on Halsey Street* is not only a story of times gone by but the resiliency of friendship, family, and faith. This redemptive story of two friends, Lisa and Dana, poignantly demonstrates that we need not be a product of our circumstances and that the power to change is within all of us. Miller has created a timeless tale that will resonate long after the last word is read."

—Donna Hill, author of *Confessions in B-Flat* and *I Am Ayah: The Way Home*

"Vanessa Miller serves a heartfelt and fulfilling, Brooklyn, New York, literary buffet in this 1980s coming-of-age journey through friendships and hardships, all nourished by 'the light on Halsey Street.'"

—Pat G'Orge-Walker, *Essence* and national bestselling author and creator of the Sister Betty Christian comedy series

WHAT WE FOUND IN HALLELUJAH

"Two sisters reunite with their mother in Hallelujah, S.C., in the satisfying latest from Miller (*Something Good*) . . . A dramatic plot and uplifting resolution . . . The result is a potent testament to the power of faith and family in the face of tragedy."

—*Publishers Weekly*

"Three strong women, family drama, secrets, and a setting that works masterfully with the plot—Vanessa Miller is at her best in this book! The complex, nuanced relationships between mothers and daughters captured my attention and drew me in from the very first chapters. This book is a heartwarming treat that will leave readers hopeful and singing their own Hallelujah praise!"

—MICHELLE STIMPSON, BESTSELLING AUTHOR

"In *What We Found in Hallelujah*, Vanessa Miller so brilliantly tells a heartwarming, page-turning, beautiful story about family secrets, mother-daughter relationships, forgiveness, and restored faith, and I thoroughly enjoyed this saga from beginning to end! So well done, Vanessa!"

—KIMBERLA LAWSON ROBY, *NEW YORK TIMES* BESTSELLING AUTHOR

"Vanessa Miller has created a soul-searching story in *What We Found in Hallelujah.* Her ability to weed through the hard topics with grace, humor, and family makes her stories like no other. I was invested in the characters and felt like praising with them in the end."

—TONI SHILOH, AUTHOR OF *IN SEARCH OF A PRINCE*

"Vanessa lays a solid foundation for the fictional town of Hallelujah. Her characters are rich in diverse personalities. She layers the plot with an artistic flair that [has readers racing] to the finish line for the big 'reveal.' Redemption and reconciliation are sweet in Hallelujah."

—PAT SIMMONS, AWARD-WINNING AND NATIONAL BESTSELLING CHRISTIAN AUTHOR OF THE JAMIESON LEGACY SERIES

SOMETHING GOOD

"A prayer for 'something good' brings together the three women in an unlikely friendship, changing hearts and restoring marriages . . . The triumph of faith over tragedy will resonate with inspirational fans."

—*PUBLISHERS WEEKLY*

"With bright threads of faith, resilience, and finding a way forward where there seems to be no way, Vanessa Miller weaves together the lives of three women in a beautiful tapestry of redemption and hope, friendship and found family. A story that shows, even when we think we've bolted all the doors, something good can find a way in."

—Lisa Wingate, #1 *New York Times* bestselling author of *Before We Were Yours*

"Vanessa Miller's *Something Good* warms the heart with a vivacious tale of faith, redemption, and renewal. She masterly creates a sisterhood of unlikely friends who realize that there is something good, absolutely wonderful, in accepting people as they are and believing they can be better."

—Vanessa Riley, bestselling author of *Island Queen*

"*Something Good*, by Vanessa Miller, is a literary treat that captivated me from the first page. This story of three women drawn together by the unlikeliest of circumstances had me sitting back and realizing that no matter our backgrounds, no matter our struggles, when it's for God's purpose, we can come together. With characters that I could relate to and women who I wanted to win, I enjoyed *Something Good* from the beginning to the end."

—Victoria Christopher Murray, *New York Times* bestselling author of *The Personal Librarian*

"Vanessa Miller's thoughtful and anointed approach to crafting *Something Good* made for a beautiful page-turner full of depth and hope."

—Rhonda McKnight, award-winning author of *Unbreak My Heart*

"Vanessa Miller's latest novel is a relevant and heartwarming reminder that beauty for ashes is possible. This page-turning read inspires understanding, connection, and hope."

—Stacy Hawkins Adams, bestselling author

"This real-to-life story doesn't shy away from some hard issues of the modern world, but Miller is a master storyteller, who brings healing and redemption to her characters, and thus the reader, through the power of love and faith. I thoroughly enjoyed this book."

—Rachel Hauck, *New York Times* bestselling author

"*Something Good* is much better than good. It's great! Vanessa Miller always delivers, and you know you will get unforgettable characters and a redemptive, heartwarming story that readers will find unputdownable. Get ready to laugh and to feel all the feels."

—Michelle Lindo-Rice, Harlequin Special Edition author

"Vanessa Miller's *Something Good* unveils the reality of living with guilt, shame, and the weight of unforgiveness through the lives of three women. This story will offer readers a beautiful perspective of redemptive healing and the measure of peace that comes with a forgiving heart."

—Jacquelin Thomas, national bestselling author of the Jezebel series and *Phoenix*

The Light on HALSEY STREET

Other Books by Vanessa Miller

What We Found in Hallelujah

Something Good

Dream Come True

Once upon a Dream

Forever

Family Business I

Family Business II

Family Business III

Family Business IV

Family Business V

Family Business VI

Our Love

For Your Love

Got to Be Love

Rain in the Promised Land

Sunshine and Rain

After the Rain

How Sweet the Sound

Heirs of Rebellion

Feels Like Heaven

The Best of All

Better for Us

Her Good Thing

Long Time Coming

A Promise of Forever Love

A Love for Tomorrow

Yesterday's Promise

Forgotten

Forgiven

Forsaken

Through the Storm

Rain Storm

Latter Rain

Abundant Rain

Former Rain

Novellas

Love Isn't Enough

A Mighty Love

Rain for Christmas

Blessed and Highly Favored series

The Blessed One

The Wild One

The Preacher's Choice

The Politician's Wife

The Playboy's Redemption

Praise Him Anyhow series

Tears Fall at Night

Joy Comes in the Morning

A Forever Kind of Love

Ramsey's Praise

Escape to Love

Praise for Christmas

His Love Walk

Could This Be Love

Song of Praise

The Light on HALSEY STREET

a novel

VANESSA MILLER

THOMAS NELSON
Since 1798

The Light on Halsey Street

Published in Nashville, Tennessee, by Thomas Nelson. Thomas Nelson is a registered trademark of HarperCollins Christian Publishing, Inc.

Thomas Nelson titles may be purchased in bulk for educational, business, fundraising, or sales promotional use. For information, please email SpecialMarkets@ThomasNelson.com.

Library of Congress Cataloging-in-Publication Data

Names: Miller, Vanessa, author.
Title: The light on Halsey Street / Vanessa Miller.
Description: Nashville, Tennessee : Thomas Nelson, [2023] | Summary: "Two girls' lives are irrevocably intertwined the summer of 1985 in the streets of Brooklyn, New York, and neither will ever be the same in this coming-of-age story that spans decades"-- Provided by publisher.
Identifiers: LCCN 2023007558 (print) | LCCN 2023007559 (ebook) | ISBN 9780840709936 (paperback) | ISBN 9780840709967 (epub) | ISBN 9780840710000
Subjects: LCGFT: Novels.
Classification: LCC PS3613.I5623 L54 2023 (print) | LCC PS3613.I5623 (ebook) | DDC 813/.6--dc22/eng/20230224
LC record available at https://lccn.loc.gov/2023007558
LC ebook record available at https://lccn.loc.gov/2023007559

Printed in the United States of America

23 24 25 26 27 LBC 5 4 3 2 1

This book is dedicated to my loving husband, David Pierce, who came of age in Bed-Stuy Brooklyn and regaled me with so many stories of his youth that I had to write about this beautiful place and time.

PART 1

And an highway shall be there, and a way, and it shall be called The way of holiness; the unclean shall not pass over it; but it shall be for those: the wayfaring men, though fools, shall not err therein.

Isaiah 35:8

JOURNAL ENTRY

I wish I could go back and change everything about the summer of 1985. I honestly believe the root of my discontent was fertilized that summer and has been growing in me ever since. Oh, the things I could have done . . . the life I could have led, if I had only made better decisions.

CHAPTER 1

JULY 1985

With a twenty-dollar bill burning a hole in the pocket of Dana Jones' cutoff jeans, which she had turned into shorts with fringe hanging below her butt, Dana slipped her bamboo earrings on. These things were her prized possession. Her name was engraved in the imitation gold across the midpoint of each earring.

She was about to leave the apartment to go downtown with her girls, Lisa Whitaker and Jasmine Parks. She'd been cooped up since graduating from Boys and Girls High School in Brooklyn, New York, last month.

But somewhere between the quiet in the house and "Pretty Young Thing" being blasted from a boom box outside, Dana tensed. Tensed as fear crept up her spine and lodged in her heart.

"Ma!"

It was always loud in her house, like noise would drown out the pain of stolen dreams. Her mother, Vida, would blast '70s music on her old record player in their basement apartment when the owners of the brownstone, who lived in the main part of the house, were at work during the day—that is, before her mom pawned the record player a few weeks ago.

Dana was used to loud. The quiet of the past weeks caused her knees to shake like she'd been cornered by a stick-up kid after her hair-braiding money.

"Ma, I'm heading out. You want me to bring you something back?"

Standing in front of the bathroom mirror, Dana combed through her asymmetrical bob–style haircut and parted it so her bamboo earring could be seen. She rubbed in suntan lotion on her face and arms. Her olive complexion was too light to be in the sun without sunscreen. Looking in the mirror, Dana's hazel eyes lit up, like beauty was everywhere and ugly didn't exist in the world.

She put her comb on the sink and walked down the hall toward her mother's bedroom. The last time Vida was nonresponsive, she'd had a seizure and had to be rushed to the hospital so they could pump the drugs from her mother's system. Dana's heart went *thump-thump* inside her chest as she knocked on her mother's bedroom door, then tried the knob. It was unlocked.

Her mother was lying on her back with her arms stretched out on the bed. Dana hesitated. No chest movement. No snoring either. Her mom normally snored when sleeping on her back.

"Ma! Ma!" *Thump-thump.* Dana's hand went to her heart as she forced herself forward. She touched her mother's shoulder and shook it.

Vida growled and then put the pillow over her head. She turned her back to Dana. "Go away. I'm tired."

Tired was better than dead. *Tired* was better than a seizure. Dana had watched her mother fight her demons since her boyfriend introduced her to cocaine. Dana's chest heaved as she sucked in air and then blew it out. *Tired* was good. She backed out of her mother's room and left her alone.

As Dana left her apartment, she found Lisa and Jasmine waiting for her next to the stoop. The heat hit her like hot grease popping at a fish fry. Sweat beaded on her forehead as they headed for the subway on Fulton Street between Lewis and Stuyvesant avenues. "Dang. It's hot out here."

"I'm dripping like a faucet," Lisa, her best friend since first grade, said.

When they reached the station, they went down the stairs, deposited their tokens, and then hopped on the A Train.

"Man, I get so sick of standing up every time I get on this train," Jasmine complained.

Dana and Jasmine became cool in tenth grade. Lisa couldn't hang out as much back then. She was always at the library on Lewis and Macon, keeping them grades up so she could get a scholarship.

It was a Saturday afternoon, and the subway was packed. People going here and there, basically anywhere in the five boroughs, but today, Dana and her friends were headed to the Loew's Metropolitan Theatre in downtown Brooklyn to see *Back to the Future*, starring Michael J. Fox.

"I'm glad to be on this train. I almost had to bail on y'all," Lisa said. "My dad was tripping. I didn't do the dishes, so he was holding up my allowance."

"At least you get an allowance. I had to braid all three of Mrs. Lilly's kids' hair to get twenty dollars. And I couldn't complain since my mom is late on the rent again." Dana and her mom had been staying in the basement apartment of Mrs. Lilly and Michael James' brownstone for six months.

Dana seriously doubted they would make it a whole year before getting evicted.

"Well, we're out today, and didn't nobody stop us." Jasmine held on tight to the handrail above as the train sped underground, heading toward their destination.

The train stopped at Jay Street. The moment the doors opened, a whoosh of hot, humid air blew in their faces. A mixture of urine and body odor assaulted Dana's nostrils. Nothing like a New York subway station.

Dana held her breath until she and her girls reached the stairs leading out to Jay Street. They exited the train station, then went left, headed toward Loew's movie theater at the corner of Fulton and Jay Street. It was 2:20 p.m. and the movie started at 2:30 p.m., so they had to hustle.

"Do any of these people ever stay home?" Jasmine pushed her way through the crowd.

Jasmine was always complaining about how crowded it was in the city. Dana was surprised she agreed to go to the movies since she hated being downtown. "We'll be at the theater in a minute. Once you're watching the movie, you'll forget all about the crowd out here."

"Or . . ." Jasmine lifted her arms, trying to get elbow room as they continued walking down the street. "The lookie-loos can get out of our town and go home."

Lisa told her, "We will always have tourists, so get over it."

They entered the movie theater and purchased tickets.

"I'm getting some popcorn." Dana got in line for the snacks.

"I want some candy." Lisa got in the line too. Once they had their snacks, they went to the theater where *Back to the Future* was being shown and sat down.

After several laughs and some skillful skateboarding, the movie ended and the three of them headed to The Wiz. Jasmine wanted to buy an album.

"I'm running out of money," Dana complained. "I need to go to McCrory's and get my toiletries, so I can't get anything at The Wiz."

"Girl, we'll go to McCrory's with you. Come with me to The Wiz. My mom asked me to pick up 'Raspberry Beret' since we were coming downtown," Jasmine told her.

"Prince's new record?" Lisa's eyes popped as if Prince was standing in front of the electronics store waiting on her. "Let me at it."

"Y'all acting like Prince is everything. What about New Edition with 'Mr. Telephone Man'? Now, that's a record I really want." Dana stood outside the store. She looked up at the sign, which read "Nobody Beats the Wiz." Those words were a jingle in all the store's commercials.

Dana normally avoided The Wiz when she came downtown. Walking in the store and viewing all the televisions and stereo systems only reminded her their floor-model television was broken. It weighed two hundred pounds, so she and her mother couldn't lift it to take it to a repair shop. And her mother had pawned the nineteen-inch television, so there was nothing to do at home but listen to the radio or read a book.

Her mother worked at the soul food restaurant a few blocks from their apartment, but they kept cutting her hours. So even if they could lift the floor-model TV, they didn't have extra money to fix it, and if they did, her mother's boyfriend would find a way to spend it on things they didn't need.

The three friends opened the door and went inside.

Televisions lined the shelves. Dana tried her best to ignore them and the stereo systems that blasted music throughout the store. They passed by the camera station, then took the stairs to check out the records on the second floor.

Dana glanced back, longing in her eyes as she watched a woman standing at the camera counter holding a Minolta X-700. She had begged her mother to buy the camera for Christmas during her sophomore year in high school. Dana wanted to take up scrapbooking and use the camera to make a photographic record of her final years in high school. She kept waiting, believing she'd have the camera under the Christmas tree, but she graduated from high school last month, with no scrapbook.

Lisa pointed at the New Edition poster hanging on the wall in the record section. "Look, Dana. There're your boys."

Dana turned toward the poster and smiled. "Love me some Bobby Brown. Yes, 'Mr. Telephone Man.'"

"You don't need to be loving nobody but me."

Dana heard the deep, silky voice. She put her hand on the railing to steady herself as she turned to the left and saw Derrick Little. Derrick had a high-top fade and to-die-for dimples. His light brown eyes blended nicely with his chocolate skin tone. She and Derrick had been seeing each other for a couple of months. He lived in Marcy Projects with his grandmother.

Derrick had on a blue jean jacket with matching jeans and a pair of blue-and-red Pro-Keds. The sneakers were old and worn out. Derrick was always fresh, so it surprised her to see him in a pair of run-down shoes. He wiped some sweat from his forehead as he moved closer to her.

As her girls rushed over to the record section and began

thumbing through the records, Dana finished her climb up the stairs and walked with Derrick to the R&B section.

"Why do you have on a jacket? It's too hot and humid in this city to be wearing all those clothes."

He tugged on either side of the jacket, then opened it so she could see the big pockets inside. "These are my work clothes."

"What kind of job makes you wear blue jeans with a jacket?" She pointed to his forehead. "You're sweating like crazy."

He laughed at her as he stood in front of a stack of records, fingered his way through the stack, then pulled one out. "You want 'Mr. Telephone Man,' right?"

Yes, of course she did, but she didn't have anything to play it on. "My mom sold our record player, so you don't have to buy the record."

"Got an extra record player at my place. I'll bring it to you later."

Her eyes lit up. "You'd really do that for me?"

"I got you, girl. Now, move a little to the left for me."

Dana stepped to the left.

"A little more."

Once she was in the spot he wanted her in, Derrick took the record and quickly shoved it in the inside pocket of his jacket.

Dana whispered, "What are you doing?" while glancing around.

"Don't make it look obvious. I needed you to stand in front of me so the camera wouldn't catch my movements. Play it cool, and we'll be good." Derrick then pulled out another record. He placed it in his inside pocket as well.

Lisa and Jasmine walked over to Dana. Jasmine held up

the Prince record she came in the store to get. "I'm ready to check out."

"Okay, I'm coming." Before walking away from Derrick she said, "We're headed to McCrory's to get a few things, but I'll be home later."

"I can hang," Derrick told her.

Jasmine paid for her record, and then the four of them went to McCrory's.

As Dana paid for her items at the checkout, Derrick said, "Yo, Jasmine, I'm getting ready to go to Dr. Jays for a pair of sneakers. You want to help me out?"

Dana side-eyed Derrick. Was he trying to get with Jasmine right in front of her?

"Calm down," Derrick told her. "Jasmine knows the deal."

Dana didn't know what *deal* Derrick was talking about. Derrick was new in town, so how could Jasmine know what deal he was talking about, if Dana didn't know?

Jasmine nodded. "Yeah, okay, but it's my turn next time."

"Bet that." Derrick and Jasmine fist-bumped.

They left McCrory's, then crossed over Jay Street to get to the other side of Fulton and kept walking toward Dr. Jays. A Black man dressed in a long navy blue robe with his head wrapped in a turban stood on top of a crate, shouting at passersby. "The Black man is following Western culture . . . You are descendants of the tribe of Judah. Why do you choose to live below your place in God?"

Dana glanced at the man and immediately regretted it. They made eye contact. She turned her head as the man pointed in her direction.

"Sister!" he yelled. "Why do you degrade yourself by

wearing cutoffs so short we can see the bottom of your behind?"

Jasmine put a hand over her mouth, laughing. "He clowned you."

Derrick put an arm around Dana's shoulder. "Don't pay him any mind. I like what I see, and my opinion is what matters."

Dana was mortified by the comment of the Black Hebrew Israelite. She knew better than to make eye contact, and now her friends would remember what he said about her shorts. But the way Derrick put an arm around her and pulled her closer made her feel protected. Made her want to get closer to him.

They stepped inside Dr. Jays. "La Di Da Di" by Slick Rick and Doug E. Fresh was playing on their stereo system. Lisa and Jasmine bounced to the beat of the music while Derrick searched the walls for the sneakers he wanted.

"What kind of sneakers are you getting?" Dana asked him.

"Some Pumas or Adidas." Derrick walked through the store, picking up shoes, turning them around and then placing them back on the shelf.

Lisa picked up a pair of white Nikes with pink stripes. "I'm going to tell my mom to get me this pair. I'm way past due for some new sneakers."

Jasmine smirked. "Girl, I already got a pair of those. You late."

Dana had never had a pair of brand-new sneakers in her life. Her cousin normally passed her old shoes down to her. She was thankful her cousin wasn't hard on her shoes. Although, she had to admit, she wished the flip-flops she wore today had a little more arch support, but beggars couldn't be too choosy.

The floor salesman walked over to them. Animated. Trying to act like he was their best friend to get his commission check. "What are you ladies interested in today? We've got those red suede Pumas in."

Derrick waved toward the salesman. "My man, can you get me this shoe in a size eleven?"

Dana's jaw dropped as Derrick handed the salesman a red, black, and white Air Jordan. Those were the hottest sneakers on the market since that new guy Michael Jordan started balling for the Chicago Bulls. Dana wouldn't dare ask her mother for a pair of Jordans. She knew she wouldn't get them. And she doubted her cousin would pass those down to her.

The salesman glanced down at the worn-out shoes on Derrick's feet. Dana figured he was wondering the same thing she was—why was Derrick wearing those old Pro-Keds if he could afford Air Jordans?

"Be right back," the salesman said.

Derrick held up a hand. "Bring me a ten and a half also. I need to see which one fits best."

Dana doubted the pockets inside Derrick's jacket were wide enough for those high-top sneakers, so she sat down next to him and relaxed as he took off his shoes. When the salesman brought the shoes out, Derrick tried on the ten and a half first.

"How's the fit?" the salesman asked as he watched Derrick struggle to get his foot in the shoe.

Derrick took the shoe off and handed it back to the salesman. "Too small."

As Derrick opened the box with the size elevens, Jasmine yelled for the salesman. "Hey, I need help over here. He's not your only customer."

The salesman lifted a finger. "One moment. I'll be right there once I'm finished with this customer."

"Oh, it's like that, huh? Well, let me take my business to Foot Locker." She put the Adidas back on the shelf and turned to walk out of the store.

Derrick told the salesman, "Don't miss out on your commission. Go and help her. I'll try these on." He held up the size elevens.

"Wait! Wait!" The salesman rushed over to Jasmine. "I can help you."

"I thought so." Jasmine handed the salesman the Adidas sneaker. "I want to try this in a size seven."

Derrick put the Air Jordans on and tied them. He got up and started walking around. Turning to the salesman as the man walked toward the storage room, Derrick said, "Bring me an eleven and a half. This one feels a little tight too."

"Coming right up." The salesman headed to the back to get the shoes.

Derrick bent down in front of Dana. Kissed her on the forehead. "I'll come by your place later with the record player."

The forehead kiss seemed so sweet to Dana. A smile crept across her face. She was about to ask what time he would be at her place when he took off running out of the store.

Jasmine yelled to her and Lisa. "Come on, let's go!" Then Jasmine took off running behind Derrick.

Dana looked down at the floor. Derrick's old, ruddy Pro-Keds were on the floor next to the empty Air Jordan box. All at once it registered with her. Derrick had stolen those expensive sneakers, and if she kept sitting there, the salesman was going to think she was in on it.

She jumped up and grabbed the arm of Lisa, who was looking as shell-shocked as Dana felt. "Let's go, girl." They ran past racks of sports bras, shorts, and jogging suits as they hightailed it out of the store.

Escaping the store, Dana and Lisa went left. Running down the street, headed for the A Train. The whole while, Dana's head swiveled from left to right as she tried to find Derrick or Jasmine.

The salesman ran out of the store, yelling, "I'm calling the police! Every last one of you is going to jail!"

Dana looked back. She saw the salesman shouting with an angry fist punching the air. Then on the opposite side of the street, bus number 26 came to a stop and picked up passengers. That's when she saw Derrick move out of the crowd and jump on the back of the bus, gripping his fingers into the air vents. The bus took off again, and Derrick held on like he'd been riding the back side of the bus all his life.

Dana was stuck. She stood there staring, not able to believe what she was seeing. After stealing those sneakers, Derrick was now the lone freeloading passenger on the back of a bus. He was her boyfriend. But he was a thief. And she didn't know how she felt about being with someone like him.

Lisa grabbed her arm and pulled her along. "What are you looking at? We've got to get out of here. My daddy's going to kill me if I get arrested." They started running again and managed to make it to the subway station.

Dana wasn't worried about what her mother might say. That woman had been to jail a few times herself. But Dana had never been locked up. The last thing she wanted was a prison record. She had just graduated high school, which as her mother kept telling her was something to be proud of. She had no plans to go to college and no direction for her life right now. She needed time to figure out what she wanted to do in this world.

But she absolutely, for certain knew she didn't want prison. When they got back on the train, she plopped down in her seat and breathed a sigh of relief. Then Lisa sat down next to her with the stank face.

"You should have told me your boyfriend was going to meet up with us. My parents don't like me hanging around thugs like him."

"Girl, you're eighteen. I know you're not telling me your mama still picks out your clothes and brushes your hair too."

"Shut up, Dana." Lisa rolled her eyes.

They sat in silence until the doors of the A Train opened at their stop. When they left the subway and headed down Lewis Avenue on their way home, Lisa told her, "I can't hang out with you anymore."

"Why you trippin'? It's not a big deal."

"I could have been arrested. I don't consider jail a small thing."

"Chill out, Lisa. We're good."

"If you're going to keep going out with Derrick, then I'm out." She waved at Dana and crossed the street.

Dana's nostrils flared as she blew out a heavy sigh. She wasn't happy about what happened either. But Lisa was a church kid with two parents at home who kept her on the straight and narrow. Her best friend knew nothing about the hard knocks of life. But Dana had a front-row seat to the crash-and-burn foolishness people like her dealt with on the daily.

CHAPTER 2

Lisa, girl, get out of bed right now. I don't care if it is summertime, you're not going to lay around this house all day."

Lisa heard her father call out to her, but her eyelids felt glued together. She rubbed the sleep from her eyes and then glanced over at the clock on her nightstand. It was 7:52 a.m. on a Saturday . . . a morning she had planned to sleep in, but her daddy was screaming for her.

"We need to get down to the store so we can pass out the hot dogs and hamburgers to our customers in the neighborhood," he hollered up to her. "It's good business to give back to the community on a day like this."

Lisa popped up and flung the covers off. She opened the curtain and looked out the window. She saw the sanitation street-sweeper truck as it slowly drove down the street. Mr. Rumbly ran outside in his pajamas and house shoes. He jumped in his car and made a U-turn in the middle of the street so he could get his car out of the way of the street sweepers.

A truck with DJ equipment was parked across the street. Two guys got out and started taking the gear out of the bed of the truck.

How had she forgotten? There was going to be a block party on Halsey Street today. She opened her bedroom door and stood at the top of the steps in their three-level brownstone. "Why do I have to work this morning? I want to go to the block party."

Her daddy, David Whitaker, was a tall man, about six feet four. He'd put on an extra seventy pounds over the years from all the red beans and rice he kept asking her mother to cook for him. He wore blue jean overalls to work most days. He thought it hid his girth.

Daddy was a force and didn't accept the word *no* when he wasn't the one using it. Even Pastor Jonathan down at Praise Ministries didn't like getting on Deacon David Whitaker's bad side. His big hand wrapped around the banister as he stood on the parlor level of the house where the living room, dining room, one of the bathrooms, and kitchen were. The front double-entry doors were on the same level as well. "Lisa, don't play with me. I don't have time for this today."

"I'm eighteen, Daddy. I should be able to make my own decisions."

"You should also be able to help with some of these bills. You're going off to college next month, and your mama and I are still scrounging up the money to pay for the books you need for fall semester, so you're going to help me at the corner store. That way I don't have to pay someone else to work."

Lisa wanted to object to the whole work-for-free racket her father had going on, but she knew how much her parents were sacrificing so she could attend school at New York University. She had a scholarship, but it didn't cover all her tuition, nor did it cover books. The least she could do was help her dad out at the corner store until she left for college.

"I'll be ready in a few minutes. But remember, I have to be at church this afternoon."

"I remember. Help me this morning, and then you can leave."

Despite having to work at the corner store this morning, today was going to be one of the best days of Lisa's life. When she was in junior high, her dad took her to hear Representative Shirley Chisholm at the YMCA on Bedford Avenue. And now, at the start of Evangelism Week at her church, her mother told her Elsie Richardson would be speaking at the church today.

Lisa couldn't get dressed fast enough. She had a scarf wrapped around her head, which she covered with a shower cap before getting in the shower. When she got out, she took the cap off, then untied her scarf and let her long black hair fall against her caramel shoulders. She then took her comb and ran it through the short, layered curls at the front of her head.

Lisa loved her new hairstyle, even the temple fade around the front of her ears. A lot of the girls were wearing their hair short and layered in the front but long in the back.

She went back to her room and put on her purple, ankle-length ruffled skirt with her black-and-white saddle shoes and a white tank top. The summers in Brooklyn were so hot that sweat leaked from her body like rain drizzling off the side of a house the minute she stepped outside, so even though her father thought tank tops showed off too much skin, Lisa had a different colored tank for each day of the week.

Rushing down the stairs of their brownstone, Lisa waited for her father by the front door. Besides the parlor, their brownstone also had a basement, which was more like an apartment. Her daddy rented it out from time to time. Bedrooms and bathrooms were on the top level of the house.

By the time Lisa and her father stepped outside, the street had been blocked off so there was no more through traffic. The DJ was setting his tables up in the middle of the street. Music was about to be blasted all the way down the street.

Mrs. Mabel was sitting out on her stoop. She didn't have air-conditioning in her brownstone, so it was often cooler out on her stoop than inside the house. She waved to Lisa.

"Good day to you, Lisa. I hear you're going to be leaving us soon."

"I will." Lisa nodded. "But you know NYU isn't far at all, so I'll be back home visiting plenty."

"I sure hope so. We need to see more of your smiling face around here."

"Yes, ma'am, Mrs. Mabel," Lisa said as she helped her father tote his big cooler down the street. They lived two blocks from the Halsey Street corner store, which was on the corner of Halsey and Lewis.

Neighbors were bringing out barbecue pits and placing tables and chairs in their front yards. Charcoal smoke permeated the air.

"Good morning, Mr. Whitaker." Cal Johnson stood behind the cast-iron gate that closed off the front area of his brownstone. He pointed toward his grill. "I'm getting it ready for the burgers and dogs."

Her father smiled and waved. "Hurry on over to the store before we run out. Wouldn't want you to fire up your grill for nothing."

"Don't you worry. I'll be right there." Cal sprayed lighter fluid on his charcoal.

They set up their table outside the store. Customers came

over to collect the hamburgers or hot dogs for their grills. A party was going on in the neighborhood. People were laughing, smiling, and having a good time. The DJ started playing "Party All the Time" by Eddie Murphy. Lisa didn't like the song. She couldn't figure out why Eddie Murphy didn't stick to telling jokes.

A guy with MC Hammer pants, the kind that were baggy and saggy in the middle and tapered at the ankles, started break-dancing in the middle of the street. Lisa turned to her right and caught sight of the "In Loving Memory" mural on the wall next to her father's store.

It had been commissioned a couple of years ago by a drug dealer, mourning all the friends from the neighborhood he had lost. The faces of the dead were painted on it in between clouds and gravestones. It was no longer just for gangbangers but for anyone who passed away in the neighborhood. Lisa found the mural creepy. She didn't like walking past it, let alone standing near it.

Once they passed out the last of the meat, Lisa waved to her dad. "I've got to meet Mama at the church."

A grin spread across Lisa's face as she walked from Lewis Avenue to Praise Ministries on Decatur. No longer thinking about the block party, Lisa was practically giddy about church service. Her mother, Brenda, was waiting for her in the fellowship hall.

"Do you think I can sit on the front row with you today?" She normally sat in the back of the sanctuary with her friends.

Brenda patted her hand. "Of course, baby. I told the pastor how excited you were to hear Mrs. Richardson speak. I already saved you a seat on the front row."

Beaming, Lisa sat down and turned her attention to the pulpit.

Pastor said, "I present to you Mrs. Elsie Richardson, one of the cornerstones in Bed-Stuy Brooklyn."

"Thank you, Pastor," Mrs. Richardson said as she stood in front of the podium, adjusting the microphone. The sanctuary could seat a thousand people, and it looked like they might have to set extra chairs out for the overflow if people kept coming.

Elsie Richardson began. "Good afternoon, everyone. I am so thankful for this opportunity to speak to you as you begin Evangelism Week. Now, I truly understand the reason we evangelize is to bring wayward sinners to the Lord, but I want to challenge you this week to also encourage those you minister to to become advocates for change in our community.

"And I pray you understand you're not too young or too old to make a difference. I was a teenager living in Harlem when I took part in the 1941 New York City bus boycotts led by Adam Clayton Powell Jr. We were years ahead of the bus boycotts led by Martin Luther King Jr."

Leaning forward in her seat, Lisa soaked in every word. Elsie Richardson had done so much for this community back in the sixties. Lisa was determined to do a great work for her community once she graduated from college. Elsie Richardson and Shirley Chisholm were like royalty to her. She felt how Martha and Mary of the Bible must have felt as they sat in the same room with Jesus . . . mesmerized.

Mrs. Richardson continued. "I have always been a fighter for human rights. My parents frequently told me I was as good as anyone else. So when the powers that be in this city tried to treat us as if we weren't worthy of anything, something in me stood up and demanded they recognize our humanity.

"Look around, young people. I, along with so many other people, fought to bring revitalization to this neighborhood. But the crack demon has taken over much of the Bed-Stuy community . . . destroying it. It doesn't have to be this way, my brothers and sisters.

"Help me revitalize our community once again. If you see someone going down the wrong path, and you know it will eventually destroy him or her—along with our beloved Bed-Stuy—lend a helping hand to them." Elsie Richardson spoke a few more minutes, then when she was finished, she walked to the back of the sanctuary and shook everyone's hand as they left the church to begin walking the community, telling the neighbors about Jesus and handing out flyers to invite the people to church tomorrow.

Lisa got in line and tried to be patient as everyone else shook Mrs. Richardson's hand and said their piece. But now she was wishing she had sat in the back with the rest of the teens; she would have been at the front of the line by now if she had.

"Stop fidgeting, Lisa. Mrs. Richardson isn't going anywhere."

"I know, Mama." There were about fifteen people in front of her. "I'm grateful I get a chance to meet her. So glad I came."

"Of course, child. But don't forget, I need your help passing out these flyers." Brenda laughed.

"Oh, so you want to put me to work too. Just like Daddy . . . trying to get as much work out of me as you can before I leave for college."

Putting a hand on Lisa's shoulder, Brenda told her, "We only want to teach you responsibility before you're all grown up and taking care of things on your own."

"You don't have to worry about me. I'm going to make you proud when I come back and help rebuild our community."

"Where are you going, young lady? And why do you have to wait until you get back to do something for our community?"

Lisa swung around. She had been talking to her mother and hadn't noticed the line had cleared. She stepped closer to Mrs. Richardson. Butterflies fluttered in her stomach as she stuck out her hand. "H-hi, M-Mrs. Richardson. I loved your speech."

"Then why are you leaving?"

Lisa's eyebrows furrowed. "Huh?"

"I heard you say you were going to do something for Bed-Stuy when you get back. Why not now?"

"Oh." Lisa relaxed a bit. "I'm going to college in a month. But I plan to become a community organizer like you when I return from college."

Mrs. Richardson smiled at her. "I went to college while I raised my children and took care of my husband. So if you see a place where you can make a difference, even before you graduate from college, I admonish you to do it."

"I will, Mrs. Richardson. I've always helped out at the church and will continue as long as I can."

Lisa headed outside with the rest of the ladies who were getting ready to walk the blocks to pass out Praise Ministries flyers. Taking a stack of flyers from her mother, Lisa began walking up Decatur Street, heading toward Lewis Avenue.

"Good afternoon. How are you doing?" she said to a woman who was headed down the street, holding on to a little girl's hand.

"Doing fine," was the woman's reply.

Lisa stuck out her hand, offering the woman the flyer. "This is Evangelism Week at our church. Can I give this information about Praise Ministries to you? I'd also like to invite you to church on Sunday."

The woman didn't respond, but she did take the flyer as she continued on her way. She looked like she was in a hurry, but most New Yorkers walked at a fast pace, like they were always trying to catch up to life—or get away from something.

She handed a flyer to the next person who zoomed past her. But before she could say a word, he said, "Can't talk. Got to get to the library." He had a backpack strapped to his back, loaded down with books.

Some of the choir members had joined them. As Lisa reached the corner of Lewis and Decatur where they were standing, she smiled as they started singing "Jesus Can Work It Out." This was a new praise song, but it was quickly becoming one of Lisa's favorites.

Lisa raised her hands in praise and started singing along with the choir. Her voice was not meant for solos, but she could give praise to God in a group sing-along. She was enjoying the song so much she almost forgot about the flyers she was supposed to be passing out.

Until someone tapped her on the shoulder. Lisa lowered her arms. She turned, taking a flyer from her stack, getting ready to hand it to the person who sought her attention, but then she saw it was Dana.

"Oh, hey. I didn't see you walk up."

"I bet you didn't. You had your eyes closed. By the way, you may want to take a few singing lessons if you're going to be out in the open singing for all to hear."

Lisa wasn't offended. She knew she couldn't hold a tune.

"God doesn't care how bad I sound. It is all sweet music to Him."

"Whatever." Dana smirked. "You are such a cornball."

Lisa did take offense to those words. Her hand went to her hip, lips twisted to the left. "Call me a cornball if you like, but I'm not the one who's always finding trouble and hanging with the wrong crowd."

"You still mad?"

"You're hanging around thieves, Dana. That's a problem for me."

"I didn't mean to get you caught up with them like that." Dana nudged Lisa's shoulder. "But you're my girl, so don't be mad. Okay?"

Lisa wanted to stay ticked and keep her distance from Dana's situation, but Dana had been her best friend since first grade. And when a friend was in need, the Christian thing to do was to lend a hand.

Who knew, maybe Dana would come to realize she didn't need to hang out in the streets and would instead register for college. That would certainly be making a difference in someone's life, as Mrs. Richardson said.

CHAPTER 3

Derrick knocked on Dana's door about six in the evening. Dana stepped outside and closed the door behind her. She didn't know whether she was happy or mad about him showing up at her place after leaving her to fend for herself at Dr. Jays.

"That wasn't cool what you and Jasmine did the other day. Me and Lisa could have gotten arrested."

"Ah, baby, you're worrying about the wrong stuff. You weren't going to get arrested."

Crossing her arms over her chest, Dana pursed her lips. "How do you know? You took off running so fast, you didn't even look back to see what happened to me."

"You should have been closer to the front door when I took off. Keep hanging with me . . . you'll understand how I move."

Derrick was fine and all, but the boy had sticky fingers. She didn't want to understand how he *moved*. She didn't want to be a part of his band of thieves. She was about to tell him she didn't think they should be together anymore when he held up a plastic bag.

"I brought you something."

Dana took note of how Derrick said he *brought*, not *bought*. Then he pulled a record player out of the bag.

Her eyes widened. He took the New Edition record out of the bag also. Dana's first thought was, *Derrick kept his word.* He told her he would bring her a record player so she could play New Edition's new song on it. Most of the people in her world said one thing but did another.

Her second thought . . . *Derrick must have stolen it like he stole the record and those Jordans he still has on his feet.* Dana's lips twisted. "I don't know about this. It doesn't seem right. What if you got caught?"

"That would mean I'm bad at my job." He smiled, showing off his deep dimples as they dipped into his chocolate cheeks. "And trust me, I'm too good to be bad at anything."

"Not funny. I'm serious. I don't want to be responsible for you getting arrested."

Her mom opened the front door, took one look at the record player in Derrick's hand, and said, "I've seen you around here before. You after my daughter?"

"I like her very much," he answered while looking at Dana like she meant something to him.

Vida pointed at the record player. "You selling or giving?"

"Dana told me she didn't have a record player. Since I have a couple at the crib, I thought I'd bring this one to her."

Vida opened the door wider, gave a sweeping motion with her hand. "Well, come on in here. I've got a nice spot for Dana to put her new record player." Vida directed Derrick over to a mahogany table in the living room, where the last record player had sat.

Dana wondered how long she would have this gift before

her mother took it to the pawn shop. She didn't want Derrick leaving his stolen goods at her place. But even if she told her mother he stole the record player, Vida wouldn't care. So she let him set it on the table and plug it in. Thank God the electric bill had been paid this month. She would be mortified to have anyone see them sitting around the living room with candles burning.

"Are you hungry?" Vida asked him. "I made a pasta salad. On hot nights like this, you need something cool to eat."

Derrick grinned, patted his stomach. "I ate a hero sandwich before I came over. I'm on my way to 262 to shoot some hoops, and I was hoping Dana would come hang out and be my cheerleader."

Dana glanced in her mother's direction.

"Don't look at me. You're old enough to make your own decisions. Not that you've listened to me in these last few years anyway."

People used to tell Dana she looked like her mother. They had the same light coloring, the same hazel eyes. But her mother's eyes had lost their luster as she'd become more and more skeletal with sunken-in cheeks.

Vida Jones had once been beautiful and sought after by the single men in the neighborhood. Dana remembered how her mother used to tell guys to stop bothering her when she was with her daughter. Told them it was disrespectful to push up on her like that. Dana wished Vida had thought Sam was disrespectful and had told him to leave her alone. If she had, Vida wouldn't be standing in the middle of the living room scratching her arms like she had fleas.

Dana couldn't stand seeing her mother like this, so even though she didn't want to watch Derrick play basketball, it beat sitting in this apartment with her mother, wondering how long it would be before her record player disappeared and Vida acted as if she had no idea what happened to it.

"Come on, Derrick. Let's go."

The 262 was the elementary school for Bed-Stuy students, but it was also the place where hood legends were born. Anyone who thought he could dribble like Magic Johnson or shoot like Bernard King, the Brooklyn native who was now playing for the New York Knicks, could be found at the 262.

Dana often hung out in the back of the school, cheering for one would-be superstar after another. She loved the game of basketball and she had fond memories of this school.

Her mother used to walk her to school almost every morning on the way to catch the A Train for her job at McCrory's. She lost her job during Dana's last year at the 262. But Dana still loved the school. She and Lisa became friends during those years. And when she had problems at home, Dana had a true friend she could talk to.

"What are you daydreaming about over here? You missed my dunk." Derrick wiped the sweat from his face with the bottom of his shirt.

Laughing at herself for totally ignoring the game, Dana told him, "It's the school. I loved elementary school, so whenever I come over here, I always think about the good old days."

Derrick glanced at the brownish-red brick building with the massive red doors. "I went to elementary in Connecticut, so the only memories I have of this school is . . ." He turned his head toward the court and shouted, "When I'm dunking on fools!"

"Oh, you dunking on us, huh? Well, come on back and see if you can get it off again," the tallest player on the court said while cracking his knuckles.

Derrick turned back to Dana. "You think I can take him?"

Dana looked Derrick up and down. Derrick was tall, but he wasn't Hakeem Olajuwon–tall, like the guy standing on the basketball court waiting to take him down at the hoop. "I don't know. You might want to shoot some jumpers."

"You don't believe in your man, huh?" He leaned in close and pressed his lips to hers. "Well, I'll take that as my good luck charm."

Derrick gave her a dimpled smile as he went back to the court. Dana pressed her fingers against her lips. He actually kissed her in front of everyone, and he'd called himself her man. Derrick had never said or done anything like that before. What did this mean? Were they a serious couple? Did she want to be a couple with Derrick?

"Dana!" Derrick yelled her name.

He had the ball; he dribbled it as he raced down the court. The seven-foot guy was on his heels as Derrick went straight for the hoop. He caught up with Derrick and stood with his arms up.

Derrick moved to the left, then the right. Someone in the stands hollered, "Did y'all see what happened? He crossed him and broke his ankles."

Dana jumped out of her seat. "He can't check you. Go, Derrick!"

Derrick was about six foot three, but it seemed like wearing those Jordans gave him some kind of superpower as he leaped so high his head was above the rim and he dunked the ball.

Derrick's partner on the court put his fist to his mouth, eyes big. "Ooh, that was nasty."

Dana pumped her fist in the air. "You did it, Derrick!"

The seven-foot guy walked over to Derrick and shook his hand. "You all right with me, man."

"You almost had me," Derrick told him as he strutted off the court like a man who owned his own little piece of the world. Another hood legend was born at the 262.

"You hungry?" Derrick asked as they left the school.

Her stomach had growled a few times while she watched the game. She nodded. "I could eat something."

"Let's go get a slice."

They held hands as they walked over to Fulton Street. Dana felt a fluttering in the lower part of her belly again. She was conflicted. Derrick was being good to her, but she knew in her heart what they had was all wrong. She wanted so badly to be convinced otherwise. Maybe she could help him find a better way to make a living.

After they ordered their slices of pizza and sat down in the back of the pizza parlor, she breathed in the scent of dough baking along with the oregano sprinkled on the pizza. Her stomach growled.

Their slices were ready. Derrick grabbed them from the counter. He had cheese, and she had the pepperoni slice. Looking at the pizza, she asked, "Why me, Derrick?"

"What do you mean?" Derrick took a bite of his cheese pizza and chewed it.

"You could be with any girl in Brooklyn. Why you coming for me so hard?" She lifted her slice, folded it, then took a bite and almost closed her eyes to savor the deliciousness of the ooey-gooey cheese and pepperoni.

Derrick used his index finger to lift her chin. "You really

don't know how beautiful you are." He laughed. Leaned back in his seat. "Maybe I shouldn't be telling you this. I don't need my woman getting the big head, but I had my eye on you from the moment I moved here."

Dana had been told countless times how beautiful she was, but beauty faded. Her mom was the living example. She wanted someone to see more than her face when they looked at her. "I got really good grades in school until the tenth grade, when I stopped studying for tests. But I still passed with Bs and a few Cs. If I had studied, I could have graduated with honors."

"I'm sure you could have. I like that about you. I need a woman with brains and beauty." Derrick turned his head and looked at the guy behind the cash register. He then glanced around the small parlor.

"What are you looking for?" Dana thought they were having an important conversation, but she didn't have Derrick's full attention.

"What?" He turned back to her. "Oh, I need a napkin." He waved the busboy to their table. "Yo, man, can I get a napkin?"

The busboy pulled some napkins out of the pocket of his apron and handed two of them to Derrick.

"You're not even listening to me." Dana poked her lip out in a pout.

Derrick wiped his hands with one of the napkins, then he looked at the other napkin, grinned, folded it, and slid it into his pocket.

Derrick then turned his attention back to Dana. "Stop being so sensitive, girl. You caught my eye when I first saw you, and I promise . . . you have my attention."

She smiled at him. She wanted his attention. Needed

someone in her life who was all about her. Her mother used to be . . . but that was a long time ago. Dana had been left to fend for herself. The abandonment had made her feel alone in this world. Maybe she had finally found someone who cared about her.

"I'll get you the rent money, but you have to give me some time."

Dana had been sleeping, but she heard her mother yelling at someone, and it woke her up.

"You ain't right, Mr. James. You and your wife always talking to me about taking better care of Dana. How you think I'm gon' do that if y'all throw us on the street?"

Dana got out of bed, threw on a pair of shorts, and was rounding the corner to the living room when she heard Mr. James say, "The eviction has already been processed with the courts. You need to be out of here by next week, or the police will put your stuff on the curb."

"Well, the place is still ours for another week, so you can get out of my face."

Dana could see people walking past their apartment, looking toward their place. "Ma!" she yelled. "Why you talking so loud? Everybody can hear what's going on."

Vida put a hand to her chest, then slammed the door. "Girl, don't sneak up on me."

"Why do we always have to be the talk of the neighborhood? This stuff is embarrassing."

"I'm not trying to embarrass you."

Dana's eyes bored into her. "We're getting evicted again . . . right? How embarrassing."

Vida's hands went to her hips. "Don't give me your guff today. As far as I'm concerned, you're grown, so if you don't like the way I'm handling things"—Vida made a sweeping motion with her hand—"then get on out there and show me how much better you can do this."

Her mother was insufferable. Sometimes Dana didn't even want to go outside. She couldn't stand the look of pity on the neighbors' faces. Worse yet was when the neighbors sat on the stoop and Dana heard them talking about her mother.

But at this moment, Dana couldn't stand being in the same room with her mother. She stomped to the front door and went outside. The neighbors might be gossiping about what they'd heard from Vida and Mr. James, but she sat on his stoop anyway. She kept her eyes averted and her head low as she tried to imagine a world where things were good. A world where people were stable and took care of their children.

After she'd sat out there for about thirty minutes, Derrick came over and sat down next to her.

"I brought you something." Derrick reached behind his back and pulled out a camera.

Dana's smile dimmed a bit. Derrick had said *brought* again. She shook off the thought, focusing on the camera. It was the exact one Dana had wanted for Christmas during her sophomore year of high school. The Minolta X-700. It was an all-black 35 mm camera with a flash and a roll of film. It fit snugly in her hand, and Dana was absolutely beside herself with joy.

"I begged for this camera when I was in high school. I can't believe you're actually giving this to me." Looking at Derrick with adoring eyes, she asked, "How did you know?"

He pointed toward the apartment. "Your mom told me, so I went and snatched it for you."

So her mother was encouraging her boyfriend to steal. Dana sighed. She wanted to give the camera back to Derrick so he would get the message. She didn't like the fact he'd chosen being a thief as his profession, but she'd begged for this camera and had been so disappointed when she didn't get it.

"Thank you, Derrick."

She leaned forward and kissed him, then snapped his picture.

Derrick said, "I'm glad you like it. It's good to see a smile on your beautiful face."

"I love it." She might not have been able to make her scrapbook during high school, but she was going to take as many pictures of friends as she could before she and her mother had to move again.

Derrick leaned back against the concrete step, looked around, then said, "I'm going to need you next week. I'm planning something big."

She sat up straight, put the camera down. "What's that supposed to mean?"

"I'll tell you more once I have it all planned out, but this will set us up for a while. I might even be able to get us an apartment and move you out of here."

He wanted to take her away from her mother. She wanted to get away from Vida too. But she wasn't the stealing kind. "I don't know, Derrick. You've got to give me more time."

"The time is now, Dana. Don't you want to get out of here?"

She did. Seeing Vida in this haphazard condition every

day tore at her heart. The only problem was, Dana hadn't bothered to come up with any kind of plan to get her own place. She was planning to put in job applications at a few places, but nobody was going to pay her enough money to live on her own. She didn't have much work experience.

CHAPTER 4

Lisa spent the following week shopping for school supplies and bedding since she would be staying in the dorm at her college. She and her mother used her father's credit card like it had no limit. That is, until Daddy started yelling so loud through the house the walls vibrated.

"Brenda, why on earth would you go out and spend over a thousand dollars in one week like this?"

"Lisa needs things for school. We can't send her off to college without supplies and things to make her dorm room feel homey."

"I'm not made of money," he exploded, "and I'm not the government. I can't go and print up more money when we run low."

Lisa had been in her room folding all her new clothes and packing them in her new suitcases when her dad started yelling. Her parents rarely argued, but Lisa hated the few times she heard their disagreements. While her mother always tried to remain calm and reasonable, her dad would raise his voice, shouting and jumping around like a buffoon.

Lisa couldn't let her mom endure the disagreement by herself, not when the money was spent on her. She opened her bedroom door and took the stairs two at a time until she reached the parlor. Her parents were in the living room.

Her mom said, "Will you keep your voice down before Lisa hears us?"

"I already heard Daddy screaming." Lisa was standing in the parlor, a step or two away from the entry of the living room. Her parents swung around, looking as if she had caught them misbehaving. Daddy was definitely cutting up, and he needed to chill.

Her mother motioned her hands as if she was pushing Lisa away. "Go back upstairs. This is between me and your daddy."

"But, Mama, you bought those things for me—said you wanted me to have some nice things to take with me to school so the other kids would know I come from a good family."

"You do come from a good family," her daddy interjected. "New clothes and shoes don't determine what kind of family you have."

"But, Daddy, most of my tuition is covered, so why is it such a big deal for me to have a few nice things? My roommate will probably have a nice cover set and trash can."

David's head swung back around to Brenda. "You bought this girl a trash can? Doesn't that high-priced college have their own trash cans?"

"They have trash cans outside, but the students have to bring their own smaller trash cans for their rooms," Brenda answered.

David shook a finger at Lisa. "You don't have a full ride, young lady. Your mama and I have to fork over three thousand each semester, so don't tell me about no scholarship when I'm talking about all this extra money your mama spent, when we don't have it like that."

Lisa's mouth tightened. Her dad was so cheap, she never got any of the things the other kids had in school. She and her mother normally shopped at thrift stores so they could save money for college. She always got good grades. She didn't want her parents to pay her tuition. Was it her fault NYU didn't give her a total free ride?

"And another thing," David Whitaker said, continuing his tirade. "Why does this girl have to stay in the dorms when she is going to a New York school? Why can't she bring herself home every night and save us some money?"

"Why do you have to be so cheap all the time, Daddy? Can't you be happy for me?"

David puffed out his cheeks, blowing out hot air. "Don't you disrespect me, young lady," he said, finger still wagging as he approached her.

Brenda grabbed his arm. "David, calm down. I'll work some overtime and pay off the credit card."

"Didn't you hear how this girl talked to me? She might be going off to college and thinking she's grown." He looked pointedly at Lisa when he said "*thinking she's grown.*" "But I'm not going to let her disrespect us in our home."

"Apologize to your daddy, Lisa," her mother said.

Lisa's eyebrows scrunched. "For what? All I said is he's cheap. I'm not lying, Mama . . . if he wasn't cheap, you and I wouldn't always be shopping at thrift stores."

"What's wrong with thrift stores?" David demanded.

Lisa raised her voice. "The other kids at the Boys and Girls High School were always going to Macy's to shop. I never asked for that. I knew we were trying to save money." Lisa's nostrils flared, the same way her dad's flared when he got angry. "Why are you giving us such a hard time about this?"

"Keeping a roof over your head and paying the rest of

your tuition is more important to me than whether or not you have brand-new clothes or the latest sneakers."

"But, Dad—"

He shook his head. "Don't 'but, Dad' me. Your mother offered to work overtime at her job to help with this bill, so unless you want to give up dorm living, I suggest you put in some extra hours at the store before we drive you to school."

Nostrils flaring again, Lisa's fists balled as she yanked her arms in a downward motion. "Fine!" she shouted before running upstairs and slamming her bedroom door.

She was so amped up about her father threatening to not pay for her dorm room she couldn't sit down. She paced the floor of her room. Took pillows off her bed and threw them at the wall. The four walls of her room felt as though they were closing in on her. She had to get out of the house.

Lisa's billfold was on her dresser. Next to it was her Social Security card. Her mother had given it to her when she went to get her state ID.

"You're eighteen now, so I'm trusting you with your important documents, but if you don't think you can handle it, I need you to return your birth certificate and Social Security card to me after you get your ID."

"I can handle it, Mom. You gotta start trusting me with stuff."

Her mom kept her Social Security card in her billfold. So Lisa took her Social Security card off her dresser and put it in her billfold, along with her new state ID. She threw her billfold in her purse and opened her bedroom door.

Her dad was standing there with his hand raised as though he was about to knock. "We need to talk about your schedule at the store."

Lisa lifted her hands to halt him. "Daddy, please. I'm angry right now, and I need to cool off. Let me take a walk and then we can discuss it, okay?"

Her father nodded. Stepped out of her way. "A walk might do you some good."

Stepping out of her room, she rushed down the stairs. Her father was behind her. She loved him dearly, but right now she was so mad she didn't want to be anywhere near him. All this fuss over some school clothes and items for her dorm room.

Her father said, "Your mother tells me I should apologize for all the yelling."

Lisa opened the first set of entry doors. She turned to her father. "Mom told you to apologize, but do you really believe you owe me an apology?"

"No," he admitted. "I actually think you and your mom owe me an apology for spending our money on frivolous things without consulting me."

"Okay, Daddy. I'll see you at the store later." Lisa opened the second set of entry doors and left the house. It was weird to her that brownstones had two sets of entry doors. But Daddy told her the doors were built to keep the heat out in the summer and the cold out in the winter.

She walked down the block, kicking at rocks and sticks on the sidewalk. She turned on Lewis Avenue and headed for Dana's place. The *beep-beep-beep* of car horns, which she hardly paid attention to on Halsey, was blaring in her ears as she walked down Lewis Avenue.

When she reached Dana's place, Lisa opened the gate to the lower level, knocked on the door, and waited. Music was playing inside the house, so she knocked again. The door opened, and Dana's mom stood in front of her holding on to the door with an irritated look on her face, like Lisa had interrupted her.

Dana's mom looked so different from the way she had when they were kids. Everyone used to say Ms. Vida was the prettiest woman on Halsey Street. That had been when Ms. Vida and Dana lived above the barbecue spot on Halsey. Lisa had not liked those comments. She thought her mom was pretty also, but everyone kept talking about how all the men were after Ms. Vida.

Ms. Vida's skin looked like it was lacking in lotion and a good vitamin—it was ashy. Her cheeks were sunken, and her eyes looked bigger now since her face had lost the effect of the roundness it once had.

"Yeah. What you want?" she asked Lisa.

"Um, hi, Ms. Vida. I'm here to see Dana."

Without saying hello back, Vida hollered over her shoulder, "Dana, you got company. And keep it down. I have a headache."

"Okay, Ma, dang." Dana rolled her eyes, then gestured for Lisa to come inside and closed the door behind her.

Vida turned off the record player and walked to the back of the house. Dana and Lisa sat in the living room. "I thought you were packing for college."

"Girl, I had to get out of the house. My dad was trippin'."

"I'll take your dad over my mom any day of the week." Dana headed for the door. "This place is wack."

They walked up the stairs from the basement unit. Dana pointed toward the stairs of the main house. They sat down.

A group of kids from the house next door got their jump ropes out and started doing double Dutch. Lisa pointed to them. "Remember when we used to jump rope at the 262?"

"Yeah, I remember. Sad to say, but elementary was the

best time of my life. Seems like everything has lost its beauty since then."

Lisa pointed toward Dana's apartment. "What was up with your mom? Did I do something to her?"

"You didn't do nothing. Vida is mad at herself." Dana's lips tightened. "We're getting evicted again."

"What!" Lisa hugged her friend. "What are you going to do?"

"I don't know." A tear trickled down Dana's face. "I need to find a job."

"You've been putting in applications. Have you heard anything?"

Shaking her head, Dana told her, "I gave them Mrs. Adams' phone number, but she hasn't told me about any callbacks."

"Give them my number. I'll let you know if anyone calls back."

"You're leaving in three weeks."

"Gives us three weeks to find you a job."

Dana stood, wiped off her pants, and started walking. "Let's go."

"Where we going?"

When they reached the corner of Halsey and Lewis, Dana pointed left. "Let's go to Tompkins Park."

Three blocks down, they came upon a group of men playing chess. A few guys were drinking next to the chain-link fence that surrounded the park. Dana and Lisa went into the park and sat down on one of the benches. The legs of the bench were made of concrete, with wood planks nailed into the seat and back of the bench.

Dana waved toward the basketball court; Lisa turned to see Derrick waving back. "You knew he was going to be here?"

Grinning like a fool with no good on the brain, Dana said, "He's really good. Let's watch him play."

Lisa watched the game for a few minutes, then snapped her fingers. "You know what? I'm going to ask my dad if you and Vida can move into our basement apartment."

Dana's eyes brightened. "You'd do that for me?"

Lisa shoved Dana's shoulder. Tears were now in her eyes as well, as if Dana's pain was her pain. "You're my girl. I'm not going to let you end up on the street with no place to go."

"Derrick said he wants to help me get a place, but I don't know."

"Do you hear yourself?" Lisa's eyes shifted to the basketball court. A guy dunked, then Derrick grabbed the ball and headed to the other hoop. "Derrick's a criminal. You need to pump the brakes with him."

Dana turned her head, looking away from the court like she was in deep thought about something.

Lisa said, "Come to church with me on Sunday."

Dana gave a bitter laugh. She turned back to Lisa. "Church isn't my thing."

"I know. But you need to focus and figure out what God wants you to do with your life. Maybe attending church will help you do that."

With a twist of her lips, Dana asked, "When has God ever had me on His mind? I seriously doubt He is directing my life."

"God allows us to choose our way. Ask yourself, are you choosing the right way? From what I saw of Derrick, it doesn't seem like it."

"You don't know anything about him. He is a real cool guy. And with as much as I have to deal with around here, I need someone in my life who cares about me."

Lisa had been praying about the situation with Dana and her mom, but she didn't know how to help her friend.

"I'm sorry things have gotten so bad," was all Lisa could say.

Dana nodded. "As bad as things are with me and my mom, the one thing I miss is how she used to hug me. Man, one hug from my mom, and I used to think my whole day was going to be good." Her lips twisted. "Now I wake up to the same terrible day, like it's on repeat or something."

Lisa saw the wetness at the corners of Dana's eyes and understood the disappointment she must feel in the way things turned out for her. Then she thought about her anger issues with her father. He was a hard taskmaster, and he was cheap, but she'd also heard her mom say countless times that Deacon David Whitaker was a good man. Maybe she needed to cut him some slack.

CHAPTER 5

Why can't they stay here, Daddy? That's not right."

"Lisa, girl, you better go 'head on with this mess. I'm renting the room out to the Parkers. Him and his wife both have jobs and they can pay the rent."

Lisa sucked her teeth. "Dana needs help. Her mother is being evicted."

David turned to Brenda. "Will you tell your daughter we pay our tithes and you volunteer down at the homeless shelter and at church, so we're all caught up on our charity work?"

Brenda side-eyed David and then turned to Lisa. "Hon, I'm sorry to hear this about Dana and her mother. I wish we could help, I really do, but your father has already promised our apartment to the Parkers."

Lisa was about to give up, but then an idea struck. "What about my room? I'm going to be away at college. Can Dana use my room?"

Lisa had directed the question to her mother, but her dad shook his head. "Absolutely not."

"I'm sorry, Dana, my dad already rented out the basement apartment."

Dana's stomach dropped, but she kept a straight face so she wouldn't make Lisa feel bad. "No biggie. But thanks for looking out. My mom's out right now. Hopefully she's looking for a place. I know she's not going to be able to pay Mr. James so much back rent."

Lisa's lips twisted like she wanted to say something else.

Dana pointed to the newspaper on the kitchen table. "I've seen a few jobs that only require a high school diploma."

Lisa's eyes lit up as she glanced at the newspaper. "Really? Do you know what you want to do?"

"I like doing hair, but you need a certificate to get into a hair salon." Dana hunched her shoulders. "I need a paycheck."

"It's already late in the afternoon, and since tomorrow is Saturday, I don't think you'll have much luck with applications. Maybe we should go to a couple of those places on Monday or Tuesday."

"Yeah, you're right." Dana closed the newspaper. "Let's go sit outside."

They sat on the stoop watching people walk by. Others were out on their stoops talking to neighbors.

Mrs. Smith from down the street ran out of her house, chasing Mr. Smith with a broom. "Get away from here, Jerry. Go on somewhere."

Dana and Lisa laughed. Then Dana said, "This is the second time this week she chased him out of the house. It's a shame to see. They used to be so happy."

"Mr. Smith has a drinking problem. I've seen him sitting out by the store with some of the other winos."

Rolling her eyes, Dana asked, "Have you decided on a major yet?"

"I'm doing liberal arts with a minor in social work."

Dana lifted an eyebrow. "You not going to college to be some broke social worker. Naw, not for you."

"I don't see it like that," Lisa told her. "There are people out here who really need help. Need someone who can guide them in the right direction and get things done to build up the community."

"Yeah, but why social work?"

"I believe God is directing me toward this path." Lisa smiled. "And like Elsie Richardson told me, somebody has to be a change agent in our community. Why not me?"

Dana scrunched her nose. "Why would God care what you do with your life?"

Lisa nudged Dana with her shoulder. "Instead of asking me all these questions, you should come to church and get a word from God yourself."

Dana thought about it for a moment. She admired how Lisa seemed to know what she wanted to do with her life. She didn't think social work was for her, but maybe she did need a revelation on what came next. "I might attend with you Sunday."

"I'm serious, Dana. This is the last time I'm going to ask you. And I won't be here much longer."

Dana put her elbow on her thigh and then a fisted hand under her chin. "I'm thinking on it. Chill. I might come down there."

They continued sitting on the stoop until Derrick came over. Lisa stood up. "I guess I'll get to the store. I need to put in some hours."

"You don't have to leave. Why don't you stay so you can get to know Derrick?"

"Can't." She waved at Dana as she headed up the street. "See you tomorrow or at church on Sunday."

"You're going to church?" Derrick asked as he sat down next to Dana.

"I'm thinking about it. Lisa invited me, and she won't be here much longer since she's leaving for college soon."

Derrick put an arm around her. "Don't go getting all holy on me. I'm not with all that church stuff."

"What's so bad about church?"

Derrick smirked. "I told you what I'm about. I don't need no guilt trip coming from my woman."

God help her, she liked hearing him call her his woman. Dana grinned and snuggled close to him.

Lisa loved coming to church the Sunday after Evangelism Week. She was able to see how many new faces showed up for service. Most of the people who came to church after Evangelism Week were like the ones who attended on Resurrection Sunday—here today, gone tomorrow. But a few received the word Pastor Jonathan delivered, and it stuck like hot caramel to popcorn.

Lisa was always so happy for the ones who discovered joy in Jesus. She prayed Dana would walk through the church doors this morning. Maybe something in Pastor Jonathan's sermon would give her friend the motivation needed to change her life.

Praise and worship started. The choir at Praise Ministries was anointed. They could sing you into a happy place even if you were feeling down. Lisa glanced around the sanctuary. Still no Dana.

Please, Lord. Let Dana experience worship and come to know You in a special way, she prayed as the choir sang "I Give Myself to You" by Rance Allen. Lisa sang along in her seat at the back of the church.

When the choir began another song, Lisa glanced around the church again. Still no Dana. She left the sanctuary, went into the fellowship hall, and opened the back door to look out. She glanced up the street in the direction Dana would walk from, but she didn't see her.

Lisa's shoulders caved in as she went back to the sanctuary. She had prayed for Dana, hoping her friend would come to realize her way was not the right way. Elsie Richardson had asked that Lisa try to make a difference, but if Dana couldn't even show up for church . . .

Praise and worship was almost over when she reclaimed her spot in the back of the sanctuary. She'd started singing again when someone scooted into the pew next to her and said, "Girl, you are not making a joyful noise. Just stop."

Lisa turned to her left and saw Dana standing there grinning at her. "You made it!" Lisa hugged her.

"I didn't have anything else to do." Then Dana whispered, "And you did say there would be dinner after service, right?"

Lisa laughed. As the last praise song ended, they sat down and enjoyed the rest of the service. Pastor Jonathan preached a message titled "Your Struggle Is About to Change Your Whole Life." Lisa wasn't sure whether Dana was listening to the sermon, but at least she sat through the service. Lisa could only hope Dana took in some of Pastor Jonathan's message.

After the benediction, Dana and Lisa went into the fellowship hall to eat dinner. A few other girls who graduated with them came over to say hello to Lisa and Dana.

Dana pulled her camera out of her purse. "Huddle up. I want to take y'all's picture."

The group struck a pose together, and Dana snapped the photo.

Lisa's mom walked over to the group. She held out her hand to Dana. "Get in there. I'll take your picture with the girls."

Dana handed her the camera. "Thank you."

The group huddled up again and posed for the camera. "Say cheese," Brenda said.

"Cheese," the five girls said in unison.

After the picture was taken, Brenda told Dana, "When you get the film developed, I'd like a copy of the photo. This will probably be the last picture of these girls together before they go off to college."

Dana nodded. "I'll bring the picture to you, Mrs. Whitaker."

"Have you given any more thought to college, Dana? You're such a smart girl. I think you can do it."

Lisa caught the look of sadness on Dana's face after her mother asked her about college, so she jumped in. "We have to get going, Mama, but thanks for taking the picture."

"Where are you going?" Brenda asked Lisa. "I thought you were supposed to work at the corner store for your father this afternoon."

Lisa waved that off. "I'll get over there later on. Dana and I were going to hang out for a little while. Right, Dana?" Lisa looked to her friend to get her out of working at the store. Her dad wanted to do inventory today. Lisa hated doing inventory with her dad. He always corrected her numbers.

Dana lifted her camera. "We were going to take more pictures with my new camera."

"Okay. You girls go on. But, Lisa, you need to get to the store later on this afternoon."

"I will, Mama, I promise. I want to hang out a little while first, though."

Her mom kissed her on the forehead and walked away.

Lisa saw Dana frown again and wondered why she would frown about something like a forehead kiss. Maybe Dana thought her mother was treating her like a baby or something. So she wiped her mother's lipstick from her face as the two of them left the church and headed down the street in the heat of the day.

CHAPTER 6

Dana went to Lisa's house with her so she could change her clothes. The cool air caressed their bodies as they opened the front door. "Oh my goodness, it feels good in here."

"After walking them blocks and sweating every step . . ." Lisa sighed. "I wish we could put an air conditioner on our backs before we leave out again."

Dana laughed. But Lisa put one of her mother's accordion fans in her purse before they walked to the game room on Halsey Street. It was a spacious building with three floors. The game room was on the first floor and apartments on the second and third floors. Pac-Man and Centipede, along with pinball machines, lined the walls, with pool tables and table tennis in the middle of the floor. Games were only a quarter, so even Dana could afford a few when she wanted to play.

"Do you know how long it's been since I've been in this game room?" Lisa asked Dana as they took turns on the Pac-Man machine.

"Years. You never come here with me."

Lisa nodded. "Not since you and I played this very game the summer of our last year in junior high."

Lisa took her turn behind the machine. "I'm not as good as you are. I'm rusty."

"Give it your best shot."

As Lisa played Pac-Man, Dana brought up the past again. "If your daddy hadn't stopped you from hanging out in here, you'd know how to play the game."

"He doesn't like it here. Says there's too many kids hanging out, doing nothing, around here." Lisa then glanced over at Dana. "And you had a new group of friends anyway . . . girls that didn't like me."

Dana protested. "None of my friends ever said they didn't like you."

"They made fun of me, Dana. That's not being friendly where I come from." Lisa lost the game, and they moved over to Centipede.

Dana hadn't stood up for Lisa back then. She was trying to fit in herself. And having a friend like Lisa, who was the do-no-wrong kid of the neighborhood, made it difficult for Dana. She wasn't a church kid, but she hadn't been a street kid—until she started hanging out with her new friends.

Back then, Dana figured there was no reason for her to go to church with her mother, who was usually high, so she made her choice. She and Lisa stayed friends, but she also hung out with people like Jasmine. "I could have stood up for you back then, but my head was in another place. I was dealing with my own stuff."

"Hey, are y'all going to play or talk?" a guy standing behind Lisa asked.

"We're talking, so I guess we'll move out of the way since it's such an emergency," Dana said to the guy, then grabbed Lisa's arm and moved away from the Centipede machine.

Lisa pointed back at the Centipede game. “I thought we were going to play.”

“Come on, girl.” They walked over to the pinball machine. Dana whispered to Lisa, “He’s Jo-Jo’s son. He’s one of the biggest gangsters in Bed-Stuy, so we don’t want no trouble from them.”

Lisa looked back at the guy who made them move away from the Centipede game. He was short and stocky, with baggy jeans and tattoos on his arms. “No wonder my daddy told me not to come to this game room anymore.” Lisa started walking toward the door.

Dana caught up with her as they stepped outside. “You’re being a big scaredy-cat.”

“Oh, I’m the scaredy-cat, huh? You’re the one who moved me away from the game so some gangster’s son could take our spot. Looks like these thugs around here have put some fear in you.”

“I’m not scared. I know the deal, is all. You don’t be out on these streets, so you don’t know what’s up.”

They were getting ready to turn on Lewis Avenue and walk to Dana’s place when they ran into a group of men leaning against the outer wall of the game room. A guy in the group stepped forward and handed a woman a small packet. The woman, who looked like she should be somewhere holding an “I’m homeless, will work for food” sign, handed him some money.

Running her hand through her hair, Lisa said, “A lot has changed since we were younger.”

Dana wished things were different, but wishes and dreams didn’t mean a thing around here. She wished beauty existed where ugliness seemed to prevail. “Come back here for a minute. I forgot to do something.”

Dana and Lisa then stood in front of the game room while Dana asked one of the passersby to take a picture of them in front of the building.

"What's the deal with you and this camera?"

Dana glanced back at the group of guys. "I want to capture some goodness in this world with my camera. And our friendship is the best."

When Dana and Lisa arrived at the apartment, Dana didn't want to go inside and deal with her mother, so they sat on the stoop and watched the people go up and down the street. The sun beat down on their heads. Lisa took her fan out of her purse, and she and Dana took turns using it.

A guy headed up the street, blasting "You Brought the Sunshine" by the Clark Sisters on his boom box. A few kids chased each other down the street. Yelling, "You're it . . . no, you're it."

Jasmine came by and sat down with them. Then Dana saw Shayla, a girl they went to school with, walking on the other side of the street. She shouted, "Shayla, come here!"

Shayla hesitated.

"We're not going to eat you for lunch." Dana held up her camera. "I want to take your picture, that's all."

Shayla crossed the street and came over to where they were sitting. She spoke to Jasmine and then looked at Lisa. "I thought your daddy didn't like you hanging out with the riffraff."

"Who you calling *riffraff*?" Dana stood up like she was ready to defend herself. But first she had to wipe sweat from her forehead. The sun was clowning on them.

Mr. Adams, from next door, got his wrench out and uncapped the fire hydrant. His teenage son started scraping an aluminum can on the ground to smooth the edges so he wouldn't cut his hand. Then he put the can over the hole where water was flowing out of the hydrant. Water began spraying everywhere.

Dana quickly forgot her beef with Shayla. She snapped their picture, then pointed toward the fire hydrant. "Look, let's go, y'all."

But Lisa complained, "I don't want to get my hair wet."

Jasmine jumped up. "It's so hot out here, I don't care about my hair." She ran toward the water. Other kids were gathering in the street, taking joy in the relief from the heat. Dana ran into the water, then the next thing she knew, Shayla was in the water, too, jumping around and laughing.

When she noticed Lisa was still sitting on the stoop sweating like a pitcher of ice water, she went over to her, grabbed hold of her arms, and pulled her up. "Come on, girl. Act like you're being baptized."

"Okay, okay." Lisa laid her purse on the stoop and ran into the water with Dana.

Dana splashed water on her friends, and they splashed it back on her. The water dripped on her like a cold winter's rain—swept across her face as if a rushing mighty wind was sent to cool her down.

Dana twirled around in the water, wishing she could capture the moment with her camera. Mr. Adams was standing to the side, gleefully watching them. Dana pointed toward the stoop. "Take our picture," she called out to him.

"Look at my hair!" Lisa yelled.

"My hair is a mess, too, but don't you feel better?" Dana said.

"Much," Jasmine answered.

Dana posed for the camera as Mr. Adams started taking photos.

Lisa smiled, splashed some water on Dana. "I feel cooler, for sure."

Mr. Adams set the camera back down on the stoop next to Lisa's purse.

The girls let the cool water hit every part of their bodies. When they stepped away from the water, everyone was drenched. The girls started twisting their hair to drain the water.

Dana told them, "I have some towels. Let me get y'all some." Dana went into the bottom level of the brownstone. She opened the door and started walking toward the linen closet. But then she saw her mom stretched out on the floor having convulsions.

Dana's eyes did the screaming for her. She ran back to the front door, opened it, and yelled, "Help! My mom needs help!" Then she got down on the floor and tried to shake her mother.

"Ma! Ma! What's wrong? Are you having another seizure?"

Mr. Adams, Lisa, and Shayla came into the house. Mr. Adams pushed her aside. "Don't shake her. Go get me a spoon."

Dana jumped up, ran into the kitchen to get the spoon. Once she was back in the living room, she handed it to Mr. Adams, and he pressed it against her mother's tongue.

"Call the ambulance!" he shouted.

"We don't have a phone," Dana told him, eyes downcast as she spoke. "It got cut off."

"Go to my house and tell my wife you need to call for an ambulance."

Dana and Lisa ran out of the house and took the steps to Mr. Adams' brownstone two at a time. Dana banged on his front door. Mrs. Adams swung the door open and started wagging her finger in Dana's face. "Now see here—"

Lisa held up a hand. "We need help. Mr. Adams wants you to call 911."

Mrs. Adams stepped onto the porch, concern etched on her face. "Is something wrong with my husband?"

"My mom is having convulsions." Dana ran back down the steps as she shouted, "Mr. Adams is trying to help her now!"

"Please call the ambulance." Lisa stood next to Mrs. Adams, wringing her hands.

"Okay, y'all go back to the house. I'll call right now."

Dana and Lisa ran back into the apartment. Shayla was still there, standing in the entryway with tears rolling down her face. Dana's mother was propped against the wall next to the table where Dana's record player had been. The convulsions had stopped. Dana noticed her mother was dazed and still looked like she was out of it. She also noticed her record player was gone.

Dana sat on the floor next to her mother. "Ma, what did you do?" Tears streamed down Dana's face as her mother labored to breathe. Her head leaned to the side like she was about to nod out.

"You can't keep doing this stuff, Vida. You have a daughter to think about," Mr. Adams told her.

Vida's head bobbed back and forth. Her eyes opened and closed like she was trying to regain her focus.

Dana kept crying. She held on to her mother's hand. She didn't care about the record player. She wanted her mother to be okay. "Don't die on me, Ma," she whispered into Vida's ear.

Lisa put a hand on Dana's back. Dana could hear her friend praying for her.

The sirens of the ambulance could be heard outside. Mr. Adams told them, "The paramedics are here. Y'all need to move so they can get to your mother."

Dana swallowed hard as Lisa helped her stand. But she kept her eyes on her mother while the paramedics checked Vida's vitals.

"Looks like an overdose," one of them said as they put her on the stretcher.

Dana followed behind the stretcher as they wheeled her mother to the ambulance. She grabbed hold of her mother's hand and begged, "Please get better. Please don't die on me."

The tears kept coming. They lifted Vida into the ambulance. Dana wrapped her arms around herself and tried as best she could to comfort herself. Slowly lifting her head, she saw Derrick running down the street toward her. She felt so alone at this moment, she needed his presence.

When Derrick reached her, he pulled her close. "You good? You good? Jasmine called and told me about your mom."

Wiping her eyes, Dana looked around. The paramedics were locking Vida's bed in place. Lisa and Shayla were standing next to the stoop where she had left her camera. But she didn't see her camera on the stoop, nor did she see Jasmine. "Where did Jasmine go?"

Derrick shrugged. "I don't know."

Vida moaned.

Dana reached out her hand. "Ma!" She turned back to Derrick, tears streaming down her face. "I've got to go."

Derrick asked the paramedic where they were taking Vida

as Dana climbed into the ambulance. "I'll meet you at the hospital."

"Thank you." She needed someone and was so thankful Derrick was willing to sit at the hospital with her. As the doors on the ambulance were closing, Dana heard Lisa say, "Where's my purse?"

CHAPTER 7

By the time she made it to the house, Lisa had worked herself into such a frenzy that she was crying when she opened the front door. Her parents were seated at the dining room table. It looked like they were in the middle of a serious discussion with the way they were looking at each other and shaking their heads.

Lisa hated interrupting them, but she had a problem and needed their help. "Mom, Dad!" she bellowed as she stood in front of them.

Brenda jumped out of her seat. "Lisa, what in the world?" She rushed over to her daughter and wiped the tears from her face. "What happened, honey?"

"It—it was terrible." Lisa's shoulders shook. She wrapped her arms around her mother. She was so grateful to have a mother like Brenda Whitaker. Her mother went to work and church and kept her house clean and her family fed. Her mother volunteered at the homeless shelter and at the 262, helping young kids learn to read. She was a good mother and Lisa admired her. "Dana's mother was taken to the hospital. She overdosed."

"Oh, my sweet Lord. How is Dana doing?" Brenda asked.

"She's totally distraught."

Her father got up from the table and came to where Lisa was standing. While her mother had an arm around her, comforting her, her daddy wagged a finger in her face. "You weren't supposed to be with Dana anyway. I told you that girl was trouble. But you wouldn't listen. And now you come home traumatized."

She knew he would be like this. It was going to be worse when she told him about her purse. But she couldn't keep it from them, not when her identification was in it. "Daddy, don't be so mean. Ms. Vida almost died," she bawled as more tears rolled down her cheeks. "Why can't you listen?"

Brenda lifted a hand to her husband as she rubbed Lisa's shoulder. "We're listening, dear."

"Yes, there is something else she needs to tell us," David said with his arms folded, "I need to know why she was even at her friend's house when she was supposed to be at the store."

Lisa stomped her foot in frustration. Her daddy attended church every week, like she and her mother did, but he must have been in the hallway when the pastor gave sermons on forgiveness and having grace for others. He didn't seem to have any for her.

Lisa was so distressed from the events of the day she couldn't bear the lecture that was sure to come from her dad if he found out her purse had been stolen, so she said, "You're right, Dad. I should have been at the store. I'm going to change my clothes and go down there now."

Wiping the rest of the tears from her face, Lisa turned to go upstairs. Her mother stopped her. "What else is on your mind? You know you can tell us anything."

She could tell her mom anything. Brenda Whitaker was a kind woman, full of grace, but her daddy was hard and unrelenting. She didn't want to hear more judgment from him about the decisions she'd made when all she had done was hang out with a friend who was going through a really tough time.

Lisa went upstairs to her room and changed into a pair of tan pants and a white-collar shirt and then left the house. She thought about the purse situation as she walked to the corner store. Her mother would know all she needed to do to get her identification before she left for school, but Lisa would have to figure it out herself. There was no way she was going to take another lecture from her father.

She was about to be on her own. She wished she had applied to a college in upstate New York, then she would be farther away from her parents and wouldn't be expected to come home on weekends.

Lisa prayed for Vida as she walked. She felt bad for Dana. She saw how distraught she had been when she got in the ambulance with her mother. But Lisa's mind was also on her purse.

So distracted by the events of the day, Lisa was almost at the front door of her father's store before she noticed the artist who painted the faces of people on the In Loving Memory mural.

The artist was climbing the ladder with his paintbrush and paint supplies. Curiosity got the better of Lisa. She hadn't heard about anyone dying in the neighborhood lately. Her forehead crinkled as she turned toward the ladder. She put her hand over her eyebrows to get the sun out of her eyesight as she looked up.

"I didn't hear about anyone dying."

The painter looked down at her and gave her a wry smile. "The local news don't care about a wino's liver giving out on him, but we do."

"What wino?" As Lisa waited for an answer, she thought about the three winos who normally sat on milk crates outside the store. She glanced around but didn't see any of them sitting out, drinking wine from a brown paper bag while talking all kinds of smack.

"Mr. Taylor. Cirrhosis took him out last night. I got the call this morning." The artist continued up the ladder.

Lisa went into the store, all the while thinking about Mr. Taylor. He might have been drunk half his life, but he always had a kind word for her when she saw him on the street. At that moment, she wondered why she hadn't spent more time praying for him.

"You look like you've got the weight of the world on your shoulders."

Lisa looked to her right and saw Terri Milner. She worked part-time for her dad and was stocking chips on the shelf. "I saw the artist who paints the faces on the In Loving Memory wall. He said Mr. Taylor died."

Terri's hand went to her mouth. She blew out air. "I'm so sorry to hear that. Mr. Taylor was a nice man."

A customer entered the store. Lisa stood behind the counter while Terri continued shelving the chips. After about a minute, the customer put a 100 Grand bar, a bag of barbecue Bon Tons, and a can of soda on the counter. She rang him up, then bagged his items and handed them to him.

Terri walked over to the counter with the empty box. "It's been a slow day, so I was able to refill the shelves."

Glancing out the store window, Lisa saw people going here and there, into the corner store across the street that had a meat department with a butcher on staff, but very few were coming into their store. She told Terri, "If you want to leave early, I can close up. Dad will be down shortly anyway. We're going to do inventory this evening."

Terri glanced at her watch. "Are you sure you don't mind being here by yourself?"

Lisa pointed at the cameras on the wall by the front door. "My dad has this place filled with so many cameras, I seriously doubt I'll have any problems."

"Let me go home and check on my kids, then I'll come back to help you and Mr. Whitaker with inventory."

Lisa blurted, "One day I'm going to get a community center started. It will have after-school and summer programs for the kids in this neighborhood. Then you won't have to leave them babies by themselves while you work."

Terri patted Lisa on the shoulder as she headed for the door. "I'll be the first one to sign up. Just make sure it's affordable."

"It's going to be free. I promise you," Lisa told her. Terri was one of her dad's best workers. Her husband was in the military, so she was often left to take care of their three children on her own. There was never enough money for babysitters, so her children were frequently left at home while she worked. She lived in an apartment a block up from the store, so she was able to check on them during each break.

After college, Lisa wanted to work in social services. She prayed she would be able to solve the day-care dilemma for so many of the women in their community. It was a travesty. Women had to work to take care of their families but couldn't afford proper care for their children while they worked.

A few more customers came in; Lisa cashed them out as they grabbed chips and soda. One of the customers wanted a hero sandwich with turkey and ham. Her dad had taught her how to fix those sandwiches. She made it and cashed the customer out as Dana walked into the store.

Lisa waved at her when she finished up with her customer. "How's your mother?" It had been about three hours since Dana's mother was taken to the hospital.

"She's doing better, but they're going to keep her overnight at St. John's."

"You mean Interfaith Medical Center?" Lisa corrected.

Dana gave her a raised eyebrow.

"The hospital," Lisa said. "It's no longer St. John's. Interfaith took it over a couple of years ago."

Many of the Bed-Stuy residents still referred to the hospital as St. John's. The hospital had been a staple in the neighborhood. At one time, it had been the largest employer in Central Brooklyn. But as the white, affluent residents fled the area as Black and brown residents moved in, St. John's began to struggle, with so many of the new residents relying on Medicare and Medicaid. Government insurance paid less than private health insurance companies. So Interfaith was able to take over the hospital.

This government-sponsored-insurance-versus-private-health-insurance issue had come up in her political science class during her senior year in high school. Lisa didn't think it was right for hospitals and doctors to overcharge private insurers and then be in dire straits when forced to accept government-backed insurance. This was one reason lower-income families didn't always receive the best care available. Doctors would take only a limited number of patients with government insurance. Another thing that needed to be changed.

Dana tapped her forehead with her index finger. "I keep forgetting the name of the hospital changed. Anyway . . ."

She then lifted Lisa's purse and handed it to her. "I stopped in to bring you this."

Lisa's eyes got big. "Oh my goodness. Where did you find it?" Lisa unzipped her purse and pulled out her billfold. Her state ID and her Social Security card were there, but no money. She turned back to Dana. "I had twenty dollars in my wallet."

Dana shrugged. "Jasmine must've taken it. I went by her house after I left the hospital. I figured she took our stuff, and sure enough, she had your purse and my camera." Dana's mouth curved upward to the right as she added, "Talking 'bout how she grabbed our stuff so it wouldn't get stolen."

"Then why'd she steal my money?" The whole ordeal was stupefying to Lisa. Why did people put their hands on things that didn't belong to them?

"Because Jasmine steals. I've seen her in action. That's why Derrick and I went to her house after we left the hospital."

"What am I supposed to do about my money? Sheesh, the people you hang around are wack."

"Well, dang, you'd think you would say thank you or something." Dana rolled her eyes.

Lisa wasn't really mad at Dana, but she was upset about the choices Dana made. "I wish you wouldn't hang around those people."

"Neither of you should be hanging around with people who steal from you."

Lisa's and Dana's heads swiveled toward the door, where Lisa's father was standing with a scowl.

Dana waved. "Hi, Mr. Whitaker."

He nodded. "How is your mother?"

"Pray for her, please," Dana said woefully. She turned back to Lisa. "I'll see you later." She left the store.

Lisa put her purse under the counter and did her best not to look her father in the eye. "You ready to do the inventory?"

He loomed over her. "Right after you tell me what's going on with you."

CHAPTER 8

Vida came home from the hospital Monday afternoon. Dana was sitting in the living room holding the vacate order issued by the police this morning. She handed it to her mother. "What are we going to do? The police are going to throw our stuff on the street if we don't pack up and get out of here in three days."

"Well, hello to you too," Vida said as she took the notice out of Dana's hand.

Her mother stumbled backward as she raised the notice to her face.

Dana put her hands to her head and pulled her hair. "How could you do this to us again? We were doing fine before you decided to smoke crack and ruin our lives."

Lowering the notice, Vida sat down next to Dana. She put a hand on Dana's cheek as a tear trickled down her face. "I'm sorry, baby. I know I need to do better."

Dana let go of her hair but started pacing the floor while rubbing her temples with her index fingers. When she was young, her mother would put her arms around her and pull her into a hug. Back then, after a hug from her mom, Dana knew her day was about to be special. But as Vida put those skin-to-the-bone arms around Dana today, it didn't bring her comfort. "Where are we going to live now, Ma?"

Vida wiped her face. "I'll go down to the county and see if they can help us. Don't worry. I'll take care of this."

But Dana was worried. She was still waiting on callbacks from some of the applications she put in.

She went outside and sat down on the stoop. This was supposed to be a good summer. She had just graduated high school. Dana didn't have money or any scholarships to go to college, but she still thought she would figure out some things and get her life on track. She did have a high school diploma, and that had to count for something.

Where were they going to live once they left this apartment? Dana's elbow was on her knee. She lowered her head and put her hand under her chin as she watched people walk by.

Why did she have to live with a mother who couldn't take care of herself, let alone a child? But then again, Dana wasn't a child anymore. She was eighteen and needed to make some moves.

As she was full of thoughts and wonder, Derrick came up the street and sat down next to her. "How's your mom?"

Rolling her eyes, Dana told him, "She's back home, but now we're getting evicted."

"Word?" He shook his head. "Yo, Dana, don't sweat it. After we do this job tonight, there will be plenty of money to pay rent."

Job? Dana scratched her head. Then she remembered. Derrick expected her to help him rob a store tonight. "Look, Derrick, I'm not like you and Jasmine. I'm not comfortable with taking things that don't belong to me."

Derrick leaned his head back and laughed like he'd never

heard anything so funny. "It's called stealing. I told you how I earn my living. You can't get all squeamish on me now."

"It's not my thing."

"You need the money, babe. This is for you too. And anyway, you don't have to go inside the place. I need you to be outside and signal me if you see anyone coming."

Derrick was looking at her with those gorgeous brown eyes. He put a hand on her arm. His hand felt good . . . warm. Maybe Derrick had the right idea. Nobody was giving her anything in this world. She needed to get out there and start taking things.

"I want to help you, babe, but you gotta help me too." His hand moved in circular motions on her arm, then he leaned in and kissed her like a man who was hungry for everything she had to give. "You know how it is around here."

Yeah, she knew. It was Bed-Stuy, do or die. But was she ready to do what he was asking?

"You in?"

She loved being with Derrick like this. She loved how he wanted to help her out of the jam her mother had gotten them into. And she did need the money. "I don't have to go in the store, right?"

"No, babe. I wouldn't put you in harm's way."

What was she doing? Why had she agreed to be Derrick's lookout? Dana didn't want to be a part of any theft, but when she was around Derrick, he made her feel loved. She felt special in his presence, felt seen. No man had ever looked at her the way Derrick did. With things falling apart for her, she needed Derrick.

A car pulled up as Dana sat on the stoop waiting on Derrick. It was a gray Chevy Caprice with tinted windows. The passenger-side door opened, and Derrick stepped out. He was wearing a black hoodie with black jeans and a pair of black-and-white Nikes.

He smiled at her, and she melted.

"You ready?"

A moment's hesitation, then Dana pushed herself up from the stoop. He opened the back passenger door for her. Dana climbed in, but as Derrick closed the door, she glanced toward the driver's seat and saw Jasmine behind the wheel. "What are you doing here?"

"I'm getting my cut, that's what I'm doing," Jasmine told her.

"Whose car are you driving?"

Jasmine giggled. "My uncle took a nap, and I snatched his keys. He'll be out for a while, so we don't have to hurry."

Dana had been friends with Jasmine for only a couple of years. Honestly, she didn't know the girl stole so much. But she was starting to understand why so many things came up missing in some of the classes they had together.

Lisa had told Dana she hung out with the wrong people. Since she had signed on to be the lookout for a robbery with these two professional thieves, she could no longer deny the truth of Lisa's words.

Jasmine nudged her head to the right, then told Derrick, "Look in the glove compartment."

He popped open the glove compartment. "Oh snap."

Dana heard the excitement in Derrick's voice as he lifted a gun with his right hand, then high-fived Jasmine with the left. "I knew you could score. Girl, you got skills."

"So I've been told." Jasmine pulled onto the street. "We getting ready to get paid."

Everything in Dana screamed *Noooo!* Warning signs flashed before her eyes as sweat beads gathered on her forehead. "Let me out," Dana demanded. She was done with Jasmine when she stole her camera and Lisa's purse. Now she was stealing cars and bringing guns. This wasn't Dana's speed.

Derrick turned around in his seat and looked at Dana like she was a child who needed to be scolded. "Don't get scared on me now. You know what's up."

"I'm not getting scared. But you never said anything about a gun."

"Ain't nobody gon' get hurt. Chill with that," he told her and then turned back around in his seat.

Dana kicked the seat.

"Quit tripping, Dana, and don't tear up my uncle's car."

"Forget you, Jasmine. I don't have anything else to say to you. Matter of fact, y'all can let me out right here." Dana grabbed hold of the door handle.

Jasmine pulled the car in front of the pizza parlor Derrick took Dana to last week. Derrick turned back to Dana. "Babe, look . . . me and Jasmine are going to hit this spot." He pointed toward the pizza parlor. "I need you to calm down and sit in this car with the window rolled down. If you see any cops or anything that looks suspicious, then holler as loud as you can, "Time's up!"

"Why do you have a gun, Derrick? You never said anything about shooting nobody." Dana was scared. What had she gotten herself into? Derrick was a stick-up kid, and Jasmine was cut from the same cloth. But she didn't want to steal. And she certainly didn't want to hurt anyone.

"You need rent money, don't you? You better get it together so we can make this money," Derrick said.

"It's a pizza shop. They don't have enough money to make any difference."

He pulled a napkin out of his pocket. "They have a safe in the back, and I have the combination." He waved the napkin in her face.

Dana thought back to the day Derrick brought her here to get a slice of pizza. She thought he was being good to her. But she remembered when the busboy handed him those napkins and Derrick put one in his pocket.

Now she wondered whether Derrick had taken her out. Had he truly wanted to be with her or was she just a decoy for his scouting trip.

Jasmine opened the driver's side door. "Are we going or not?"

Derrick leaned toward Dana. He planted a kiss on her forehead, then looked in her eyes. "I'm doing this for us, babe." He pointed at her door. "Roll down your window and look out for your man."

Jasmine looked at Dana and rolled her eyes. Stepping out of the car, she reached under the driver's seat and pulled something out. It wasn't until Jasmine stuffed the item in the top of her pants that Dana realized Jasmine had a gun too.

Derrick got out of the car. He and Jasmine walked into the pizza parlor and went right up to the checkout counter like they were getting ready to order a slice. Dana rolled the window down. From where she sat in the back seat of the car, in front of the big glass windows on the double-door entry, she could see every inch of the pizza parlor. She started shaking as Derrick and Jasmine pulled out their guns simultaneously.

What was she doing? Why was she here? Dana was terrified. She put her hand on the door handle, seriously thinking about leaving her post. She saw the clerk open the register and hand Derrick the money while Jasmine had her gun trained on the busboy. The same busboy who handed Derrick those napkins last week.

Dana started looking around, trying to see whether anyone was paying attention to what Derrick and Jasmine were doing. But most people walked on by, not looking anywhere but straight ahead. Then she saw Derrick point toward the back door. The clerk moved from behind the cash register and opened the door to the back of the shop. Derrick disappeared behind the door with the clerk.

Dana's stomach tied itself in knots. Yes, she and her mother needed money, but they didn't need it this bad, did they? She opened the door and got out of the car. She was going to walk home. Dana didn't care if Derrick broke up with her. This was not the life for her.

Bang! Bang!

Dana dropped down at the side of the building and craned her neck so she could peek into the parlor. She saw Jasmine moonwalking toward the door. The busboy ducked behind one of the tables. Jasmine opened the door and ran out. Then she got back in the car and quickly started it.

"Wait!" Dana yelled. She jumped up from her spot against the wall of the building. "Where's Derrick?" she yelled at Jasmine.

Jasmine sped off.

"Wait!" Dana screamed again. But Jasmine kept going. Dana swung around and saw the door to the back room of the pizza parlor open. Derrick shuffled out, holding his chest as he ran toward the entrance. Blood was on his shirt and dripping from his hand as he pressed it against his chest. He struggled to push open the glass doors. Dana's mind was telling her to flee, but her heart prompted her to help her man.

Her heart won the battle. And as the clerk came out of the back, chasing after Derrick, Dana pulled the door open so Derrick could escape. She saw a gun in the clerk's hand. He raised it and fired a shot.

Derrick dropped to the ground, blood splattering everywhere. Dana screamed. "D-D-Derrick. Oh my God!" Her face was an ocean of tears as she fell to her knees next to Derrick's bloody body.

She put his head on her lap. "Derrick, Derrick, can you hear me? Please don't die. Don't die, okay?"

Dana rubbed his face with her now blood-soaked hands. His eyes fluttered. "I'm here, baby. Don't die on me."

She heard sirens. Dana prayed someone had called an ambulance for Derrick. Her heart was so heavy at seeing him fall to the ground covered in blood. But when she glanced up, the clerk was standing above her, pointing the gun at her.

"Don't move. The law will take care of you."

Derrick jerked in her arms. "Call an ambulance!" she screamed at the man.

Dana's hands trembled, not only because someone was holding a gun on her, but Derrick jerked again. His stomach heaved, blood trickled from his mouth as the light in those gorgeous eyes of his dimmed, and he went still.

"*Noooo!*" She held on to him and hugged him tight, not wanting to let him go or acknowledge he was really and truly gone. Her tears dropped on his face as she was roughly snatched away.

"Stand up. Put your hands against the wall."

Dana's head swiveled around. A police officer was holding on to her arm. He shoved her against the wall. "Hands up."

"I didn't do anything!" Dana screamed. She pointed at the clerk. "He's the one with the gun."

The officer took her hands and roughly placed them against the wall. He then kicked her legs out and began patting her down. He read her rights, handcuffed her, and put her in the back of his police car.

All the while, Dana was screaming, "Why are you doing this? I didn't do anything wrong!"

The officer slammed the door and then went back to stand next to Derrick's lifeless body. Tears like a river cascaded down her face. Derrick was dead. She would never see him again. She was in the back of a police car, and she had no idea what was going to happen. Dana only knew she wanted to go home.

But where was home for her? Could God really be so cruel as to trade the bad situation her mother created by getting them evicted for a worse one? She'd rather sleep on the streets than spend one night in jail, but who would help her? Who could she turn to?

CHAPTER 9

It was Tuesday afternoon and Lisa was getting ready to leave the corner store when she noticed a crowd gathering outside.

Her daddy was standing behind the checkout counter. "What in the world is going on out there?"

"Who knows?" Lisa said as she stepped outside. She scanned the area. To her left was the memorial wall. The artist was on his ladder painting another face on it. A group of kids who looked to be about her age gathered on the sidewalk, looking up as the artist painted.

Lisa wanted to know who had died, but she didn't want to stand out there with the crowd. She knew her dad would come out of the store and tell her to go home, so she started walking toward the house.

Shayla approached her. She hadn't seen Shayla since that hot day they jumped in front of the fire hydrant and let the water cool them off.

"Hey, girl. Did you hear what happened?"

Lisa kept walking; Shayla walked with her. "What happened when?"

"Oh my goodness, you really don't know, do you?"

Lisa lifted her hands, shrugged her shoulders. Then she

glanced back at the crowd of people and the artist as he painted. "Don't tell me one of our classmates died."

Shayla said, "Derrick Little got shot and killed last night."

Lisa glanced at the wall again. "Dana's Derrick?"

"Yes, girl. He tried to rob a pizza parlor, and the owner shot him."

Lisa turned to look at the crowd again. Where was Dana? She would expect to see her out here if her boyfriend had gotten shot. Or maybe she was at home crying her eyes out. She asked Shayla, "Have you seen Dana? How is she doing?"

Shayla rolled her eyes heavenward. "You're not going to believe this, but Dana was with him."

Sharp intake of breath. "Dana didn't get shot. Please don't tell me she did."

"No, but she got arrested. They're saying she was the lookout person."

Lisa widened her eyes in horror. Her hand went to her mouth. She couldn't speak. She had no words. *Dana . . . what have you done? Why?* Her eyes glistened as a tear trickled down her cheek.

Dana never should have dated a guy like Derrick in the first place. She wasn't the type of person to steal. Lisa had told her to get away from Derrick. Now her friend was paying the price of being with a man like him.

"I'm sorry—I thought you knew." Shayla hugged her and then stepped away.

"I didn't."

Shayla hesitated a moment, then said, "I feel bad, but I've got to go. My mom's taking me shopping. I leave for college tomorrow."

"I'm happy for you, Shayla. You go on." Lisa started

walking up the street with a heavy heart. All the way home, with every step Lisa took, she called out Dana's name to the Lord. *Help Dana, Lord. Bring her out of this situation and bring good people into her life. Thank You, Jesus.*

Dana spent the rest of the week crying herself to sleep on the dirty cot she had been instructed to lie on in her cell. A cell she shared with three other girls. This was the week some of her friends were going off to college, while she waited to go to court to find out how much time they would give her for being in the wrong place at the wrong time.

And better yet, being in love with the wrong guy. She still couldn't believe Derrick was dead. Somehow she expected to see his smiling face again, telling her he was going to get her out of this jam.

But as she sat up on her cot and rocked back and forth, Dana knew Derrick wasn't coming to rescue her. No one was. Not even her mother.

Vida had visited her once in the entire week she'd been locked up like a caged animal. "*I'm going to get you out of here*," Vida had told her as they cried together.

Dana hoped her mother would come through for her, but after not hearing from her the rest of the week, Dana felt her hope begin to wane, as it did with every promise Vida had ever made to her.

She made two collect calls to Lisa's house, but neither call had been accepted. Dana began to face the cold, hard truth. She was alone in this world. And no one was coming to save her. She would have to save herself. Dana made a promise to herself. When she got out of prison, she would do whatever it took to be successful. She wasn't going to let anything or anyone get in her way ever again.

She didn't need anybody . . . only herself. She was crying now, but one day she would be smiling. She was going to climb to the top, by any means necessary.

PART 2

Looking diligently lest any man fail of the grace of God; lest any root of bitterness springing up trouble you, and thereby many be defiled.

Hebrews 12:15

JOURNAL ENTRY

If someone had told me I would endure so much drama, I don't know if I would have even tried to step out and do more with my life. Some days, however, I wonder whether I could have done more, been more, before the bottom fell out.

CHAPTER 10

2000—NEW CENTURY, NEW BEGINNINGS

John! You won't believe it!" Lisa exploded into their apartment in the lower level of her father's brownstone on Halsey Street. Arms pumping the air.

John peeked his head out from the kitchen, wiping his hands on a dish towel. "What's got you so excited?"

Lisa met John Coleman during their junior year of college. They married right after graduation and moved into the lower-level apartment of her dad's brownstone. John was not a New Yorker. His family was from Ohio. He had planned to be in New York only for college, so Lisa was thankful he agreed to stay with her in Brooklyn. There was no place on earth she would rather raise a family.

"You are looking at the new director of operations at Liberty Advocates." Liberty was a social services organization. The company provided training for people reentering the workforce, and they also helped clients find affordable housing and paid clients' utilities when needed.

This was Lisa's dream job. The one she'd been vying for while she put in the work at the county welfare office. Now she would be the face of the organization, the one reporters would talk to during press conferences. She had spent years crossing every *t* and dotting every *i* to even get the chance to interview for this job.

John picked her up and swung her around the kitchen. "Oh my goodness. You've been waiting for an answer from them for months."

"Tell me about it." When John put her down, she fixed her jacket. "I thought Kennedy would be in high school before I heard whether I got the job or not."

They sat down at the kitchen table. John asked, "When do you start?"

"I have to give the county a two-month notice so we can hire a replacement and I can train them."

John hugged her. "I'm proud of you." He glanced over at the stove. "I was making a white-bean chili, but with news like this, I think I should take you out to dinner. How's Royal Rib House sound?"

"You know I love their food." She rubbed her hands together and licked her lips.

John put the kitchen towel on the table. "Should I tell Kennedy to get dressed, or do you want to go on a date night? It has been a while."

They had now been married for eleven years. Ten years ago they welcomed their beautiful daughter, Kennedy, who was named after John's grandmother. The name also reminded Lisa of the thirty-fifth president. Since her husband's name was John, she was all in. But if Lisa had known her mother would pass away five years after the birth of her granddaughter, she would have named her child Brenda. The death of her mother stung like nothing she could have imagined, but John and Kennedy brought her comfort.

Lisa leaned close to her husband and pressed her mouth

against his moist lips. "We've both been busy building our careers. It will pay off for us, wait and see." She stood up. "Let me see if Daddy will watch Kennedy so we can have our long-overdue date night."

"Tell him there's a bowl of white-bean chili in it for him."

"Oh, he'll definitely agree to watch his only grandchild for some of your chili." Lisa laughed at her husband's attempt to bribe her father. Truth was, Deacon David Whitaker was semiretired since he suffered a heart attack last year, but he loved spending time with his granddaughter. Said she reminded him of Mama.

Lisa didn't see her mother in Kennedy yet, but her father smiled every time he set eyes on the girl. She brought him joy, so Lisa let him talk about how his granddaughter was a miniature version of his Brenda.

She left her apartment and climbed the stairs to the main part of the house. The way the brownstones were set up, she also could have entered the main house by opening the door to the hallway on the parlor level, but she had asked her father to keep the door locked so he didn't feel as if he could enter her apartment anytime he felt the urge.

She rang the doorbell, then looked to her left and saw a young couple entering Mrs. Mabel's house. Actually, it wasn't her house anymore. Mama was gone, and Mrs. Mabel was gone. Mrs. Mabel's children had decided to sell her brownstone. Sighing deeply, Lisa looked on the other side and saw a For Sale sign on the brownstone next door. Things were changing in Bed-Stuy. Not all the changes were good. They were losing the community feel.

It sure was taking her father a long time to come to the door. She rang the doorbell again. She heard him on the stairs but didn't understand why he was taking so long. She put her face against the windowpane of the double-entry front door. He was putting both feet on each step and slowly making his way to the door as he held on to the banister like it was a security blanket. When she was younger, she would jump down those stairs two at a time.

Lisa was now thirty-three years old. Her father was sixty-two. He should have been able to take those stairs with no problem, but all the heavy lifting at the corner store had caught up with him. He'd been having knee and back problems lately.

He finally made it to the door and opened it. "Sorry it took me so long to answer the door. I went upstairs for a nap. You should have used your key."

"I left my purse in the apartment. Are your knees still bothering you?"

Lisa followed David inside, and he sat down on the sofa in the living room and rubbed his knees. "They're swelling on me again."

"Oh, Daddy, I'm sorry you're in so much pain lately."

David pointed toward the front of the house. "Those stairs don't make it any better. I seriously need a bedroom on the first floor."

"Why don't you have your bed moved into the living room? It's not like you have tons of visitors anymore."

Still rubbing his knees, David smirked. "Your mother would roll over in her grave if I destroyed her showpiece living room like that."

Lisa laughed. The plastic was still on the sofa and chair her mother purchased in 1980. Her parents rarely allowed anyone to sit on the furniture. And if someone did sit in the living room, her father made sure they knew there would be no horseplay—no jumping up and down.

When Kennedy was three, she took pink, purple, and black markers and drew on Lisa's sofa. Lisa then realized how much of a genius her mother had been for understanding that kids will tear your stuff up. "But Mama wouldn't want you suffering going up and down those stairs."

"The Rumbleys are selling their home," he told her.

"I saw the sign in their yard." Lisa bit down on her lower lip. "The neighborhood is changing, and I'm not sure if I like it."

"People are getting older. The Rumbleys are moving to Florida to get out of this cold weather. And Mrs. Mabel died."

Lisa didn't like thinking about Mrs. Mabel not being next door anymore. When she was a kid, Mrs. Mabel would always give her candy. She would always encourage her. Lisa barely knew the names of the couple who moved into Mrs. Mabel's house and doubted very seriously if they had said an encouraging word to Kennedy.

"Doctor says this cold weather is causing my arthritis to act up." He pointed to his knees. "And this swelling is not helping matters either."

"Oh, Daddy." Lisa sat down next to him and put a hand on his back. "I feel so bad for you."

He nodded before saying, "Truth is, this house is too big for me. I've been thinking about selling this place ever since your mama passed. Maybe I need to move down to Florida too."

Lisa jumped out of her seat. Hands to her hips. "Now you are talking foolish, Daddy. You know Mama wouldn't want you to sell this house to some strangers. It needs to stay in the family."

David sighed deeply. "I wish I could, but I can't afford two houses."

Lisa felt sick to her stomach at the thought of losing the home she grew up in. Things were changing so fast in her neighborhood she could barely keep up. Her father's lease was up at the corner store, and the owners wanted to turn it into a restaurant.

She put her hands to her face as she stood in the living room, staring at the steps leading to her childhood bedroom. Everything about this house was familiar to her. She still felt her mother's love in every room. She couldn't let some stranger buy their home and wipe away all her memories.

The income from the new job Lisa would start in two months would allow her and John to afford to purchase this house from her father. She had to talk to John, but she was sure he would be on board. "Let me buy the house from you, Daddy. I'm getting a new job, so John and I will be able to afford it."

"This house really means a lot to you, doesn't it?"

Lisa looked around. Every room held a memory she never wanted to forget. No one could have prepared her for how her heart would ache for Brenda Whitaker every single day. But when she was in this house, it was as if she felt her mother's presence. "It does, Daddy. It really does."

CHAPTER 11

Dana spent four years in prison paying a debt she didn't owe. When she got out of prison, her mother was in worse shape than she'd been in when Dana was sent away.

"You can't stay here, baby," Vida said as they sat in the bedroom she was renting from a couple.

"What? Why not?" Dana didn't have anywhere else to go. She had $300 to her name, thanks to her monthly pay from Rikers Island. She could buy her own food while she looked for a job, but she sure couldn't pay rent with so little money.

"My landlord says she only rented this room to me. And if you don't leave, then I've got to go."

"What am I supposed to do, Ma? I've only been out of jail two days. I don't have anywhere else to go."

Vida didn't respond. She jumped up and pulled a tote from the side of her dresser. "Look what I kept for you. I've taken this tote with me no matter where I've moved."

Dana opened the lid and looked inside. Her clothes and shoes were packed inside. "I can't believe you kept this stuff."

She looked through the things and noticed there was a case with film in it, but her camera was gone. Of course it was gone.

Vida patted Dana on the arm, then said again, "You can't stay."

Realizing yet again she couldn't count on her mother, Dana packed the things Vida had saved for her and caught the train to Flatbush. Once there, she walked to her friend Yolanda's place.

"Thanks for letting me crash with you, Yolanda."

"I got you. Us felons have to stick together," Yolanda said as she showed Dana around the small two-bedroom apartment.

Dana had shared a prison cell with Yolanda Pierce for two years. Yolanda had been released six months ago and was now in need of a roommate.

Dana set her bag of clothes in her bedroom and then walked the block, putting in applications. She wouldn't be able to stay with Yolanda forever. She needed to get some money in her pocket so she could get a place of her own.

She stopped in a corner store and asked, "Are you hiring?"

The manager handed her an application. "We are. One of my best workers took another job. How soon would you be able to start?"

"I'm available immediately," Dana said, feeling excited about being in the right place at the right time. She took out her pen and started filling out the application. It wasn't until she reached the part that asked if she had a felony record that she began to doubt herself. She marked yes to the felony, then wrote below it, "I'd love a chance to explain." Even though she really didn't know how to explain a robbery charge.

Dana then went into a local pharmacy. She wondered whether the film from her old camera was still any good. She hoped she wasn't wasting her money, but she had to take the chance. Those were her memories, and she wanted them. She desperately needed to see something good and beautiful about this world. She handed the film over to the clerk at the photo station, then asked, "Are y'all hiring?"

The clerk pointed to the back of the pharmacy. "You might want to ask my manager. He's behind the pharmacy counter today."

Dana started walking toward the back of the store. The clerk stopped her. "Do you want double or single photos?"

Doubles probably cost more. "Single is fine." She then found the manager and put in an application. But no matter how many applications she put in, the felony question kept rearing its ugly head.

Dana had spent several months putting in applications but not receiving any callbacks. Dana knew she would have to do something different. So she signed up for cosmetology school and finally found a job as a waitress.

After cosmetology school, the struggle was still real, so after thinking long and hard about it, Dana decided to do something drastic to change her circumstances.

She'd been able to convince a landlord to rent her a building to open a hair salon. Dana had worked the business for eight years, trying to make a success of it. But the rent on the building and the credit card bills to purchase equipment for the salon became too much for her.

She turned the keys into the bank in 1999 and spent the rest of the year planning and implementing her next move. The coming new millennium had given her the courage she needed to try something new. While she had her salon, Dana had experimented with her own brand of hair-care products. She developed a shampoo, conditioner, and hair-growing grease, and they worked. So Dana used the money she earned from selling off the inventory and furniture in her salon before it closed down to purchase the supplies needed to brand her own hair-care line: jars, lids, labels, a computer, and the ingredients needed for the shampoo, conditioner, and hair grease. Then she wore out several pairs of shoes walking the blocks, introducing herself to salon owners. She even knocked on doors and gave out samples of her hair grease to parents who had little girls whose hair would dry out and stop growing without the right hair grease.

Dana had business cards made up, and soon she was receiving orders for her products. Business had gotten so good she now needed to hire help, but it wasn't good enough for her to be able to afford the help.

Today Dana pulled a cart up and down numerous blocks as she delivered her products.

"Thank you so much for your order, Ms. Green. I have your full set here." A *full set* consisted of shampoo, conditioner, and hair grease. Dana handed the set to Ms. Green. She had three granddaughters, and she made sure their hair was washed, greased, and braided every week.

"Thanks, girl. I've been waiting for this."

"I appreciate your business. Give me a call when you run out."

Dana left one doorstep and went to the next. She knocked on Dave Barley's door. He was a widower with a seven-year-old daughter. "Hi, Dave, thanks so much for your order." Dana handed him his full set.

But Dave pushed the bag back toward her. "I love your products, Dana, but I ordered the full set three weeks ago. When I didn't receive it, I went to the hair store."

"I'm sorry about that, Dave. It's just me right now, so it takes me a while to fill all of my orders." She handed the bag back to him. "You have been a good customer, so please take this set with my apologies."

She walked away with her head hanging low. Her customers expected delivery of their products fast, but she was mixing the products in her kitchen and bottling everything herself, so she couldn't fill orders as fast as her customers would like. She needed to get help soon, or she would lose more customers.

Dana walked into Beauty, one of the premiere hair salons in Brooklyn.

"Hey, Dana, I hope you brought a few extra jars of hair grease. My clients love it," Sheri Williams, the hairdresser and owner of Beauty, said.

Dana lifted a box out of her cart and handed it to Sheri. "I told you I would bring more in two weeks. I wish I could deliver faster." Pointing toward the box, Dana said, "This is your whole order. Three shampoos, three conditioners, and ten jars of hair grease."

Sheri was combing her client's hair. She put the comb down and pulled some money out of her pocket and handed it to Dana. "My brother will be here in a minute. I told him about you, and he wants to meet you."

Dana waved a hand in front of her face. "I'm not trying to date anyone right now. I'm too busy trying to get my business off the ground." And the fact she did prison time for dealing with a guy who promised her the moon but in the end died in her arms, leaving her to suffer the consequences of his actions, had a lot to do with those dateless nights.

Dana was still traumatized by a relationship that ended when she was a fresh-out-of-high-school didn't-know-what-to-do-with-her-life eighteen-year-old. Since starting her new life in Flatbush, she'd been out with only three guys. Two were total duds, but she was willing to admit she messed up with one of the guys. She kept thinking he was going to be like Derrick. No, thank you.

Sheri laughed at her. "Dang, girl, who scared you off of men?"

"I'm not scared of men. I'm not dating right now."

The door to the salon opened. A man with a scrumptious almond skin tone, goatee, and bald head, wearing an I'm-about-my-business blue pinstripe suit, stepped in. Sheri waved him toward her, then she nudged Dana and said, "That's my brother. And I didn't ask him here for a hook-up. I think he can help with your business."

"I don't need help," Dana declared.

"Oh really? So why are you still knocking on doors and bringing your supplies to salons?"

Dana had been facing Sheri when her brother made his comment. She swung around, hands on hips. "And what do you know about my business?"

He stuck out his hand. "Hi. I'm Jeff Williams, and my sister gave me your business card."

Dana ignored his hand. He pulled her business card out of his jacket pocket and showed it to her. Dana turned to Sheri. "Why you give him my business card?"

"Chill out, Dana. Give Jeff a few minutes of your time. I really think he can help you."

Dana turned back to Jeff. She didn't understand why this man wanted to help her with her business. He didn't know her—they weren't friends. She hadn't asked for his help and didn't even know what kind of help he could offer.

But she did know Sheri. Dana had been selling her products at this salon for a year now. Sheri seemed like a nice person, and she was supportive of Dana's business. She didn't want to offend her customer, so she glanced at her watch, then told Jeff, "I have a few minutes before my next appointment."

"Great. Let's talk about it over lunch."

Dana stepped back. "You don't have to spend your money on me. Tell me what you're about, and then I can be on my way."

"I don't have reservations or anything. I was thinking we could grab a hero at the sub shop down the street."

Dana felt silly. This man was trying to talk to her about business, and she was acting like he wanted a date. She smiled. "Okay, but I'll purchase my own sandwich."

Jeff lifted his hands. "What the lady wants, the lady gets."

Dana liked the sound of his voice, but she was her own hero, and she could buy her own sandwich. She walked out of the salon with him and went down the street to the sub shop. They purchased their sandwiches, then sat down at a table in the back.

"So what exactly do you do, Mr. Williams?"

He took a bite of his sandwich, chewed, then said, "I finance small businesses for people like you. My goal in life is to see young and gifted people succeed. I help by providing the finances needed to take businesses to the next level."

"So you're the moneyman, huh? And what do people like me have to do to get our hands on this money?"

Jeff put a hand to his chest. Shook his head. "I make a good living, but I certainly don't have enough money to fund businesses. I'm more like the middleman. I help my clients find the right lender to fund their business."

Dana leaned back in her seat. She squinted as she tried to size Jeff up. Was he truly a man of the people, out to help small businesses in the community, or was he a snake in the grass?

Dana did need to partner with a bank so she could

manufacture enough of her products to be able to court Walmart and beauty-supply stores.

But what bank would do business with her once they discovered her first business went belly-up and she couldn't even pay the rent on her salon? But then she remembered the loss of her business and salon was not listed on her credit report. Maybe things would be different if she was able to receive a business loan. She had to try, right?

"Look, Mr. Williams—"

"Jeff. Every time you say Mr. Williams, I want to look around for my daddy." He smiled at her.

She laughed. Conceded. "Okay, Jeff. I'm not sure what your lenders require to process a loan, but I'm going to be honest with you. I don't have much credit. Only one credit card, which is maxed out."

"I work with lenders who are sympathetic to the struggles in our community. Most of my clients didn't have perfect credit files at the time they needed to expand their businesses. But if you have records showing consistent earnings with your hair-care products, I should be able to find a lender for you."

The man sitting in front of her exuded confidence as he leaned back in his chair and finished off his hero. Dana wanted to be confident, but too many things had gone wrong in her life for her to ever be confident something was about to go right.

She wondered whether she should disclose her background to Jeff. Was it right to ask him to do this for her without knowing who he was doing business with? But there was nothing of her past she wanted to share. Nothing she cared to remember.

What if this guy was for real? What if he could get her

the money needed to ensure her business thrived, rather than crashing like the salon business had done?

"So what information do you need in order to make money appear in my bank account?"

CHAPTER 12

One of Praise Ministries' outreach initiatives was with a homeless shelter in downtown Brooklyn. They collected toiletries and food, then took the items to the homeless shelter once a quarter. Lisa was on the committee, so she and Sister Betty, the church secretary, delivered the items the church collected and then volunteered at the shelter the same day.

Today the manager for the shelter asked them to make the beds. "The bed sets have been cleaned. You'll find them in a rollaway bin next to the bathroom," she said.

There were thirty beds at the shelter. With the way rent and mortgage prices had gone up over the years, the homeless population in Brooklyn had skyrocketed. Thirty beds were hardly enough to solve the homeless issue they were dealing with, but it wasn't nothing. Especially since the whole goal at this shelter was to make the guests feel at home, even though their bed was six feet away from the next guest.

Lisa pushed the bin into the main room where the mattresses were already laid out on the floor. There were five beds in each row. "I'll start at the first row. If you take the next row, we can have these beds made in no time."

"Sounds like a plan," Sister Betty said. Then they got to work.

Lisa put a twin fitted sheet, flat sheet, and blanket on each mattress. Each bed had one pillow and pillowcase. When she was done making each bed, she set on top a tote bag full of toiletries and on-the-go food items like peanut-butter crackers, candy bars, juice boxes, bottled water, chips, and canned meat with pop-tops.

"How is Kennedy?" Sister Betty asked.

"Growing faster than I can keep up." Lisa started on the next bed.

"It's amazing how that happens." Betty put the fitted sheet on the bed. "One day they're looking up at you with those big trusting eyes, and the next they're taller and meaner than you ever expected them to be."

Lisa laughed. "Stop it, Betty. Your daughter is a sweetheart."

"She's twenty-seven now, but when my child was sixteen, I had to talk myself out of running away from home on several occasions."

"Well, I pray Kennedy keeps a level head."

"You did. Your mother would be so proud to see you now . . . taking over her responsibilities with the homeless shelter and all."

They continued dressing the mattresses, then stayed and helped fix plates for the people as they arrived at the shelter. The whole time, Lisa kept thinking of her mother, wishing they could have this experience together.

As they were walking to their cars after helping the other volunteers clean the tables once the guests had finished with their meal, Betty said, "Did you hear about Councilman Brown?"

Lisa had worked on the campaign to get their councilman elected. She thought he would do great things for their community, but he'd been in office for three years and hadn't done anything to help Bed-Stuy. "I don't keep in touch with Councilman Brown anymore."

"Watch the news tonight. He's being investigated for misappropriation of funds."

Somehow, Lisa wasn't surprised. Councilman Brown was shady, and she had made a mistake backing him.

Dana went into her kitchen and pulled out her soup pots and her double boiler. She then put all the ingredients needed for her products on the counter. To make her shampoo, she combined organic castile liquid soap, organic aloe vera gel, and sunflower oil, along with rosemary oil and lavender oil. She set the pot on the counter and used a long-handled spoon to thoroughly mix all the ingredients together.

Her doorbell rang. She wiped her hands on the kitchen towel and let Jeff in. He'd told her he wanted to see how she made her products so he could have a better idea how to market her to potential investors.

"Look at you," Dana said as Jeff stepped into her living room. He was wearing a pair of jeans and a baby-blue polo shirt underneath his winter coat. "I would have thought you'd be in a stuffy old business suit."

"Since it's Saturday afternoon and I'm working overtime, I figured you wouldn't mind if I dressed comfortably, especially since I brought"—he lifted the bag in his hand—"shrimp fried rice."

Dana smiled. "Did you bring egg rolls?"

Jeff reached in the bag and pulled out the egg rolls. "Would I show up with Chinese food without the egg rolls?"

"I hope not." She laughed as she directed him to the dining room table. "Set the bag here. The kitchen is cluttered with my supplies."

The dining room was to the left of the kitchen. Jeff glanced over at the kitchen counter. "You've got a lot of stuff over there. How many ingredients go into your hair grease?"

Standing in her kitchen, Dana's hand swept the length of the counter. "These aren't only for the hair grease. I have shampoo and conditioner as well, remember?" Dana put her double boiler on the stove, turned the burner on, then began heating up her shea butter. She added sesame oil and olive oil to the mixture and stirred.

She then pointed to the items she had put in the double boiler. "These are the items I use to make the hair grease."

"Sesame oil can be used to make hair grease?" His lips pursed together as he stood behind her, watching her stir the ingredients together.

Dana turned the stove off and nodded. "Sesame oil reduces frizziness and prevents split ends."

"Learn something new every day," he said while peeking over her shoulder at the mixture. "Is that all, or do you add anything else to the mixture?"

"I let it cool for a little while, then I add lavender oil before putting the grease in jars." She pointed to stacks of boxes toward the back of her kitchen. "The jars are in those boxes."

Jeff shook his head. "You need a factory and an assembly line. This is too much work to be doing in your kitchen."

Dana rubbed her hands together. "If you find an investor, I might be able to afford a factory."

Jeff took her hand and walked her over to the dining room table. "Let's sit down and eat while your hair grease cools."

When he took her hand, she almost pulled back, as she got a flashback of Derrick holding her hand as they walked to the pizza parlor. But she exhaled and reminded herself she wasn't that same girl. She sat down at the table with Jeff and enjoyed her shrimp fried rice right out of the container since Jeff had purchased two.

"This is so good." Dana savored the flavor of the shrimp mixed with the rice and soy sauce.

Jeff tossed an egg roll over to her and then slid the hot mustard in her direction. "Now let me see if you can handle this."

Dana puffed out her chest. "Oh, you don't think I can handle the hot mustard, huh? You must not know about me. I'm the hot food champ." Dana pulled her egg roll out of the wrapping, dipped it in the hot mustard, and took a bite.

As she chewed, Dana felt the rush of heat go straight to her head, then explode out of her nose. She blinked and then blinked again. "Whew! That stuff cleans out your sinuses."

"I know, but I love it." Jeff dipped his egg roll in the hot mustard and took a bite. He then shook his head like it was on fire. *"Oowee!"*

"No more for me. That's a different kind of hot." Dana pushed the hot mustard toward Jeff, and they both laughed. Dana finished eating her shrimp fried rice, then went back into the kitchen and poured a few squirts of lavender oil in the pot and stirred.

Jeff closed his container and put it back in the bag. He got up and grabbed a box with the jars for the hair grease. "Where do you want these jars?"

It felt to Dana like her mouth was glued shut. She never expected Jeff to offer to help her. No one had helped her with anything for as long as she could remember. She shook it off and pointed to the dining room table. "I normally fill them over there."

Jeff moved the few things on the dining room table, then opened the box and laid out the jars on the table. "Okay. What's next?"

"You really want to help?"

"Absolutely," Jeff said. "I truly believe I can connect you with an investor. By watching your process, it will help me see all the needs of your business, and then I'll know which investor is best for you."

Dana nodded. "Makes sense." She then pointed to other boxes. "If you really want to help, take the bottles out of those boxes. I'll put the grease in the jars, and you can pour the shampoo into the bottles."

"Don't trust me with the hair grease, huh?"

Dana smiled. "It's easier to pour the liquid into the bottles. Getting the hair grease in the jars takes a little more time."

"Okay. I'm down for whatever. Let me see your process." He looked around the kitchen. "How long will it take to make the shampoo?"

She pointed to the big soup pot on the counter to the left of the stove. "It's done. Take the pot to the table." Dana took her pot to the table, too, then grabbed the water pitcher and handed it to Jeff. "You'll have to pour some of the shampoo from the pot into this pitcher so you can pour the liquid in the bottles."

They started working on filling the containers, then Jeff asked, "How long does it take you to fill your orders?"

Scooping some of the solidified grease out of the pot with a spoon, Dana put the product into the jar. "I normally get about thirty to forty orders each week. And it takes about two to three weeks to fill my orders, depending on if my supplies are available when I order them."

Jeff held a bottle with his left hand as he poured the liquid into it from the pitcher in his right hand. "This shampoo smells nice."

"It's the lavender and rosemary oils."

"How long have you been getting thirty to forty orders a week?"

"About a year now. I have a lot of repeat customers."

Nodding, Jeff told her, "I think you've got a winner here. You have to find a way to streamline your processes and hire a marketing team to get your product in front of more people."

"That's the dream," Dana said.

Jeff set the pitcher on the table and turned to her. "I'm serious, Dana. If you can deliver a business plan to me that shows how you can ramp up production, you'll be a multimillionaire in a few years."

Dana had been filling the jars with hair grease, thinking no further than this moment, but when Jeff got serious, she realized this man believed in her. His words caused her to wonder what life would be like if her hard work finally paid off.

She wanted to give herself permission to dream . . . to believe, but when Jeff left and she turned out the lights and went to bed, it wasn't Jeff's face she was seeing as he said, *"You'll be a multimillionaire in a few years."* It was Derrick's.

Derrick was sitting on the side of her bed, saying, "Girl, why you tripping? I'm ready for a big score, and you laying there sleeping."

"Leave me alone, Derrick. I don't trust you."

"Hey." Derrick put hands on her shoulders and sat her up in bed. "What's this talk? It's you and me, baby. I'm the best thing you've got going."

"No, you're not. You never were!" she shouted at him.

He shook his head. Stood up. "Get dressed. I told you I would get you out of here. Now stop trippin' and help me with this score."

His back was to her as she stood up. "Don't do it, Derrick. You're going to get killed."

Slowly he turned toward her. As she stood facing him, she saw the blood running down his shirt. His eyes rolled back in his head and she screamed.

Panting, Dana shot up in bed. Her chest was heaving as she looked around the room. She wasn't eighteen anymore. She wasn't being led around like a puppy in love anymore, and Derrick was dead.

CHAPTER 13

Lisa had two days left before she would officially be the director of operations at Liberty Advocates. She was excited about her new position. This was the same type of work Elsie Richardson, the woman who helped to revitalize Bed-Stuy in the sixties, had done. Lisa would now be working in the same building as the Bedford-Stuyvesant Renewal and Rehabilitation Corporation at Restoration Plaza.

The plaza occupied a full city block and contained businesses, nonprofits, banks, and cultural venues. The building Lisa was going to work in had been purchased by Elsie Richardson and her business partner after their corporation received millions of dollars in grants from the government, with the support of Senators Robert Kennedy and Jacob Javits, to revitalize the neighborhood.

Lisa would not be working for the Bedford-Stuyvesant Renewal and Rehabilitation Corporation as Elsie Richardson had, but she would be working for a nonprofit that leased several offices within the building. Still, this was the dream for Lisa. Instead of passing out checks and working with her clients at the county office to get their Medicaid in order, she was going to be responsible for helping the community residents rebuild their lives.

"Mrs. Coleman, your two o'clock is here." Her assistant handed her a case file.

Lisa placed the file on her desk, then picked up a stack of papers from her desk and put them in her top drawer. "Send her in."

As the manager of her department, Lisa didn't normally take appointments, but since she had only two more days on the job and she had already trained her replacement, she figured she'd make herself useful and take the load off the other caseworkers.

Lisa opened the case file. The first thing she looked for was the name of the person she would be speaking with today. She thought it was important to show respect by addressing her clients formally. When Brianna Russell sat down in front of her, she greeted the woman with a smile and said, "Good morning, Ms. Russell. What brings you to the Department of Social Services today?"

The woman's shoulders lifted and then dropped as she let out a long-suffering sigh. "My Medicaid and food stamps got cut off again. My daughter has a doctor's appointment next week, and I need to feed my kids."

Brianna's attitude was at a seven at the moment, but Lisa knew it could quickly escalate to a ten if she didn't handle this situation with care. She understood Brianna's frustration. If Lisa's child was hungry, she would do anything to feed her. Lisa glanced at the file and pulled out the letter they sent to Brianna two months ago. She showed it to her. "Did you receive this requalification letter from us?"

Brianna quickly reviewed the letter, then handed it back to Lisa. "Yes, but I work. I don't have time to come down here to keep reapplying for stuff I already applied for."

A common misconception people had about folks

receiving government assistance was that they were lazy and didn't work. But the truth was, it wasn't a lack of employment but underemployment that was the problem. Many welfare recipients showed up to work every day and tried to get by on minimum wage. And there was no getting by when housing and food costs continued rising while income growth remained stagnant for the people in this community. "We understand you have to go to work, Ms. Russell, but we require information from you for continued services."

Brianna rolled her eyes. "Well, what do you need, because my child needs this doctor's appointment, and I can't afford to pay for her monthly prescriptions."

"All we need is your bank statements and your paycheck stubs for the last two months."

Brianna opened her purse and pulled out the documents requested. "I have to bring the same thing down here each and every time y'all make me reapply. I'm still making the same amount I made six months ago." She handed the paperwork to Lisa.

"I know this is a pain, but our hope is our clients one day find employment paying enough so you no longer need our assistance, which would be a good thing, right?"

Brianna's lips smacked together as she cut her eyes at Lisa once again. "You think I like coming down here groveling for the little bit of assistance I receive from the government? It's not like y'all giving me a monthly check. All I've asked for is assistance with medical costs and food for my kids."

Lisa held up a hand. "I wasn't trying to offend you. I do understand the circumstances of the people in our community with low-wage jobs." She reached into her purse, took out the new business cards she'd received back from the printer, and handed one to Brianna.

"I will be working for Liberty Advocates beginning next week. We help our clients with job skills so they can obtain better-paying jobs. If you are interested, give me a call at the number on this card."

Brianna's eyebrow lifted as she looked at the card. She put it in her purse, then glanced back at Lisa. "You're not like most of the caseworkers in this place. I mean, you act like you care."

"I do care, Ms. Russell. I want the best for you and your family, maybe not as much as you want it, but my desire for the people in our community to succeed is way up there."

Brianna nodded. "I'll give you a call. But as far as my benefits, do you think I can get help?"

"Yes, ma'am. Absolutely. I have your paperwork and will get your information into our system immediately. Have the doctor turn the insurance claim into Medicaid as normal."

"Awesome." Brianna was smiling now. "And will you be able to reactivate my food assistance?"

"I will take care of it today as well."

Lisa stood, shook Brianna's hand, and walked with her to the door. As Brianna walked down the hall, Lisa was thankful she had been able to lighten a few of her worries. The next step would come when Brianna Russell upped her skill game and was then able to demand higher wages.

Lisa was itching to get started with an agency that was doing more than handing out checks, insurance, and food assistance, but was instead giving a hand up in this world.

Lisa took her coffee cup off her desk and headed to the break room before her next appointment at 3:00 p.m. It was going to be a long afternoon. She needed another jolt of java. After work, she had plans to meet John at the bank so they could see whether they qualified for enough of a loan to buy her father's brownstone.

She saw her coworker's head peek out of the break room as she got closer. She waved at the woman, but her eyes got big as she waved back, and then she turned back into the break room.

Strange, Lisa thought. She got along well with her coworkers. She wondered why Sue would turn away. But the moment she stepped into the break room her questions were answered.

"Surprise!" everyone in the break room yelled at her.

There was a cake on the table with the words *We Will Miss You* written on it. Jugs of fruit punch and chips were also on the table. Balloons floated around the room, some of them with the word *Congratulations* on them. Lisa beamed with joy as tears ran down her face. "You all did this for me?"

"Of course we did. You might be a hard taskmaster, but we enjoy working with you," one of her employees said.

"And I have enjoyed working with all of you as well." Lisa cut the cake, then they ate and laughed together until she had to go back to her office for her next appointment.

A couple of hours later, after her last appointment of the day, Lisa was getting ready to pack it in when she noticed the message light blinking on her phone. She was about to listen to it when the telephone rang. The caller ID showed it was John.

She picked up the phone. "Hey, hon. I'm packing up now. I should be able to meet you at the bank within an hour."

John said, "I just got off the phone with our lender at the bank, and things don't look good."

Lisa frowned. It was her first frown all day. "What's going on? We gave them all of our paperwork last week."

"Right," he agreed. "But he ran our credit reports this morning, and it appears you have defaulted on a lease agreement and a few credit cards. Your credit rating is trashed."

Lisa glanced around the room as if she was looking for the person John was talking to. It couldn't be her. "What lease? I don't owe anyone."

"That's what I told him, but he said we can't move forward until we can get your credit file straightened out."

"This doesn't make sense to me, John. Why would debt on a lease be on my credit file?" She didn't understand it. The only credit she had was two credit cards, and she paid them on time every month. Knowing they wanted to buy a home someday, she and John had been saving for years. Their dream had obviously moved up in priority since they were planning to buy her childhood home.

"We'll figure it out. I'm going to order our credit reports so we can see everything on it."

"I didn't do this, John. I swear I didn't." Another call beeped in. It was her new boss. "Let me call you back. I need to take this call."

"Okay. I'll see you when you get home."

They hung up, and she accepted the call. She tried to clear her mind of the news her husband just gave her and put a smile on her face. Lisa believed people could see a smile, even over the phone. "Hi, Sam. This is a nice surprise. I didn't think I'd be speaking to you until next week."

"I didn't expect to be speaking with you today either," Sam said.

His voice sounded dry to Lisa. Not at all like the jovial guy she interviewed with a few months ago. "Don't tell me you're calling with an assignment already. You can't wait until I arrive at work on Monday," she joked.

"HR left a message for you to call them, but I wanted to talk with you myself."

Something wasn't right. Lisa was getting an uneasy feeling. "Is there something I need to know?"

"Well, the thing is . . ." He paused for a moment, cleared his throat. "I was informed by HR you didn't pass the background check."

Lisa's head whiplashed. What was going on? Was she being punked? Wait. Today was April 1. People were playing April Fools' Day jokes on her. Then she realized April 1 was on Saturday. Nobody was playing a joke on her. This was really happening. "There should be no reason on God's green earth I can't pass a background check." She shook her head, trying to shake this moment away. This was not her reality. She had lived a good life, done right by others. "I'm no criminal. There shouldn't be anything alarming in my background."

"It's your credit file."

Her credit file? Hadn't John said her credit file showed she had defaulted on a lease?

"The way HR sees it, a person in debt to creditors cannot run a department where they have access to the grant money we receive. I'm sorry, Lisa, but we can't hire you."

"But I'm not in debt to anyone. I'm sure there has been some mix-up. Maybe they pulled the wrong file." That had to be it. Maybe someone else in the city had her name and their credit files had gotten mixed up. "You have to give me some time to check into this. I need to find out why my credit file has the wrong information."

"I'm sorry, Lisa, but we have to move on."

"No!" She stood up, held out her hand as if Sam could see her. "I quit my job already. You can't rescind your offer over a mistake. It has to be a mistake. The only credit I have are the two credit cards in my billfold."

"I wish there was something I could do, Lisa. You came highly recommended by Elsie Richardson, but I can't hire you. I've got to go."

"Wait!"

He hung up, leaving Lisa standing behind her desk, scratching her head. Everything had been going in the right direction. How could it end like this?

CHAPTER 14

Dana had spent the past week scouting buildings and working on her business plan. She and Jeff met at a deli so he could look over her work.

"I think I have an investor for you," Jeff said and then took a bite of his sandwich.

Dana's eyes lit up. "Are you for real? Don't play with me, Jeff."

"I'm not playing with you. My investor has loads of money. The thing is, his grandmother used to be a hair-dresser. He has fond memories of her, so he wants to add a hair-care business to his portfolio."

"Wow! Thank you, Granny." Dana pumped her arm in the air.

Jeff held up a hand. "One step at a time. He'll need to review your business plan first, so let's make sure you have everything together." Jeff spent a few minutes glancing over the plan. He flipped a few pages, then lifted his head. "Where's the information about the building?"

Dana scratched the tip of her nose. "Oh, I didn't know you needed location info."

Jeff laid the business plan back on the table. He rubbed

his chin, looking pensively at her. "Do you know the number one reason most Black-owned businesses fail?"

"Not enough customers," she guessed.

He shook his head. "Lack of funding. So it's not enough to get a few thousand from an investor. You have to receive an amount substantial enough to put you in position to be successful. Therefore . . ."

"We have to include the cost of leasing the building in the business plan."

"Exactly."

Dana was so impressed with Jeff's business savvy and the way he seemed to want her to win, she opened a door and let him peek into her world. "The building I looked at is in Bed-Stuy, not too far from where I grew up."

"I didn't know you grew up in Bed-Stuy. I thought you were a Flatbush kid like me."

"Nah." She told him, "When I was a kid, I lived on Halsey Street and then on Lewis Avenue when we had to move because my mom couldn't pay the rent."

"Tough break."

"Yeah, it was." Dana cleared her throat and sat up straight. "I'll get the numbers from the building owner and update the business plan."

True to his word, Jeff lined up a lender for Dana's small business. She wasn't able to qualify with a traditional bank, but Jeff's investor came through and was willing to put two million dollars behind the building of her enterprise. Dana couldn't believe this was happening to someone like her and shared as much with Jeff when the two next got together.

"Why not you?" Jeff said as the two clinked glasses and toasted in celebration of her newfound wealth.

She had a million reasons why this shouldn't, wouldn't, and couldn't happen for her, but she wanted to share none of them. Dana took a sip of her apple cider—alcohol had never been her thing. She'd tried it once but didn't like the way it made her feel. And after her childhood, Dana was against anything that altered her perception.

As she put the glass on the table, a giggle bubbled up, and she released all the joy she was feeling. "I absolutely can't believe I am a millionaire."

"Well, not yet," Jeff told her. "All of this money will need to go toward building your business. Your investor expects to be paid back on a faster track than a normal lender, so you need to get busy producing your Hair Fabulous products."

"Oh, I'm already there. I've talked with a manufacturer who will be able to put me on their schedule, and I'm hiring a marketing professional so we can put Hair Fabulous products into as many stores as possible. I'll be able to pay this loan back. I'm confident I can do it."

Jeff put his glass down and stared at Dana from across the table as if she were a puzzle he was trying to put together.

"What?"

Jeff shook his head. "Nothing. You seem different from the first day we met."

Dana pursed her lips; she leaned back in her seat. "I'm still Dana from the block. Having this money doesn't change who I am. Trust me on that."

"I hope you do stay the same. But I'm not talking about your personality." He explained further. "When we first met, you were guarded, as if you didn't know whether you could trust me. I thought it was the Brooklyn in you, but you've relaxed around me lately."

Nodding, she admitted, "You've put me at ease. I see that you're a man of your word."

Jeff smiled, then put a hand over his face. "Look at me, blushing after a woman said something nice about me."

"You're not blushing. Stop lying." Dana watched as Jeff lowered his hand. He first seemed to be in a joking mood, but his facial features took on a more serious note as the smile left.

He cleared his throat, sat up a bit straighter in his seat. "In all seriousness, when we first met, I did want to take you out to dinner, but you were set on paying for yourself. Now I can't ask you out, and I'm a bit bummed."

She hadn't been on a date in years, too busy trying to recover from her first business venture going belly-up. But Jeff was real easy on the eyes, with his almond skin tone and those light brown eyes, not to mention the goatee he sported was so sexy she had to avert her eyes during a few of their meetings.

"Why can't you ask me out?" she inquired with a raised brow.

"Isn't it obvious? You're out of my league now." Sweat beads formed on Jeff's upper lip. He wiped them away. "I don't want you thinking I'm after you for money."

Dana laughed. "If it wasn't for you, I wouldn't have a dime to expand my business. I would be in my apartment with all my ingredients spread out over the kitchen, trying to fill my orders."

"Now you can hand all those ingredients over to a manufacturer and get a distributor to deliver your products to stores like Sally Beauty Supply and Walmart."

"Well, I no longer have to mix all my ingredients in my kitchen, sooo"—Dana dragged the word out as she looked into Jeff's eyes—"guess I have some time on my hands. I'm thinking about going out to dinner."

"You should take some time to enjoy your success."

Tapping her fingers on the table, she asked, "Do you have any suggestions for where a single girl might get a good meal?"

Jeff took a moment to think. "I have the perfect restaurant, but you will need a reservation. And they have a long waiting list. But I know a guy . . . I might be able to get you in by next week."

"Well, if the restaurant is a snazzy one, I'm going to need a date." Dana bit down on her bottom lip. "Wonder if I can find a man comfortable with dating a woman with two million dollars in her pocket."

Jeff took the bait. He waved a hand. "Hold on. If I'm getting the reservation, then I'm taking you out. I'll call you with the day and time of our meal, okay?"

Dana shrugged. "If you're sure you want to be seen out with me. I think I can tolerate you for an evening."

"Oh, you got jokes, huh?" Pointing in her direction, he said, "I got you. Well, let me say this: I'm a gentleman, so I guarantee you will enjoy a night on the town with me."

Lisa and John sat at the kitchen table reviewing the Experian, TransUnion, and Equifax credit reports. All three reports indicated she had defaulted on a lease agreement and several credit cards. "I have never had a Chase credit card or a Discover card."

"The only credit cards I am aware of are the two we have together," John said while continuing to study the credit report.

Lisa jabbed a finger at the report. "Right there it shows the credit cards we have together, and they are current . . . It's the only correct thing on this report."

"This is bananas." John threw up his hands. "Unless you're living some double life I don't know about, then there is no way you racked up thirty thousand in credit card bills and defaulted on a lease agreement."

Lisa pointed toward one of the line entries. "There's a telephone number for Chase Bank. I'm calling them right now." She picked up the receiver and started dialing the 800 number, hit several prompts, and then tapped her foot as she waited for someone to answer the phone.

Right after the customer service rep greeted her, Lisa went in on her. "Hi. My name is Lisa Coleman." Remembering the credit card was in her maiden name, she said, "Sorry, I'm Lisa Whitaker, and I need to speak with someone about a credit card that is in my name, but I didn't apply for."

"Can you give me the credit card number?" the customer service rep asked.

Lisa glanced back at the credit report. "I don't have the full number, only the last four digits. Can't you look it up with my name and the four digits on the credit report?"

"Yes, ma'am. Can you provide me with your information?"

Lisa gave the rep all the information she saw on the report. She could hear the rep clicking a few keys, then she said, "I have your loan pulled up. Before we go any further, I must tell you this is an attempt to collect a debt and any information received—"

"This is not my debt," Lisa tried to explain.

"Your name is Lisa Whitaker, correct?"

"Yes, but—"

"Then you currently owe us fourteen thousand two hundred sixty-seven dollars. How do you plan to pay? We haven't received a payment in the past two years."

Kennedy walked into the room with her history book and notebook. "Mom, are you ready to help me with my homework?"

Lisa put her hand over the phone. "Ask your father to help. I'm taking care of something." Then she spoke back into the phone. "I don't think you understand what I'm telling you. I am Lisa Whitaker, but I do not have your credit card, nor did I apply for it or ever use it."

"Are you claiming to be a victim of identity theft, ma'am?"

The way the representative said those words, it sounded like people called them all the time, trying to get out of paying a bill by saying someone else made the charges they were being billed for. And maybe people did stuff like that on the regular, but Lisa wasn't like one of them. "Yes, ma'am, I am a victim of identity theft. I'm hoping you can help me sort some of this out."

After a few minutes on the phone, she was finally able to get the address where the bills were being mailed. "I don't live there and am hardly ever in Flatbush," Lisa told her.

"Can you provide me with your address?" the rep asked.

Lisa gave her address on Halsey Street, then saw John waving to her. He was shaking his head as if she'd done something wrong. She put her hand over the phone again while looking in John's direction. "What did I do?"

"Don't give them any more information."

"We have to get to the bottom of this." She understood

her husband's concern, but this credit issue had cost her a dream job and the ability to purchase the family home from her father. She needed someone to do something.

When she hung up with Chase Bank, she gave John the address the bank had been sending monthly statements to. "I think we should borrow Dad's car and drive over there."

"But, Mommy, I need to get my homework done for my history class," Kennedy whined.

John looked at the address. "This is in Flatbush." John flipped a few pages on the credit file, then jabbed a finger at the report. "The address for the rental property is listed right here. It's in Flatbush too."

"I know." Lisa rubbed her forehead. "I have been in Flatbush all of two times in my entire life."

Kennedy lifted her book in the air. "Will somebody please help me?"

"Sit down next to me, Kennedy. Let me see if I can help," John told her.

Lisa normally helped Kennedy with her homework. But not today, not when someone in Flatbush had ruined her well-made plans. Now she needed a plan for what they would do once they found this person.

CHAPTER 15

Lisa sat in the passenger-side seat as John drove them over to where the building she supposedly rented was located. They parked in front of a small building. It looked to be no more than about five hundred square feet. There was no signage on the building. A few of the windows had boards on them.

John got out of the car. Lisa opened her door and got out as well. They walked up to the building, peeked inside the one window that wasn't boarded up.

"It's empty." Lisa didn't know what she expected to see, but she had hoped something would at least give them a clue about the business operating at this location.

"We should have expected this," John told her. "Based on the credit report, the person stopped paying the rent a little over two years ago. The owner probably hasn't been able to rent it out since."

Lisa looked around, saw parents holding their children's hands as they walked down the street. Other kids were hanging out. She turned to John and said, "If I was going to rent a building like this, I would open a community center for after-school programs to benefit kids in this area."

John looked frustrated. "We need to find out who owns

this building. I don't understand why they haven't rented it out again."

"They have me on the hook for it, that's why." Steam formed in Lisa's nostrils as she blew out hot air.

A few men and women were passing by. They went along their way, not even waving a greeting to anyone. Lisa turned to a woman who was pulling a cart full of groceries. She was walking as fast as she could while pulling it. Lisa went over to her. "Excuse me, ma'am. Do you live around here?"

The woman looked as if Lisa had asked her to donate a kidney and kept walking. Lisa rushed after her. "I'm not trying to get in your business." She pointed to the building she and John had been standing in front of. "Do you know anything about this building?"

The woman gave Lisa the hand and kept walking.

Lisa was about to ask one more question, but John grabbed her arm and moved her back toward the car.

Lisa pointed to a man who walked past them. "Sir, sir, can I ask you a question?"

The man shook his head, made a motion with his arm as if he was getting in a running stance. "I'm late. Can't stop to talk."

"Get in the car, Lisa." John walked around to the driver's side and opened the door.

"But . . . but . . ." Lisa waved a hand toward the no-name building.

"We can't stand out here accosting people on the street. We have the address where the credit card statements were sent to. Let's go see where this person lives."

Lisa nodded. "Oh, oh yeah, I like the way you think." She got back into the car, and they drove over to 315 Flatbush Avenue. Lisa squirmed in her seat at the excitement of tracking down the person who stole her identity. Her fist clenched and unclenched. She was mad enough to kick some butt today.

This person's senseless actions tore down everything Lisa had spent years building. She didn't even have a job with the Department of Social Services anymore. After they threw her the going-away party, Lisa was too embarrassed to admit her job offer had been rescinded, so she packed her office up and left her job, letting the new manager take over as planned.

When she was younger, Lisa had mapped out her life. She'd planned everything: college, marriage, career, and children. She always knew she wanted only one child . . . kids were expensive. And she wanted to give Kennedy every advantage in the world, as her parents had done for her.

Lisa wanted to solve this mystery, restore her good name, and then get her life back on track. Kennedy needed to see her mother taking action rather than sitting in the house moping about how she had been done wrong.

John pulled up to the address they had been given. Lisa's face dropped. It was a UPS store. She turned to her husband like he could provide the answers she sought. "What . . . what is this? Why did the credit card company give us the address to the UPS Store?"

John put a hand on Lisa's shoulder. "Honey, I'm sorry this crappy thing happened. It's not fair how someone can pretend to be another person and buy all this stuff and leave us holding the bag."

"But we shouldn't be holding the bag. We've lived good and faithful lives. We attend church, we're raising our child to be a responsible adult. We pay our bills." She beat a fist against the car door. "This shouldn't be happening to us."

Rolling her eyes heavenward, Lisa opened the car door as an idea struck. "I bet the UPS Store has the real address on this fake Lisa."

"Good thinking." John opened his door, and they walked into the store.

Lisa stood in line while the three people ahead of her were served. When it was her turn at the counter, she said, "Can I speak with the manager or the store owner, please?"

"Sure thing," the clerk said. "He's in the back. Let me get him for you."

Lisa turned to John as the clerk walked to the back. "Now we're going to get some answers."

John crossed his fingers.

A tall man with dreadlocks came from the back. He had on a UPS uniform and a name badge that read *Gary.* He walked over to Lisa and said, "I was told you're looking for the manager."

"Yes, I am. I need your help with something."

"Do you have a mailbox at this location?" Gary asked.

"No," Lisa answered, then immediately corrected herself. "I mean, yes, sort of."

Gary's eyebrows dipped as creases in his forehead appeared. "I don't understand."

"Let me explain." Lisa glanced back at John, then turned back to Gary. "What I'm trying to say is, someone opened a mailbox at this location using my name, but it wasn't me."

He held up a hand. "We require identification before opening a mailbox."

Lisa was almost giddy as she clapped her hands. "That's what I was hoping for. You see, whoever used my name for the mailbox also used my name to purchase things on credit that I'm now on the hook for. So my husband and I were hoping you'd be able to provide us with some information so we can find this person."

He scratched his chin. "Can you give me your ID, please?"

Lisa opened her purse, took out her state ID. She'd never had need of a driver's license since she didn't drive. John, however, couldn't imagine not having one.

Pointing toward the name on the ID, Lisa said, "My married name is Coleman. The name on the mailbox would be Lisa D. Whitaker."

Gary went to the computer, which was directly behind the checkout counter, and began typing on it. After a few seconds he turned back to Lisa. "The mailbox was closed last year for nonpayment."

"Figures," Lisa said to John. Then she asked Gary, "Can we have the home address for the person who opened the account with you?"

Gary shook his head. "I feel for you, if this person did what you said, but I can't give out personal information."

"Then what am I supposed to do? If I can't find this person, then there's no way I will be able to clear my name."

John put a hand on Lisa's shoulder as he asked Gary, "Is there anything we can do to get this information? There has to be some way. People can't go around posing as others and have no repercussions."

Gary nodded. "You need to get the police involved. File a report and have them request her records. We will then turn over our files to the police."

"So I have to go through all these extra steps because someone created a whole new identity using my information?"

"I hate to say it, but yeah," Gary said.

Her shoulders slumped. "Well, thank you for your help." If she needed to get the police involved in order to get answers, then she was headed to the precinct.

CHAPTER 16

Jeff was becoming everything to Dana. She could hardly believe she had let another man into her life and had actually grown comfortable with the idea of loving someone again. They had been dating only three months, but they had been inseparable after the first month, and she was ready for a lifetime with this man. He was good to her.

Today she was meeting his parents, and Dana was a little nervous They were meeting up with them at church before they went to his family's home for dinner. She put on a form-fitting aqua-blue dress, but as she looked at herself in her full-length mirror, Dana's eyes zeroed in on her boobs.

She couldn't meet Jeff's parents in a dress like this. Dana was headed back to her closet when the doorbell rang. She'd told Jeff she would meet him at the church. Why was he ringing her doorbell instead of waiting for her at Brooklyn Tabernacle Church?

But when she opened the door, she was surprised to see Vida standing on her stoop looking like a good wind could blow her away at any minute. And she smelled as if she'd never had a soap-meet-Vida, Vida-meet-soap moment in her entire life. "Ma! Oh my goodness, I haven't heard from you in months. Where have you been?"

Vida started crying. Her voice caught as she said, "It's good to see you, Dana. You're so beautiful. I can't believe how well you've turned out."

Dana waved her in. She wanted to hug her mother, but Vida's clothes were filthy. "Come in, Ma. You need to change out of those clothes and take a bath."

"I haven't eaten. I'm hungry," Vida told her, still standing on the stoop.

"I have food. Come in and let me take care of you."

Vida wiped her feet on the mat and stepped into the house. She didn't make eye contact with her daughter. "I'm sorry I came here looking like this, but I didn't have anywhere else to go."

"I'm glad you came to me. I have something for you, but first I need you to go run yourself a bath. I'll fix you some breakfast."

Vida stared at Dana a moment, then pointed at her dress. "Looks like you're getting ready to head out."

Dana glanced down at herself. "I was going to church with Jeff, but I can cancel."

"Who's Jeff?"

The last time she had seen her mother was about three months ago. Dana ran into one of Vida's old friends at the grocery store and the woman told her where her mother was living.

Horrified at the condition of the house she was told her mother was in, Dana stiffened as she knocked on the door and then side-eyed the two men who were sitting on the porch. They smelled like they didn't have access to running water. The men had unruly beards and knotted afros.

One of them laughed as he told her, "You don't have to knock. Open the door and go inside."

Dana looked over her shoulder at the man who spoke to her. "You own this place?"

He laughed again, showing his rotting teeth. "Nah. We all sort of stay here."

Rolling her eyes heavenward, Dana wondered what her mother had gotten herself into now. She pushed open the door. Her hand went to her nose as a whoosh of hot, smelly air assaulted her senses.

She stepped into a room with brown carpet. It had black patches of dirt in so many spots it looked like they had skinned a leopard and laid the skin on the floor as a rug. A woman was sitting on the couch nodding. Two other women were sitting on the floor passing a pipe.

Dana's skin crawled as she walked through the house. She wanted to leave and forget this whole experience. But as she was contemplating walking back out the front door, she tripped over something, looked down, and widened her eyes in horror at the dark circles around her mother's eyes and the bruises on her cheek.

She bent down on the dirty floor. She shook Vida. "Ma! Ma! Wake up!"

Vida moaned as if in pain as she turned over. Dana saw the dried blood on the other side of her face. Her mind flip-flopped, as if she was seeing Derrick lying on the ground bleeding out. Screaming, she backed up against the wall.

She was shaking like the wind from outside had swept through the house and sent a chill through her body.

Pictures of Derrick's lifeless body kept flashing through her mind. Her trembling hands were in front of her face as she tried to calm herself so she could think. Her mother was on the floor. She pulled out her brand-spanking-new cell phone and called 911. "I need an ambulance. My mom has been beaten." Dana had wondered if she was wasting money when she decided to purchase her cell phone. She was so used to having only a house phone, but she was thankful she made the purchase and didn't have to run around looking for a phone to call an ambulance for her mother as she had years ago.

The paramedics took Vida to the hospital. When Vida came to and discovered where she was, she tried to get out of bed.

Dana stopped her. "Mom, I found you on the floor in a dirty house. You had been beaten unconscious. Do you know how scared I was?"

Vida dipped her head in embarrassment. "I didn't mean to scare you. Things got a little out of control."

"You could have been killed." Dana stood next to her mother's bed. "I've asked the hospital to put you on a seventy-two-hour hold so I can find you a rehab." A tear trickled down Dana's face. She was so tired of fighting her mother's demons. "I need you to go to rehab."

Vida scratched her arms, twisted her lips. "I've tried rehab. It doesn't work for me."

"Ma, listen to me. My business is taking off. I can get you a place to live. You don't have to be in that, that . . . house. But I need you to get clean." Tears dripped from Dana's face and fell onto her mother's blanket. "You get clean, and I'll take care of you, okay? Do it for me, Ma. We deserve a chance to restore our relationship. Don't we?"

Vida nodded. Dana thought Vida would finally do something for her, but when she arrived at the hospital forty-eight hours later to tell Vida about the rehab she'd found for her, she discovered her mother had checked herself out of the hospital.

Dana hadn't gone in search of Vida after that. She had been focused on her business and getting her own life on track. And if she was being honest with herself, she was tired of being disappointed. But as she looked at her mother and saw defeat in her eyes, she realized how wrong she had been to concentrate on the things that mattered to her while forgetting about the people who mattered. "I'm sorry I didn't try to find you this time, Ma. You don't look well."

Vida waved a hand as she headed toward the bathroom. "Girl, you got your own life to live. I used to have a life, too, so I know how it is."

Dana rushed to the linen closet, pulled out a washcloth, towel, and bar of soap. She handed them to her mother, then went into her bedroom and searched through her closet to find some clothes that would fit her mother.

Dana was five feet five and 135 pounds. She and her mother were about the same height, but Vida was bone thin. Any of her size 6 or 8 clothing would probably fall off her mother. She finally settled on a nightgown and white terrycloth robe, which she hung on the outside doorknob of the bathroom.

She heard the bathwater running. Knocked on the door. "I left a nightgown on the doorknob for you. You can wear it and the robe for now. I'll put your clothes in the washing machine."

"Okay, thank you!" Vida yelled her thanks over the sound of running water.

Dana went to the kitchen and fried some eggs and bacon and turned on the coffee maker.

When Vida came out of the bathroom wearing Dana's robe and smelling fresh and clean, she looked like she had scrubbed ten pounds of road off of her. Dana handed the breakfast plate to her mother. "How do you like your coffee?" It felt strange to Dana having to ask her mother that question. But she honestly didn't remember.

"I gave up on coffee years ago. It gets me too wired and then I can't sleep."

Dana's cell phone rang. She picked it up and accepted the call. Putting the phone to her ear, she said, "Jeff, baby, I'm so sorry. My mom stopped by, and I forgot to call you."

"You haven't talked much about your mother. Is she doing okay?"

Glancing over at Vida, she said, "We can talk later, okay? But I'm so sorry I won't be able to meet your parents today."

Vida waved her fork in the air. "Uh-uh, you are not canceling your date on my account."

Dana turned toward Vida. "I can't leave you here by yourself."

Vida waved the notion off. "Thank you for the bath and the food, but I'm exhausted. I want to lay down and sleep for a while."

"But we need to talk." Dana was ashamed to admit she was also concerned about leaving her mother alone in her apartment. But she knew how important it was to Jeff for her to meet his parents.

"I'll be here when you get back," Vida said, then went back to eating her breakfast.

Dana told Jeff, "I guess I can meet your parents after all. I'll get a cab and be there as fast as I can." She ended the call, then turned back to her mother. "Are you sure you'll be okay?"

Vida used her right index finger to draw a cross over her heart. "I'm okay. Wake me up when you get back."

Since she was building her business and had investors to pay, Dana still lived in her one-bedroom apartment. She let her mom take her bed, then she changed into a brown-and-tan swing dress and headed out the door. She caught a cab to 292 Flatbush Avenue. The church was on the corner of Flatbush and Seventh Avenue. But from what Jeff told her, Brooklyn Tabernacle had purchased the old Loew's Metropolitan Theatre in downtown Brooklyn and would be moving into it once the renovations were complete.

Before Dana spent four years in prison, she and her friends loved going to the movies in downtown Brooklyn. She had been to Loew's on numerous occasions and couldn't imagine the place as a church. But if she and Jeff were still together when the church made their move, she might attend with him so she could see the changes to the place.

Jeff was waiting for her at the front of the church when she arrived. He hugged her as if he hadn't seen her in weeks, then took her hand as they headed into the sanctuary. "I'm so glad you made it."

Every single time she was with this man, he made her feel special. Like she was the only woman in the world who mattered to him. She hoped his parents would like her but was terrified they might see her for who she used to be and decide she wasn't good enough for their son.

They stopped at an aisle where there were two empty seats. Jeff looked at her before they sat. "Your hands are trembling. Don't be nervous."

"*Can't help it*," she mouthed as they sat down.

The lady next to Jeff reminded her of Mrs. Brenda Whitaker. They had the same arch in the eyebrow, the same caramel complexion, and the same kind of smile. It made Dana feel warm all over. The woman leaned toward Dana and stuck her hand out. "I'm Patricia."

Dana was full-grown, had experienced a lot of life's ups and downs, but she was not prepared to call Jeff's mom by her first name. She shook her hand. "Nice to meet you, Mrs. Williams."

The man sitting next to Jeff's mom nodded in her direction. Dana figured he was Jeff's father and was about to speak, but then Sheri, Jeff's sister, poked her head out from the other side of Jeff's father. "Hey, girl."

Dana smiled at Sheri. Jeff's dad smiled at her. The preacher stepped behind the podium, then everyone stood. The last time Dana attended church was the Sunday she attended with Lisa when she was eighteen. Dana would have liked to think she would have gone again if prison hadn't gotten in her way.

The preacher's message was about better days. Dana liked what she was hearing. She was stepping into those better days and feeling like she was making some boss moves. But if she was being honest, her attention waned a bit about halfway through the message.

When service was finally over and they stood to leave, she noted Jeff's father was several inches taller than Jeff. Which was fine with Dana. At five feet five, when she put on her three-inch heels, Jeff was still a couple of inches taller than her. He didn't need to be six feet—as long as he was taller than her in heels, she was happy.

When they stepped outside the church, Jeff's father came over to Dana and put an arm on her shoulder. "Well, I guess we know why Junior has been missing around our house lately."

"Leave Junior alone, Jeffrey. He brought this nice young woman to meet us, and I for one don't want to run her off," Patricia said.

But Jeff wouldn't let it go. "Dad, can you blame me? She's beautiful and savvy in business. I was in love at first sight."

Dana blushed. But then her mind went back to what Jeff said. Did he use the *L* word? He'd never told her he loved her. Was that what this was? Were they in love? Dana knew one thing for sure, she wasn't going to have this conversation in front of his parents. "Okay, Jeff, now stop it, please."

"You're making her blush." Patricia pulled Dana to her side. "Come with me, dear. Instead of cooking, we are going to make these men pay for our meals. Do you like Junior's?"

"Love it," Dana admitted.

"Then Junior's it is." Patricia patted Dana's hand.

Dana couldn't help it; she stood there staring at the woman. She was dressed in a lime-green jacket and skirt set. The skirt came down to her knees. The color went well with her complexion. This woman looked regal and of substance, nothing at all like Vida.

Jeff put an arm around his mother and then the other arm around Dana's shoulder. "I would be happy to take my two favorite ladies to Junior's."

Sheri stepped over to them. She had on a red dress with a pillbox hat. "What about me, big brother? I thought I was your favorite girl."

"Not anymore."

Jeffrey Senior put an arm around his daughter. "You'll have to be thankful you're still your old man's favorite girl."

Sheri playfully shoved Dana in the back. "You're not right. You can't come up in here and steal my big brother's heart like that."

"It's not stealing if I willingly give it to her." Jeff planted a kiss on Dana's forehead. "Ignore my bratty sister."

Dana turned in Sheri's direction and stuck her tongue out. "You're the one who introduced us in the first place.

Don't blame me if you made a business connection as well as a love connection."

Jeff waved a hand as cabs passed by. Two stopped in front of the church; she and Jeff got in one while his parents and sister got in the other.

She snuggled up next to Jeff as they rode in the back of the cab on their way to Junior's. For the first time in her life, Dana was truly happy.

Her business was doing well. She was about to lease a building to streamline production and delivery of her products. She was beginning to be recognized in the business world. But she found herself wondering whether this church-going family with their easygoing smiles would welcome her dating their son if they knew her mom had showed up at her apartment with a month's worth of dirt on her, smelling like a dumpster, and was at this very moment sleeping off a bender at her apartment.

There were many things she wished she could talk to Jeff about. But Dana didn't know whether he would use the *L* word again if she was to sit him down and tell him her truth. So she kept silent. She would have to tell him her story one day but didn't know when she would find the right time for such a conversation.

CHAPTER 17

Dana was having a good time conversing with Jeff's family over a meal. Jeff's parents were easy to listen and talk to. And Sheri was even funnier than her brother. Dana would never know what it was like to grow up in a two-parent household or to have a sibling. But from the outside looking in, it seemed like a Disneyland trip compared to what she had experienced.

After dinner, Jeff ordered a whole cheesecake for the table. They each took a slice and dug in. It was creamy but not heavy—light and airy with a sponge-cake bottom.

Dana took one bite and moaned. "This is simply the best cheesecake on the planet."

There was another slice left on the serving plate. Jeff said, "Why don't you take the last slice to your mom?"

Dana glanced around the table. "Does anyone else want another slice?"

Jeff's parents said no. Sheri said, "Girl, if you don't hurry up and take this slice, I'm going to stick my fork into it."

Everyone laughed. Dana thanked Jeff for being so thoughtful. Her eyes misted a bit when the server brought the box for the extra cheesecake slice.

Jeff leaned over and whispered to her, "It's just a cheesecake."

She turned to him. A tear fell from her eyes as she put her hand on his face. "It's not about the cake. I'm amazed at how good your heart is."

He wiped the tear from her face. "Hey, stop that. You have a good heart too."

"Not like you. Your parents obviously raised you and Sheri right. I wish . . ." Her words trailed off; she was embarrassed she was being so emotional over a dinner with her boyfriend's family and a slice of cheesecake she could have bought for her mother herself.

She stood. Glanced around the table. "It was so nice spending time with you all, but I did leave my mother at my apartment this morning, so I need to go check on her."

"We understand, dear. It was wonderful fellowshipping with you today," Patricia said.

Dana didn't think she could stand in Patricia's presence a minute longer without falling apart. If she had been raised by a mother like Patricia, things would have been so different for her. Yes, she finally made it, but there was a cost to every scrap of success that came her way.

She tried to hold herself together and walk with her head held high. She made her way out of the restaurant with the small box holding a piece of cheesecake. Jeff came out of the restaurant behind her.

He grabbed her arm and stopped her. "Hey, what's going on? I thought you were enjoying yourself."

"I was. Please don't let me spoil the time you have with your family. I'm not used to stuff like this."

"Stuff like what? All we're doing is having dinner."

"Yeah, I bet y'all are the type of family that has dinner

together every Sunday after church." Horns were blowing as cars raced by them.

"We do have dinner together on most Sundays. What's wrong with that?"

"Nothing is wrong with it. Nothing at all. But I don't know what that feels like." She turned away from him, then turned back. She loved this man, but it seemed like they were from different planets. "Do you want to know how I grew up?"

"Of course I want to know. I keep trying to get you to open up to me, but you change the subject whenever I ask about your family."

People were walking up and down the street. Some were close enough to hear their conversation, but it didn't matter to Dana. Right now, all that mattered was that she opened her mouth and said, "I don't know who my father is. I've never once met any man who claimed to be my dad."

She tried not to cry, but at that moment, she admitted to herself how much that hurt. As the tears flowed down her face, she said, "It didn't bother me at first. My mother and I had a good relationship, but when I was in the eighth grade, she got involved with this man who was all wrong for her."

Jeff reached out for Dana, but she pulled back, gulping back sobs. "He got my beautiful mother hooked on drugs, and nothing has been the same since. I can't even say that she's beautiful anymore. She looks scary to me with the way her cheekbones cave in."

Dana's chest heaved as she fanned herself. It was hot outside and the temperature within her was rising. "I've got to go."

"Okay, but first I need you to calm down." He pulled her close.

In his arms, she felt safe enough to cry for the little girl who wanted a daddy . . . the little girl who lost her mother to drugs. In his arms, she felt safe enough to just be. She relaxed, wiped the tears from her eyes, and stepped out of his embrace. "I'm sorry I ruined the dinner."

He shook his head. "Don't be. I'm glad you finally told me about your mom. But I want you to know everything wasn't perfect in our house. You see my parents now, after they've weathered many storms together."

"I know." She held up a hand. "I'm being silly. Please give my apologies to your parents."

Jeff was about to say something else when a woman bumped into him. He grabbed Dana and tried to move out of the way, but the woman stayed in front of them. She held out her hand. "Can you spare some change?" she asked.

She was dirty, like Dana's mother had been when she knocked on her door this morning. Her eyes were bloodshot, and she looked like the whole world had turned against her. It had been fifteen years since she'd seen her, but she still recognized Jasmine Parks, the streetwise kid who'd been down for anything. But the streets hadn't been kind to her.

"Jasmine?" Dana squinted, trying to make sure she wasn't seeing things and this was truly the girl she hung out with back in the day.

Jasmine had been looking at Jeff, but when she heard her name, she glanced over at Dana. Her eyes bulged and her head flopped back. "Dana? Girl, is that you?"

"Yes, it's me." Dana's eyes shadowed with sadness. She had been angry with Jasmine for many years for everything—introducing her to Derrick, stealing her camera, and driving away from the scene of the crime. A crime Jasmine was never

arrested for since Dana didn't snitch. But she wouldn't wish what was standing in front of her on her worst enemy.

"Hey, you're looking like a million bucks. Life is sure treating you good these days," Jasmine said.

"How have you been?" Even as she asked the question, she could see for herself how her old frenemy had been. She'd always thought, of the three of them, Jasmine had gotten off easy. But the streets had a way of bumping heads and leaving lumps. So she added, "Is there anything I can do for you?"

Jeff pulled at her arm. Moving her a few steps back, he warned Dana with his eyes. "Be careful."

Jasmine popped off. "She don't have nothing to fear from me. Me and Dana went to school together. Right, Dana?"

Dana nodded, still taken aback by the state Jasmine was in. Not knowing what else to do, she reached into her purse, pulled out two twenty-dollar bills, and handed them to her. "I hope this helps."

"Thanks, old buddy." Jasmine smirked at Jeff as she walked away from them.

"You know she's going to get high with the money, right?" Jeff said.

"I know, but I'm hoping she will at least buy herself something to eat as well." She hated the way Jeff was looking at her, like she was a fool for caring about a drug addict.

Dana wondered how many people had seen her mother out on the street and refused to give her any money. Maybe her mother wouldn't be so thin if someone had offered her a meal. "I'll talk to you later. Let me go home and check on my mom." She hailed a cab and got away from him and his perfect life and his perfect family.

When she arrived home, her mother was still sleeping

in her bed. Dana took off her dress, jumped in the shower, and changed into a pair of pajamas. She'd left the house this morning before telling her mom about the cell phone she had purchased for her. She was tired of not knowing where her mother was or how to get in touch with her, so when she purchased her cell phone, she had also purchased one for her mother and kept it in her dresser drawer, hoping she would see her mom before the phone was out of date.

Having a cell phone was a whole new experience for Dana. She'd seen others with the device but hadn't had the money to get one for herself. Her money situation was right, so she was thankful to be able to purchase a cell phone and keep up with her mother.

She opened the dresser, moved her T-shirts to the side, and pulled the flip-phone box out. She put the box on the kitchen counter and was about to take a nap on her sofa in the living room but decided she wanted to be close to her mother, like she used to be before everything changed.

She climbed into her king-sized bed and lay on the right side, facing her mother's back, remembering how she used to snuggle against her mom while listening to Vida sing a lullaby.

"Close your eyes, go to sleep, my little baby." Dana sang the words softly with tears in her eyes. Why was she so emotional today? *Go to sleep, girl . . . close your eyes*, she silently chided herself. Her eyelids got heavy, and she finally drifted off to sleep.

A few hours later, when she woke, she noticed her mother was no longer in the bed. Dana yawned, stretched, then threw the covers off. The robe she had given her mother was thrown on the floor along with her jewelry box. Her dresser drawers were hanging open with clothes spilling out. "Ma?"

Dana rubbed her eyes as she tried to focus. What was going on? She got out of bed and walked into the kitchen. "Ma?" Still no answer.

The flip phone was no longer on the kitchen counter. The contents of Dana's purse were strewn on the floor with the billfold laid open on the sofa table. "Oh, Mom." Dana's heart sank as she sat on the sofa and started picking up the pieces her mom had left behind.

CHAPTER 18

Lisa had contacted the police about the identity theft situation she was dealing with. The police officer assured her he would investigate, but it had been months, and she still hadn't heard a word from them. There was nothing she could do until the police found out who had stolen her identity. The creditors weren't taking it off of her report. The only thing she was able to do was make a notation with each credit bureau that her identity had been stolen.

For now, she was stuck working temp assignments while trying to find another job. She had to clear her name and get on with her life. After church on Sunday, she went down to the altar and prayed. What had been done to her wasn't right, so God needed to come through for her. And she trusted He would.

She and her family left church and went home for Sunday dinner. Lisa made a meatloaf with mac and cheese, green beans, and cornbread. This was one of her father's favorite meals. She and John had to break the bad news about the house to him, so she fixed it for him. They had been putting him off with claims of saving enough money for the down payment. But after months with no further word from them, she was sure her father was suspecting something.

"It's smelling good in here," her dad said as he entered the lower level of the brownstone.

"All your favorites, Granddaddy." Kennedy rushed into her grandfather's arms.

David Whitaker hugged his granddaughter, then bent down and kissed her forehead. "My favorite food and my favorite people."

Lisa walked into the living room. She noticed her father rubbing his knees as he sat on the sofa. "Did you enjoy service today, Daddy?"

"You know I did. Pastor Jonathan set the place on fire today. I saw you at the altar." He rubbed his knees again. "I've been praying for you, so I hope you got what you needed from the Lord today."

She couldn't actually say yes to that. God hadn't been showing up for her lately. But her parents had taught her to pray until something happened, so Lisa was committed to continuing to bring this issue before the Lord.

John came into the living room carrying a glass of iced tea. He handed it to her father. "We're happy you could join us for dinner, Dad."

"Y'all mention meatloaf, and I'm here. Lisa makes meatloaf like her mama used to make it." He rubbed his hands together. "I can't wait."

"Well then, why don't we sit down at the dining room table and eat," John suggested.

Lisa turned toward the kitchen. "Give me a second. I need to plate the food." She waved toward her daughter. "Come help your mama."

"Do I have to?" Kennedy whined.

"Only if you want to eat," Lisa joked with her daughter.

Kennedy left her grandfather's side and joined Lisa in the kitchen. "Get the serving bowls out of the cabinet for me." Lisa pointed toward the cabinet next to the stove.

Kennedy did as her mother requested. Lisa filled the bowls and then plated the meatloaf. They took the food to the dining room and set it on the table. "Let's eat," Lisa said.

She sat down. John said grace over the food. Then they passed the food around the table and began eating.

Her father took a couple of bites of the meatloaf, then rubbed his belly. "Tastes like home."

Lisa gave a nervous laugh as she looked at John then back at her father. "Well, you are at home, Daddy."

"Not for long," he said and then went back to his plate. "This is so good."

Lisa put her fork down. Her stomach was doing flips. He had always been proud of her, so sure she would make something of herself. But he had also been hard on her during her formative years. Therefore, Lisa hadn't told her dad about the identity theft or the problems with the bank loan. She kept holding him off, hoping something would change, but it had now been three months since her nightmare began.

Right now, she felt like that teenage girl still looking for her father's approval. How could she tell him she couldn't buy the house?

"Oh, did you hear about Councilman Brown?" her daddy asked her.

"Please don't tell me he's in the news again." He had been spending more time at his mistress' house than at the city council. The police had been called to his house when his wife threw him out. It was all caught on film and handed over to the local news.

"He resigned," David told her. "There's going to be a special election for his seat."

"Wow! I hadn't heard anything about it, but I'm not surprised. His secretary took me off the mailing list after I called to complain about the lack of support the council was giving to Bed-Stuy."

"Don't get on the team for the next one wanting to run for office." Her dad pointed his fork in her direction. "You need to run for it yourself."

"I don't know, Daddy. I don't have the experience needed to run for public office."

John added his thoughts. "It's not like you're trying to get a senate seat. This is a local office. You've helped with the councilman's campaign and the mayor's campaign, so you have campaign experience and can pull on some of your contacts for help."

"I can't even think about city council right now." Lisa took another bite of her meatloaf.

"Why not, Mom? You've always wanted to help the community. Have you changed your mind about that?"

The way her daughter was looking at her made Lisa feel like she'd be taking something away from her if she didn't run for city council. Like the person who stole her identity had taken from her. She couldn't do that. "No, hon, that's not what I'm saying. I'm not sure if I'm the right person for the job."

They ate in silence for a few more minutes, then Lisa cleared her throat. She had been looking over at John during the dinner, hoping that he would take the hint and start the conversation about the issue with the house, but he hadn't said anything, so Lisa finally said, "Daddy, we invited you to dinner to tell you what's going on with the loan for the house."

Her father put his fork down and pushed the plate up so he could put his elbows on the table.

Lisa looked at John one more time. She ran her hand through her hair, stalling. John also put his fork down, then said, "Dad, as you know, Lisa and I were supposed to meet with a banker about three months ago to finalize the loan on the house."

David nodded. "I waited for you and Lisa to tell me when to come to closing, but Lisa said y'all needed to save more money before you could close on the house." He glanced at his daughter. "I'll admit, I was wondering why it was taking so long, but I figured you would tell me soon enough."

His tone told her that he expected her to be adult about the situation, but Lisa wasn't equipped with whatever it took to be an adult about something like this. For it seemed to Lisa that her whole world was crashing in on her, and she hadn't done a thing to deserve it.

Somehow Lisa found her voice. "The bank notified us that there were things on my credit file that indicated I had defaulted on a lease and that I had two large credit card bills that hadn't been paid on in the last two years."

David's eyebrows furrowed. He turned to John and then back to Lisa. "Doesn't sound like you at all. Did the bank pull the wrong file or what?"

Lisa was grateful her father gave her the benefit of the doubt on this issue. She had worried he would accuse her of being irresponsible, as he had when she was younger. "It doesn't look like a mistake. Apparently, I'm the victim of identity theft, but the problem is these creditors won't take the items off my credit report on my word alone."

David's jaw swelled as he puffed out a bit of air. "Don't tell me they expect you to pay it."

"I filed a report with each creditor and with the police." Lisa shrugged. "I haven't heard anything back yet, so it looks like we need more time before we can buy the house."

Her dad shook his head.

"I know you're anxious to move down south before the weather changes, but do you think you can give us a little more time to get this matter with my credit straightened out?"

Empathy was in her father's eyes as he spoke to his daughter. "It's not so much about the cold as it is about me climbing up and down those stairs. At this point I'd be happy with a one-bedroom flat, so long as I didn't have to take those stairs night and day."

John held up a finger, looking like he was having a lightbulb moment. "Why don't you take our apartment, and we can move into your side of the house?"

"I can't ask Daddy to do that. He worked so hard to buy this brownstone, I don't want to shove him in the basement apartment."

But her dad was smiling. "I like it . . . great idea. It's just me, so this apartment is plenty big enough, and I won't have to climb stairs to get to my bedroom or if I need something from the kitchen." David then used his index finger to poke at Kennedy's nose. "And I'll still be able to spend time with my granddaughter."

Lisa never would have thought to ask her dad to move

into the basement apartment so she could have the house, but he seemed happy with the idea. "If you really mean it, then okay, but I don't want you lifting a thing. We'll get a moving company to switch out the bed and the furniture."

"And we will take over the mortgage and pay your utilities," John suggested. "You won't have to come out of your pocket for anything."

David was still smiling. "I appreciate you, son. You're a good man. I trust you with Lisa and Kennedy, so I don't mind helping you all out in your time of need."

"Thank you, sir. We won't let you down. You have my word," John told him.

Later that night as Lisa and John were preparing for bed, she told her husband, "I don't think I say this often enough, but I agree with my dad. You are a good man. Thank you so much for what you did today."

He turned down the covers on his side of the bed and climbed in. "I know how important this house is to you. If we have to pay it off and then take out a home equity loan to give your father the money due to him for the house, then we'll do it."

"He only has two years of payments left on the mortgage, so I'm thankful he's willing to let us take those bills off his hands." Lisa climbed in next to her husband.

He turned off the light on his nightstand. She reached up to turn her light out, but then turned back to John. "Do you really think I could win a city council seat?"

John reached for her, brought her so close she could feel

the heat between them. "I do, baby. It's your calling. All you've ever talked about is how much you want to do for this community. Maybe this is the time for you to go after your dream from a different angle."

CHAPTER 19

Since Vida pulled that most recent disappearing act, Dana closed herself off to everything but growing her business. Jeff was a great guy, but he would never understand her struggles, nor did she want to put him in a position to be taken advantage of by her mother.

She had received an order from a major grocery chain. They were placing orders for all eleven hundred of their stores and featuring her in the Black hair-care section. The marketing people she hired had earned their pay almost immediately. Now she was working to get her production up.

Dana found a building available for lease in Bed-Stuy on Nostrand Avenue. When she left Bed-Stuy eleven years ago, Dana had no desire to ever see this side of Brooklyn again. It was the place where life went so wrong for her. But when all was said and done, she couldn't pass up the opportunity to bring a business to the community she grew up in. It was like her old friend Lisa once told her: somebody had to be a change agent in their community.

She was now purchasing all the equipment needed to produce her products in her own building as she did when she began this business. Granted, Hair Fabulous had started in her kitchen. And she had been the only worker. She now had a product development team and a marketing team, and as soon as she had all her equipment in the new location, she would hire a few manufacturing employees to produce the products in-house and ship them out to their new grocery chain account and beauty supply stores all over the country.

Dana could have reduced her costs by a small margin if she continued to outsource production, but providing a living wage for the people in her community was another part of being a change agent. No doubt, Lisa would be proud of her.

Jeff had taken a chance on her and helped her find financing for her business, so she was going to pay it forward. As long as she was making money, her employees would be able to feed their families and not have to turn to the streets in order to survive.

Thinking about Jeff caused her heart to hurt. She had been ignoring his phone calls for weeks. She told herself she couldn't do romance while building her business, but every single day she woke up, she felt that familiar ache in her heart until she set her nose to the grindstone. When she was working, she wasn't thinking about her feelings.

"Ms. Jones, are you ready to review the commercial?" Sierra, the marketing manager, asked as she stood outside Dana's new office.

Dana was sitting behind her desk reviewing the reports her accountant had provided. The accountant did not work in her office. Jeff had set her up with someone she could outsource her accounting to so she didn't have to focus on the numbers and could work on growing the business. She looked up and waved Sierra in.

"The commercial is done already?" One of their marketing strategies—and the reason they had convinced the grocery chain to distribute Hair Fabulous products—was to not only do commercials but also put ads in magazines like *Essence*, *Ebony*, and *Black Enterprise* to promote the products.

"The production company we're working with is a beast. They get stuff done." Sierra sat in the chair across from Dana and handed her the CD.

"We cut this commercial last week. I didn't expect to see a final until the end of the month."

"Well, let's be happy that things are going our way," Sierra told her. "If you approve this version, we can have the commercial running within two weeks."

Dana put the disc in her computer and watched the thirty-second clip of a girl using the products to wash and condition her hair, then walk down the street with bouncy hair and a man smiling and snapping her photo as she passed by.

The image of the camera and the photo of the woman brought back fond memories of the last summer Dana spent hanging out with her girls. It was like beauty in motion. Dana missed her camera.

At the end of the commercial, the scene switched to a set with Dana holding the shampoo and conditioner in one hand and a jar of hair grease in the other. She smiled and said, "I created these products to help you look fabulous." Then the commercial ended with the logos of everywhere the products could be purchased.

"Is it really necessary to have me in the commercial? I thought it was fine without the ending."

"Did you see how they put your name on the screen and the CEO title as you spoke? A Black-owned business is gold in the markets where we'll be running those commercials, so yes, we need you front and center."

Dana was nervous about being the spokesperson for her brand. What if someone recognized her from the time she spent in prison? What if they trashed her and turned people off her products? Her employees knew nothing of her past. She wished she could confide in someone and get some advice on how to handle her past as she moved forward in the business community.

Jeff was so savvy about business, she had wanted to confide in him, but she still remembered the look on his face when she handed Jasmine that money. It was as if he thought Jasmine didn't deserve anything in life due to her current situation. What would he think of her if he knew the things she had done?

Better not to think about Jeff—keep working.

Dana approved the commercial. Sierra left her office and Dana went back to reviewing the reports her accountant had sent over.

"How long do you think you'll be able to avoid me?"

The rich baritone of his voice sent shock waves down her spine. She'd been replaying one of his recorded messages from her answering machine at home each night for weeks so she could hear the voice she had grown so attached to.

But now he was standing at her office door, looking as scrumptious as a piece of Junior's cheesecake. Why was he here? Didn't he know by now she was not the one for him? With a calmness in her voice she didn't feel within, she said, "Jeff, what brings you to this side of town?"

"You." He sat down in the spot Sierra had vacated.

Dana put her hands on the desk. She sat ramrod straight. She was becoming a woman of power; she now had five in-house employees and would soon have at least twenty when they added the manufacturing piece. She was strong, focused, and totally in love with the man sitting across from her.

"Why have you been avoiding me?"

She glanced around at the walls of her office, then back at her computer—anywhere, everywhere but into those eyes that spoke of love. "I have a lot of work to do to grow this business. I thought I could do both—date you and run my business—but it's too much."

She glanced at him as she finished her sentence. His eyes radiated with sadness. She looked away.

"Is that all we're doing . . . dating?"

Why was he doing this to her? She was trying to protect him. Couldn't he go find some nice girl who didn't have the baggage Dana carried? But he had a point. "We weren't just dating. You and I had a relationship. But it's not a good time for me . . . I'm busy."

"You're hiding, Dana. I wish you would talk to me. Don't you know I want to be with you forever? I want to marry you, but if you won't talk to me, things will never work between us."

His words ripped her heart. She wanted to be with him, too, but how could she? His people were good and kind . . . stable. But all she had known for such a long time were people who destroyed rather than built up. She heaved a sigh as she leaned back in her seat. "I'm not the one for you. You deserve so much more."

Jeff stood, walked over to her door, closed and locked it, then turned back to Dana. "Talk to me."

She lowered her head and wrapped her arms around her chest, trying to block out what she was feeling and what she knew about the love she had for this man. She would destroy him. And she loved him too much to do to him what the people in her life had done to her.

But Jeff wasn't taking no for an answer. He walked around

her desk, got down on a knee in front of her, unwrapped her arms, and took her hands in his. "I'm here, babe. I'm not going anywhere, so talk to me."

"You wouldn't understand." Dana was convinced that no one could understand her pain unless they had been through the things she had.

"Try me."

He was so persistent, so unyielding. He wouldn't let it go, so she decided to give him a dose of what life was really like for her. "My mother didn't eat the cheesecake I took home for her."

He shrugged. "No big deal. I hope you ate it. You loved it so much."

Dana nodded. "I left it on the kitchen counter for her along with a cell phone I purchased so I could keep in touch with her." Dana's chin quivered as she looked at him. "My mom is on drugs so bad she disappears for months on end. I wanted to be able to reach her."

"You did a good thing, hon. Why are you so upset?"

Dana closed her eyes tight. She wished she could block out her past and everything that had ever brought pain into her life, but she wasn't living a fairy tale, not with a mother like Vida. "My mom was still asleep when I arrived home. I climbed in bed with her, like I used to do when I was a kid." Dana didn't want to cry; she wanted to harden her heart so her mother's actions didn't affect her anymore, but the tears kept coming.

"I had planned to tell her about how you helped me get the loan so I could grow my business. I wanted her to meet you, but she woke up before I did and ransacked my house, stealing my jewelry, money from my purse, and the cell phone. I doubt she realized it was hers anyway."

Jeff pulled Dana into his arms. She felt so comfortable in his embrace, like this was where she belonged. As her face nestled at the curve of his neck, she inhaled his scent of lavender and sage and got lost in the smell she had come to know so well.

"I'm so sorry that happened to you, but you can't shut yourself off from the world because your mother keeps hurting you."

He wiped the tears from her face. Dana nodded. "I know I shouldn't, but I don't want to hurt you. All I've ever experienced has been disappointment. You deserve someone better than me."

He broke their embrace and stood. "You've experienced more of life than disappointments." He waved a hand around her office. "Look at you. You are the CEO of your own company. Has your business been a disappointment?"

"No, but . . ."

"There's no buts about this. You are not your mother, and we deserve each other." He took her hands again, lifted her out of her seat. "I want to marry you. I love you and we belong together."

Dana lowered her head. She wondered whether he would still say this if he truly knew her. She wanted to tell him about all her struggles, but something told her he would look at her like he looked at Jasmine when she approached them outside Junior's. And Dana didn't know how she would get back up from a knock like that.

He lifted her head with his index finger. "Take a chance on me. I promise I won't hurt you."

She wasn't worried about him hurting her as much as she was worried about all the bad in her life rubbing off on him. "I know you won't hurt me."

"Then let's do this, baby. Marry me." He greedily kissed her lips as he added, "I want to do life with you."

He was so beautiful to her. He had made this life she was now living possible. She wanted him. Needed him. Dana still felt as if she was all wrong for him, and he deserved a woman who didn't have so much baggage, but now that she was in his arms again, she couldn't give him up. She couldn't go back to life without Jeff. "Okay." Laughter bubbled up in her heart. "I will marry you."

CHAPTER 20

Since losing the position with Liberty, Lisa had been working temporary assignments that she found unfulfilling. Her dad and her husband's encouragement to run for the city council had been a godsend.

In order to get on the ballot, she had to collect signatures from the people in her neighborhood, but she easily received double the signatures needed.

Then, after she registered with the Campaign Finance Board, her name was officially added to the ballot. She was running on the Democratic ticket for the special election, which would be held in late September, three months away.

John was the first contributor to her campaign. She used his money to purchase flyers. They read, *If you care about change in your community, vote for Lisa Coleman.* She took those flyers to her church.

"Hey, Sister Lisa, how are you doing?" Sister Betty asked when Lisa walked in.

"I'm doing really well. I'm excited about running for city council." She handed Betty a stack of flyers. "I brought these to see if we could put them in the fellowship hall."

Sister Betty's lips pursed. "We can't support one candidate

over the other, but nothing says you can't put these flyers on cars in the parking lot during Sunday service."

Smiling, Lisa took the flyers back from Betty. "I like the way you think."

Betty winked at her. "We need you on the council. And I'm sure several people in our church will help you pass out flyers around town."

Lisa snapped her fingers as an idea struck. "We can turn this into an event like we do during Evangelism Week."

"Absolutely," Betty agreed. "And don't forget to stop in at all of the local corner stores and bodegas. Leave some of those flyers."

"Sister Betty, it sounds like I need to hire you as my campaign manager."

"You're running for local office. You won't be able to collect enough donations to pay for a campaign manager, but I'd love to volunteer my time to work on your campaign."

Lisa stepped behind Betty's desk and hugged the woman. "Thank you so much."

"I don't mind at all," Betty told her. "And from what I've heard, Mike Barnes is running in this special election also. You're going to need as much help as you can get to beat that snake."

Mike Barnes was well known in the community. He had been a police officer and the county commissioner. He left Bed-Stuy to take a job in another borough a few years ago, but he was back and Lisa was about to go against him in the primary in order to win the seat. Mike Barnes had been involved in a lot of dirty politics, but if she truly wanted to help her community, then she would simply have to beat him at his own game.

Lisa left the church and headed home, making stops at each store she passed by.

"Hey, Mr. Phillips. How is business?"

Mr. Phillips owned the only store with a butcher within a five-mile radius, so most of the meat business in the neighborhood came to him. "I'd be doing a lot better if the city stopped allowing these discount grocers to take business away from me," he grumbled.

Small, family-owned stores couldn't compete with the chain stores popping up outside of the neighborhood. Lisa handed him her flyers. "I can help you with that. I'm running for city council, and like you, I want things the way they used to be in our neighborhood."

"Wonderful news, Lisa. You've got my vote for sure."

"Thank you, Mr. Phillips." She pointed to the flyers she had handed him. "Do you mind laying those out on your counter so customers can pick them up?"

"Not at all." He wiped his hands on his apron and walked around the counter to a table by the entry door. "I'll put them right here by the door. I had the pleasure of watching you grow up, so you certainly have my support."

She received similar responses with each store she stopped at. These community stores were the lifelines of the neighborhood. Word would get out about her candidacy. She prayed the voters would truly show up for her.

As she was walking down the street, she saw Mrs. James from Lewis Avenue. "How are you doing?" Lisa said as she approached. "I haven't seen Renee or Raven around town in a while."

"They were offered jobs in the South, so Renee now lives in Atlanta, and Raven is in Charlotte, North Carolina, but if you hadn't tutored them when they were struggling in high school, they never would have received scholarships for college and be doing so well now." Mrs. James put a hand on Lisa's shoulder. "Thank you, Lisa. You were truly a godsend."

"You've already thanked me, and Renee and Raven are smart. They needed a push."

"Their daddy and I could never push them in the right direction. I don't know what your method is, but it works."

Lisa smiled. "My method is called *believe*. That's it. I told them I believed in them." Lisa pulled out one of her flyers. "I'm running for city council, and I would sure appreciate your vote."

Mrs. James took the flyer, glanced at it. "You've got my vote," she said and then continued down the street.

The last stop for Lisa was a beauty-supply store. She needed some hair grease for Kennedy, so she decided to pick some up while giving the workers her flyers. On the shelf to the left of the entry door was a whole row of different types of hair grease. She normally bought Ultra Sheen, but the store was out of stock. They did have a new brand—Hair Fabulous—with a lavender scent. She purchased it, handed her flyers to the workers, and then headed home.

She and her family were now in the main living quarters of the brownstone while her father had taken the basement apartment. She climbed the steps to her home and opened the door. Even with sneakers on, her feet were throbbing. She sat down in the living room and kicked her shoes off.

Kennedy came running into the room and sat down next to her. "Did you pass out all those flyers already?"

"Pretty much. But I have more upstairs."

"I took your flyers to school today and gave one to my teacher."

Lisa leaned forward and kissed Kennedy on the cheek. "Thank you for helping out."

"Of course, Mommy. You're going to win."

Her father walked into the living room, wiping his hands on a kitchen towel. "The little one has eaten, and I left fried chicken and home fries on the stove for you and John."

"Thanks for watching Kennedy."

"Got to make myself useful in some way."

Her dad didn't know how to enjoy retirement. She pointed toward the television against the wall on the opposite side of the room. "You can turn the TV on for me."

He turned it on, then sat on the sofa with her.

Lisa leaned her head back and waited for the news to come on. She half watched a few commercials as she waited. The third commercial—for Hair Fabulous—caught her attention.

"Oh, they have shampoo also." Lisa made a mental note. If she liked the hair grease, she might try the shampoo next.

As the commercial was ending, Lisa's eyes almost bugged out of her head when Dana Jones came on the screen holding shampoo, conditioner, and hair grease. Dana said, "I created these products to help you look fabulous."

Her dad pointed at the screen. Lines creased his forehead. "Isn't that your old friend?" He popped his fingers. "The one who got arrested."

"Sure is." Lisa grinned.

"Looks like she's doing something productive with her life." David stood and headed for the door.

"Well, I'll be." Lisa leaned back against the sofa. "Prayer does change things. Dana Jones has made something of herself." She took a moment to pray for continued blessings for her old friend.

CHAPTER 21

Dana had been named Businesswoman of the Year by the National Association of Women in Business. And from the way everyone was acting, it was a big deal. And now she was lying in bed on a tropical island next to the man of her dreams. It was now late July, and Dana was winning.

"So how does it feel to wake up as Mrs. Dana Williams?"

Dana put a hand on Jeff's cheek as she lay in his arms. "It feels good, Mr. Williams." There had been no beautiful wedding, no family and friends at an elaborate reception where they cut a three-layered cake, had their first dance, and took memorable photos. Just her and Jeff at the justice of the peace, with clerks for witnesses.

Dana hadn't wanted any questions about why her mother and father weren't at the wedding. And she certainly didn't want Jeff's parents wondering why she didn't have many friends to invite. And if she were being honest with herself, if she had taken the time to plan a wedding, she might have come to her senses and canceled the whole thing.

They were now on their honeymoon on Paradise Island in the Bahamas. Since the Atlantis opened in 1998, Dana had dreamed about vacationing at a place like this but never imagined her dreams would come true two years later.

But as she lay next to the man she loved in their grand suite with its spectacular view of the Caribbean beach, she asked, "Is this for real, Jeff? Did we really get married?" She turned toward the floor-to-ceiling windows in their room and looked out at the ocean. "And are we truly vacationing at Atlantis?"

"We did." He turned her face back toward him and kissed her lips. "And we are." He kissed her again. "And you deserve to be here as much as, if not more than, all the other people at this resort."

She tried to smile, but she couldn't hold Jeff's gaze and averted her eyes.

Jeff leaned on his elbow and moved his head until she had no choice but to look directly at him. "We're not doing this." Tucking a finger under her chin, he bore down on her with those all-knowing brown eyes of his. "You're beautiful inside and out. You are special, and you are Dana Jones Williams, Businesswoman of the Year. The woman who developed her own line of hair-care products. The woman who stole my heart . . . Nothing about your past defines the woman you have become, so stop it."

"Well, when I hear you recite my accolades, I guess I am that girl."

Jeff flopped back down on the bed and pulled Dana into his arms. "No, you're not a girl anymore. You're a woman—my woman—and I'm a blessed man."

She adored him. Jeff was unlike any man she had ever met, and she truly believed one of the reasons he was such a good man had to do with his upbringing. His parents hadn't let him run wild.

During many of their nightly phone conversations, Jeff had told her about the structure his parents set in the household. No staying out late, no smoking or drinking. Homework was a priority, and college was discussed at the dinner table.

Dana was proud to be associated with the Williams family.

"So what's on the agenda today?" she asked her husband.

With his arm wrapped around her, he said, "I chartered a boat so we can go snorkeling. You and I are going to swim with the fish."

Dana propped herself up on her pillows. "Oh no we won't. Doesn't sound like any kind of fun I want to participate in."

"It's not like we're going to be jetting off to the Bahamas every weekend. We can't pass this opportunity up. Come on, Dana. You only live once. Let's have some fun."

Dana's issue was she truly understood what "you only live once" meant. She also knew how life could be snatched away when you were doing stupid stuff. "It's too risky, Jeff."

"You trust me, don't you?"

"Of course I trust you, but I don't know the crocodiles or sharks in this water you want to dive into."

Jeff got out of bed, headed toward the bathroom. "I've already paid for the excursion, hon. Go with me. I promise you will have a good time."

"No! I'm not doing it." She folded her arms across her chest. "Not me. No way, nohow."

He stopped at the bathroom door. "Okay, then you pick. What are we going to do today?"

An easy grin spread over her lips. "Let's lounge on the beach in a cabana, having food and drinks brought to us while we do nothing but swim, listen to music, or read a book."

"You do live on the wild side, wife." Jeff laughed at her as he closed the bathroom door.

"The wild side is dangerous!" Dana yelled to him. "I don't like danger."

But she did like being with her husband, so she put on her light blue and white bikini and then threw on a sundress. They went to Poseidon's Table for the best buffet breakfast Dana had ever had. With food like this, she would stay at Atlantis for an extra week if they could.

After breakfast, they rented the cabana and lounged there while Dana read a book and Jeff took a few dips in the pool. But then he told her about a stingray experience not too far from where they were lounging. Nothing in Dana wanted to do that, but she had already halted his snorkeling adventure, so she walked down the beach with him.

The moment the instructors told them they had to put on a wet suit and get in the pool of water with the stingrays, Dana backed out.

Oblivious to her trepidation, Jeff put on his wet suit, then held her wet suit in his hand, inviting her to join him. Dana stood there . . . not moving. "I can't."

Jeff rubbed her arm. "It's okay, baby. I'll do it by myself. This is something I've always wanted to do."

"I wish I was as brave as you. But too much adventure isn't good for anyone." Dana folded her arms across her chest.

He smiled as he told her, "The one thing you need to remember about me is I'm a praying man. I might not attend church every week. But God is always with me." He touched his heart. "In here. He will protect me."

Dana didn't hang her hat on God's protection. She'd seen a lot of people die in her lifetime. Maybe she was jaded. "Be careful. God doesn't have to protect you in your foolishness." Dana knew this firsthand.

"I'm good. Please stop worrying."

She nodded, lip quivering. "Don't let that stingray bite you, and I'll stop worrying."

The instructor walked over to her. "You can't get in the water without the wet suit and life vest."

She side-eyed Jeff. "Did you hear the instructor? You need a life vest for this excursion."

"It's cool," Jeff said.

Dana rolled her eyes, then turned back to the instructor. "I'm not going. I'll stay right here and wait for my husband."

"Okay," the instructor told her, "but you're missing one of the best parts of sea life you'll ever experience."

As far as Dana was concerned, she'd already seen all of the sea life she wanted or needed in the hotel lobby with the huge aquarium that was built into the walls on the first floor of the Atlantis. It was beautiful, and she loved every minute of exploring the biggest fish tank she had ever encountered. But she did not want to swim with the stingrays. She wanted to go back to the hotel, lounge in their cabana, and look out at the shimmering blueness of the water.

The instructor let them feed the stingrays, and then Jeff and a few other people started swimming with those creatures. Dana tried to take her mind away from this moment and the quiver inside her stomach each time Jeff got too close to one of those creatures. "Jeff, go the other way!" she screamed.

He glanced up at her but kept swimming toward the stingray. She wished he understood bad things happen and life could be over in an instant. Why was her husband taking such a risk?

Dana enjoyed taking risks with her business and seeing the growth with each move as she walked into her destiny, but taking unnecessary risks was not for her. She wanted to keep both feet planted on the ground . . . most times.

Jeff put a hand on the stingray, rubbing its back. Dana was about to yell at him to back away when he went completely still and started floating.

She rushed to the edge of the pool, leaned forward, and started yelling. "Jeff! Jeff! Can you hear me? Are you all right?" Her emotions were all over the place. Had her husband been stung? Was he dying?

She pulled her sundress over her head and was about to jump in the water when the instructor stopped her. "You can't go in without the proper equipment."

She swung around, eyes dripping with tears. "Go get him!" Fingers jutting toward the water. "Go help my husband! Don't leave him out there. Bring him back to me." She felt like that eighteen-year-old girl holding Derrick in her arms while blood trickled from his mouth and life left his body.

Turning back toward the water, seeing her husband still in distress, she cried out, "Jefffff!" Sound vibrated against the side of the pool, and the water shook.

Jeff shot up like a bullet. He swam toward them with purpose. Dana was shaking as she watched him come toward her.

Climbing out of the pool, Jeff rushed over to her. "I'm okay. I promise. I was having fun with you."

Dana wanted to say something, but her tongue felt dry and thick as her chest heaved. Sweat was dripping from her forehead, but she shivered as if she'd been doused by a bucket of ice-cold water.

He grabbed her and pulled her into his arms. "What's wrong, baby? Talk to me."

In his arms, seeing he was safe, Dana felt her breathing settle. She felt the warmth of him. "You came back to me."

"Yes, baby, of course I came back. I'll always be here for you."

They went back to their room, ordered room service, then went to bed. Dana had not wanted to take the excursion in the first place, but she had no idea it would cause a panic attack.

Now she was wondering whether she should have gotten some therapy since she obviously wasn't over Derrick's death.

Jeff ran his hand down her back. She was facing the floor-to-ceiling windows, staring out at the ocean. The waves were slow and calm.

"You want to talk about it?" Jeff asked her.

Dana had tried to keep her past in the past, not wanting to talk about all the mistakes she made. But she owed Jeff the truth after her reaction today. Still watching the water, she told him, "You are so brave. I'm proud of how you completely let loose and experience life. But I learned a long time ago, people who take too many chances end up dead, and I don't want to lose you."

"You're not going to lose me, hon. But I don't understand why you were so scared."

She wouldn't turn to him, couldn't face him as she said, "I had a boyfriend when I was eighteen. I thought I loved him even though he was all wrong for me."

Jeff turned her around so she was facing him. "What's caused you to be so afraid?"

Dana squeezed her eyes shut. Shut out the memories . . .

shut out the pain. But when she opened them again, her husband was still looking at her. Waiting. With a heavy sigh, she began. "He was this stupid kid who thought he could do whatever he wanted without facing the consequences, but he got shot and died in my arms."

A lone tear rolled down her face. "I try not to think about it, but it must still be affecting me. All I could imagine today was you lying on the bottom of the pool, dying, without me by your side."

"I wish you had told me this before. I never would have put you through that type of trauma if I had known."

"I should have told you, but I had no idea you'd fake your death." She punched him in the side.

"Let's make a promise to each other." He took her hands and kissed them. "Let's tell each other everything—our fears, our triumphs, and even our sorrows."

She nodded. "I promise." She said those words, but deep inside Dana wondered—if she truly opened the nightmare that was once her life, would Jeff run away screaming, looking for the nearest divorce attorney?

CHAPTER 22

Lisa had reached out to the officer assigned to her case at least once a week since she reported the crime. Early on, he assured her he was chasing down a lead, but since then, she'd left him message after message with no response. So today, as she walked the blocks passing out flyers encouraging constituents to vote for her in the special election that was now twenty-eight days away, she made her way up Tompkins Avenue.

Lisa walked eight blocks, bumping into residents and shaking hands.

"Hey, Mr. Walker. How has Mrs. Lois been doing?" she asked as he stepped out of the bodega.

He took the cigarette out of his mouth. Let it swing in his left hand. "She's still mean as a rattlesnake. Don't get too close or she'll bite you."

"Not funny. Your wife is the sweetest woman in Brooklyn."

"Yeah." He coughed. "Sweet enough to put up with me for thirty years."

"Tell her I'm running for city council and I would appreciate your votes."

As she continued down the street, passing out flyers and listening to the concerns of neighbors, Lisa made her way to her destination—the 79th Precinct. She entered the building, asked to speak with Officer Roberts, and then waited to be escorted to his desk. Officer Roberts was a little taller than Lisa—she guessed he was about five feet seven. His hair was in that awkward stage—bald on the top but hair on the sides and the back of his head. Lisa wondered why men didn't shave the whole head when it was like this. But it wasn't her business, so she let the thought drift away.

"Good afternoon, Mrs. Coleman. Please have a seat."

"Thank you, I will." She sat down in the chair next to his desk.

"I have received all your messages, and I am working on your case," he told her.

"Officer Roberts, I'm sure you have a ton of work on your plate and my issue might not seem like a big deal to you, but it is to me."

He lifted a hand. "We don't operate in that manner at this precinct. Identity theft is a crime just as if the criminal broke into your house and stole your television."

"How can we get some resolution?"

"I don't have any news to share with you yet, but I think we're going to find this person."

"Good, this has brought great hardship on me and my family. I lost a very prestigious position with Liberty Advocates. I lost out on the ability to buy my father's brownstone, and he now has to delay his dream of moving to Florida."

"I get it. Someone misused your credit, but—"

"I'm working temp assignments. My new job retracted their employment offer after learning about my credit history and my old job had already hired my replacement." She closed her eyes and took a deep breath, trying to calm herself.

"Imagine how you would feel if you had worked hard all your life to pay your bills and earn a good name only to discover someone had snatched it away from you."

"I would be angry," the officer admitted.

"I'm trying to believe some good will ultimately prevail, but I'm at the point where I need to see something working in my favor. Does that make sense to you?"

He nodded. "Makes perfect sense." He opened his desk drawer and pulled out a file. "I made contact with the owner of the UPS Store, and he provided me with the home address of the person who was using the box. The problem I have is the owner of the apartment passed away last year, and his daughter can't seem to locate the leases of prior tenants."

"So you're saying she doesn't live there anymore?" This was so frustrating, like chasing after a ghost.

"Apparently there is another family in the apartment now, but the owner's daughter does remember two roommates shared the apartment a few years ago. She is going to check the storage unit where they placed her father's things to see if she can provide me with the lease agreements from the other tenants."

Evidently the wheels of justice moved slowly and ground to a halt when the paper trail ended. Lisa pulled one of her flyers out of her bag and handed it to Officer Roberts. "I lost my job over this credit fiasco, but not my will to do something positive for the people in our community."

Officer Roberts smiled as he took the flyer from her. "You're running for city council. I think that's awesome." He stood. "Concentrate on the election, and let me run down the leads as they come in. I promise I will continue working on this case."

Lisa stood as well, shook his hand. "Thank you. I appreciate your hard work."

She had almost reached the door when Mike Barnes' booming voice stopped her forward motion. "Hey there, Mrs. Lisa Coleman. What brings you down to the precinct? Are you reporting how badly I'm about to beat you in this special election?"

"Hahaha." He was so sure of himself it made Lisa want to beat him all the more. "You'll be filing the report in twenty-eight days."

Holding on to his belt buckle as he leaned back on his heels, he said, "I know you're not in here trying to hustle up votes. The boys in blue stick together."

"You're not a police officer anymore, Barnes, and you don't get to tell people what to do with their votes. That's what democracy is all about." She opened the precinct door and walked out.

Lisa clenched her fists as she made her way back home. Barnes was too full of himself to care about the people in Bed-Stuy. But she did care. She would win this election. She couldn't afford to lose.

Sitting at her desk, Dana was left stupefied by the ten-million-dollar check she was holding in her hand. The commercials had been a hit, and the grocery chain had sold out of her products and were requesting double their last order.

What a difference a day makes, was all Dana could think as she pinched herself to make sure she was actually living this life and not dreaming it. She grew up so poor she never imagined what being rich would be like.

She'd also been deceived by love in such a devastating way she never imagined she would find a man who was good and true. But now she was rich and in love with a man she was proud to call her own.

There was a knock on the door. She put the check in her purse. "Come in."

Kim, her receptionist, entered carrying a brown paper bag. Dana still couldn't believe she was running a business that required a receptionist, marketing team, and manufacturing team.

"Lunch is here." Kim put the bag on Dana's desk.

Dana rubbed her hands together. She was getting hungry and couldn't wait to bite into the corned beef hero with sauerkraut. *Mm-mm* good. She opened the bag, pulled the hero out, and set it on her desk. Practically salivating as she unwrapped it, she picked the hero up and was about to take a bite when her belly did a flip-flop. The sour smell of the sauerkraut irritated her nostrils and assaulted her senses in such a way Dana grabbed hold of her mouth.

She dropped the hero back on the desk, pushed her chair back, stood up, and ran out of her office toward the bathroom. Her hand was pushing the bathroom door open when the contents of her breakfast spilled out onto the floor.

"Oh my goodness. What a mess," she said once she stopped throwing up.

Kim came running around the corner. "Are you okay?"

"I think so. I had a reaction to the smell of the sauerkraut." Dana went into the bathroom and grabbed some paper towels. She came back into the hallway and started wiping up her mess.

Kim said, "My mother told me she used to throw up at the smell of food when she was carrying me. She said she still can't stand the smell of taco salad and refuses to eat one."

"Well, I'm not pregnant," Dana told her as she put the paper towels in the trash. "I've only been married six weeks." But as she grabbed some more paper towels and turned on the sink to wet them, she realized her cycle was late.

She wiped the floor with the wet towels. Threw them away. Back in her office, Dana put the hero back in the bag, grabbed her purse, and then threw the sandwich in the trash. "I'm taking a break," she told Kim as she walked out of the building.

There was a drugstore a few blocks up. She went inside and purchased a pregnancy kit. On her way out of the store, she noticed a political flyer on top of the newspaper stand at the checkout counter.

Lisa's picture was on the flyer, but her last name was no longer Whitaker. Lisa Coleman was running for city council. Dana hadn't seen her old friend since they were teenagers. Hadn't wanted to see any of the gang from the old neighborhood after going to prison. Dana had been too ashamed. And Lisa had never accepted any of her collect calls or returned any of the letters she'd written. She put the flyer in her purse and went back to work.

Dana took her pregnancy test into the bathroom and peed on the stick, then tapped her foot while she waited.

They hadn't been married long. Were they ready to start a family? She didn't even know if Jeff wanted kids right now. But she was thirty-three . . . She wasn't getting any younger. Would it really be a bad thing if she was pregnant?

Her answer came in the shape of a plus sign. A smile spread across her face. Pregnant. She couldn't concentrate the rest of the day. She ordered two steak dinners, then called Jeff and asked him to meet her at home.

When she arrived at their apartment, she put the vase with the dozen red roses Jeff had given her this morning on the dining table, pulled out the china Jeff's mom had given them when they returned from the Bahamas, and set the table.

"Well, aren't you being fancy today," Jeff said as he took off his jacket and tie.

"Only the best for you, baby." She almost giggled as she said *baby.* She had to be careful—she didn't want to give it away too soon. "Go take a shower, get out of your work clothes, and let me finish setting the table."

Jeff sniffed the air as he walked toward the bedroom. "It smells good in here. What are we celebrating?"

"You hurry back before the food gets cold." She put the medium-rare steaks, garlic mashed potatoes, and mixed veggies on their plates. A basket of rolls sat next to the roses. She then filled champagne glasses with nonalcoholic champagne she picked up on the way home.

Chocolate cake with vanilla ice cream was Jeff's favorite dessert. She left the cake in the kitchen, along with the pregnancy test and the political flyer for Lisa, and put the ice cream in the freezer.

Jeff strutted back into the dining room wearing a pair of tan slacks and a black polo shirt. The grin on his face was contagious. Dana turned away from him and sat down, trying to wipe the grin from her own face. "Well, husband, we've been married six weeks now. Do you have any regrets yet?"

He shook his head. "Not a one." He pointed to the roses. "Does it look like I have any regrets?"

She grinned again. This morning had been special. He'd brought her breakfast in bed and then handed her the roses.

She truly loved this man and couldn't wait to be a parent with him. They ate their food as they talked about their day. Dana carefully omitted the most important part of her day. But when they finished the dinner, she went into the kitchen, took the ice cream out of the freezer, and put two heaping scoops of vanilla ice cream in their bowls. She then sliced two pieces of chocolate cake and placed them over the ice cream.

As she headed back to the dining room with the dessert, she grabbed the flyer and the pregnancy test. Dana set Jeff's bowl in front of him. She then sat down in her seat and slid the flyer with the pregnancy test beneath it over to Jeff.

She took a spoonful of her cake with the ice cream, then casually said, "An old friend of mine is running for city council."

"Oh yeah?" He nodded his approval. "It always helps to have friends at city hall."

Dana pointed toward the flyer. "I'd like to support her campaign, but I don't want her to know the money is coming from me. Would you mind taking care of this for me?"

Jeff picked up the flyer. He looked it over. "How do you know her?"

"We went to school together."

"Then I don't get it." He shrugged. "Why don't you want her to know you're donating to her campaign?"

Dana lowered her eyes. "Our friendship got complicated." Her lips twisted as she added, "This is a good moment for Lisa. I don't want to get in the way."

"I get it, hon. I'll make the donation." Jeff placed the flyer back on the table. He was about to pick up his spoon to take another bite of his dessert when his eyes connected with the pregnancy test.

He looked stuck, like he couldn't move, so Dana got up, put the pregnancy test in her hand, and stood in front of Jeff with the plus sign showing.

Jeff blinked and blinked and blinked. A tear rolled down his face. He looked up at Dana, questions in his eyes. "I'm going to be a daddy?"

"Facts, baby, facts." She tried to act nonchalant about it, but her face broke, and she was crying right with him.

Jeff jumped out of his seat, picked Dana up, and swung her around. "I can't believe it!" he kept saying. He kissed her lips as he put her feet back on the floor. "I love you so much!"

"I love you too, babe." Then she said the thing she hadn't believed could ever happen for her. "We're going to be happy, aren't we?"

CHAPTER 23

He wants a debate." Lisa had come down to the basement apartment to visit with her father.

"Who wants a debate?" David asked.

"Mike Barnes, the oh-so-obnoxious one who thinks I should get out of this race because he deserves to be on the city council more than anyone else."

"Does he know you were on the debate team in high school and you and your team brought the trophy back to Boys and Girls High School?"

"Obviously not." Lisa balled her fists. "I want to beat him so bad."

"Careful, Lisa. Remember: vengeance belongs to the Lord."

"I know, Daddy, but he was so sure of himself when I saw him at the 79th Precinct a couple weeks ago. And the thing that really gets my blood to boiling is he isn't even from Bed-Stuy. He grew up in New Jersey and moved over here when he became a police officer."

Her father shrugged. "Sometimes outsiders can see what a community needs better than the people who have been in it all of their lives."

Wagging a finger at her father, she said, "Whose side are you on? I mean, you did tell me I should run for city council."

He nodded. "I did, and I think you would be an asset. But others on the council will have ideas different from yours. I want you to be willing to listen. I want you to be a good leader."

This from the man who would yell and scream in church meetings when he didn't get his way. Pastor Jonathan got so tired of her dad's antics he tried to vote him off the deacon board. Her father had been saved by two votes. Lisa didn't let him get away with his don't-do-what-I-do-but-what-I-say comment. "Daddy, you never listened to anybody when you thought you were right about a matter at the church or at your store."

David looked at her with eyes full of the wisdom only age could bring. He said, "I've made a lot of mistakes in my life. The chief of them being, I once thought I knew best about everything and wouldn't listen to anyone.

"My foolish ways cost me some friends." He shook his head and grinned. "I'm thankful your mama put up with me until the end. But I think she always knew the good Lord would knock some sense into my head."

"And you think I need some sense knocked into my head now, is that it?"

"All of God's children need some sense knocked into them every now and then. I wish I had known that when I was younger. But I'm more settled now . . . I've learned to pray more and to listen for God's soft answers."

After speaking with her father, Lisa went home and helped Kennedy with her homework. She then practiced with John for the debate.

"Daddy thinks I need to be humble about it, but I want to crush Barnes in this debate."

"Don't worry—you're going to smoke him. You're really good at presenting your argument. Keep in mind the reason you want to be on the city council."

Lisa nodded. "I have a heart for the underprivileged kids in our neighborhoods. I want to make sure they have access to a quality education and access to after-school programs that will give them the tools they need for higher education."

John lifted a finger. "I know you have a heart for the kids, but what about the adults? What can you do for us?"

"A lot of the Bed-Stuy residents are underemployed. I want to bring more job-training programs to the neighborhood . . . when one rises, we all rise."

Standing up from his spot on the sofa, John clapped. "You got this, Lisa. You got it."

Lisa pumped her fist in the air. "Yes!"

They sat back on the sofa together. John took her hand in his. Hesitated for a moment, then asked, "Have you thought about what you'll say if the credit issues come up during the debate?"

With a catch of her breath, Lisa put a hand to her heart. "Do you really think someone would be so low? I mean, this is a local election. None of us have enough money to hire investigators to dig into the other candidate's background."

John nodded. "You might be right, but let's say the subject comes up. What will you say?"

Lisa tapped her chin a few times. "I guess the only thing I can say is the truth . . . I am the victim of identity theft."

Lisa prayed she had practiced enough to give the answers her constituents were looking for during the debate with Mike Barnes. The event was being televised on one of the local channels. Lisa doubted if many viewers would watch their debate, but she still put in the work.

She and John walked into the Bedford-Stuyvesant YMCA and went into the area where the debate would be held. About a hundred chairs were set out for constituents. The podium and four chairs were at the front of the room. John took a seat in the audience, and she walked behind the podium.

Besides herself and Mike Barnes, Shelly Devine and Art Stewart also were running for the city council seat being vacated by Councilman Brown. The four of them took their seats. The moderator sat behind a desk a few feet away from them. A microphone was connected to the desk, and he sat facing them. The moderator explained the format: each candidate would have an opportunity to make an opening statement, then the moderator would ask them questions and give them each two minutes to answer.

Lisa knew this borough like she knew the back of her hand. She was confident she brought heart, skill, and know-how to the table. So when it was her turn at the podium to make her opening statement, Lisa stared out at the constituents in the room. Only half the chairs were filled, but she made sure to smile and greet them as if the room was wall-to-wall with people she knew and loved. "Some of you may know me from the years I worked at my father's corner store. I may have bagged your groceries or even carried them to your home.

"Through the years, I have worked at social services and tried my best to treat our people in this community with dignity. I've tutored some of your children and volunteered at homeless shelters or wherever I was needed. I've done all this for the love of Brooklyn. No other place in the world could lure me away. I was born in Bed-Stuy; I live, love, and work in Bed-Stuy. And that is why I believe I am the perfect person for the city council seat, and I hope you will give me your vote."

She sat back down and silently prayed the people heard her heart and believed she would be the best person for this position. But then Mike Barnes took to the podium and started bragging about having been a police officer. "Bedford Avenue, Halsey Street, Lewis Avenue, Fulton Street. I walked my beat on all these streets. I've gotten to know the people in this community during good and bad times. The people have talked to me about what works in Bed-Stuy and what doesn't. I plan to take this knowledge with me to the city council if you cast your vote for me."

The moderator then asked the candidates the first question. "One of the main things members of the city council are charged with is creating a budget that reflects the needs of the community. How have your past experiences prepared you for doing such a thing?"

Shelly walked to the podium and tried to make a joke with her response. "I can barely balance my checkbook, so I'm going to need help from the other council members. Hopefully someone good with math."

The constituents laughed as Shelly sat back down.

Lisa stood behind the podium. She adjusted the microphone and said, "I balance the checkbook in my household, and I can promise you, the numbers come out right every month."

The constituents smiled and clapped.

"But seriously," Lisa continued. "Working on the budget for our community is simply about understanding the needs of our community. For one thing, we need an after-school program so our youth can receive help studying for their SATs or get tutoring on some of the subjects they don't understand.

"A lot of dropouts have simply given up. They don't think they can do the work. We need to provide our children with tools to become successful, and I certainly will be proposing such a program be added to the budget if I'm elected to the city council."

As Lisa sat back down, several audience members stood up and clapped for her. One shouted, "I'm all for it. An after-school program could surely help my son."

Yes! They were feeling her. Lisa wanted to jump back up and tell them about other plans she had for the community, but she had already used her two minutes.

Mike Barnes stepped to the podium. He hesitated a moment. Then turned toward Lisa. "You have some great ideas for this community, Mrs. Coleman." He shook his head, then turned back to the audience. "The thing I don't understand is why Mrs. Coleman has defaulted on rental property and credit cards if she truly cares about this community."

Lisa blinked. Did he say what she thought he said? She looked in John's direction. John mouthed, *You got this.*

Barnes continued. "How can we trust someone to work on a budget for our citizens when they default on their own bills and treat creditors as if paying them is not as important as taking advantage of them?"

"That's not fair!" Lisa jumped out of her seat. The cameras zoomed in on her. Her legs wobbled. She put a hand on the chair next to her. "How dare you! I am a victim of identity theft, and the police are working on my case right now."

"I've heard it all before." Mike waved off her comment. "People play the victim card all the time when they don't want to take responsibility for what they've done." He turned back to the audience; the cameras were in front of him. He gave a sad frown. "Now, I ask you, do we really need someone who is dealing with money issues on the city council? What if the money the people in the community have paid in taxes suddenly comes up missing and then my opponent plays the victim again? I say we shouldn't even take the chance!" He hit the podium with his fist to bring home his point.

The moderator tried to get the debate back on track with a few other questions. John tried to encourage her with smiles and nods every time she spoke, but it was no use. Lisa's mind kept replaying Mike Barnes' words over and over.

When the debate ended, a reporter ran over to Lisa and stuck a microphone in her face. "How much money do you owe? How many creditors have you defaulted on?"

"I didn't default on anything. I'm a victim. A victim!" she shouted.

Tears flowed like a river as she and John watched the news later in the evening. She had told John she would simply let the people know she was a victim of identity theft if the subject came up, but those words came back to haunt her as the local news picked up the horrible scene where Mike accused her of defrauding creditors, then they used the sound bite of Lisa saying, "I'm a victim. A victim!"

Her political career was over before it had begun. There would be no city council seat. Her dreams of doing something positive for her community ended tonight. How would she ever recover from this nightmare?

"*Argh!* I'm mad." She kicked the chair.

John put a hand on her shoulder. "Hon, it's not as bad as you think. Once the police find the person who stole your identity, everyone will know you told the truth."

She knew he was trying to calm her, but she didn't want to be calm. She was tired of being the calm, reasonable one while others went about life doing whatever they pleased to whomever they pleased.

She shrugged his hand off of her shoulder and stormed out of the room.

CHAPTER 24

"Yo, your girl got torched at the debate last night," Jeff said as he and Dana lay in bed watching the morning news.

Dana sat up, eyes glued to the television. "She looks shell-shocked."

"It's not like those accusations came out of nowhere. She knew about those nonpayment issues. Why'd she run for office before taking care of her issues—either by paying her bills or finding this person she claims stole her identity?"

Dana's hand went to her mouth as she closed her eyes to blot out the pain and guilt she was feeling. The hurt in Lisa's eyes was forever branded on her soul. This was someone she had once called a friend.

"Babe, you know the money we gave to her campaign is worthless now."

Dana turned to her husband. She didn't like the way he made all this sound like a business transaction. "I didn't donate to her campaign to get anything from her. I wanted to support her. I know how she feels about Bed-Stuy."

Jeff put an arm around his wife's shoulders as he laid a hand on her stomach. "You have a good heart, hon. It's too bad you can't get her out of this jam. I seriously doubt she will win the election after what we saw on the news."

Dana heard what Jeff said, and she wondered if she might be able to help. All through the day, as she sat in product development and marketing meetings, her mind kept swinging back to this morning and hearing Lisa say she was a victim. She wanted Lisa not to be a victim anymore. And she was going to find a way to make that happen.

"Dana, are you with us?" Lee Stevens, her production manager, asked.

"I'm sorry, Lee, my mind was somewhere else. Please, what were you saying?"

"Is this how it's going to be for the next six months?" he joked with her.

Dana rubbed her belly. She was almost three months pregnant, dealing with morning sickness and fatigue. "I can't make any promises. This baby is kicking my butt so far, so I don't know how I'm going to be acting in a few months."

When the meeting was over, Dana left the conference room and went back to her office. She took care of a few things, then fatigue set in, so she called it a day. If this was how pregnancy was going to be for her, she didn't know if this kid was going to have any siblings . . . this was work.

She called Jeff as she walked out of the building. She was hoping to hail a cab. She wasn't feeling the train today. Her stomach was queasy, and if she threw up on someone at the subway station, she might have to fight her way out of there.

"Hey, hon, just letting you know that I'm leaving work."

"Is something wrong? Do you need me to come home?"

"No. I'm tired again. I feel like getting into a bubble bath and then taking a nap."

"You work hard. You deserve to take it easy every now and then."

Dana was holding the phone to her ear with her left hand as she waved to a cab with her right. Out of the periphery of her left eye, she saw a woman heading down the street toward the subway.

The woman had the same olive skin tone, height, and skinny frame as Vida. She was wearing a lime-green tank top and a pair of cutoff jean shorts. Dana yelled, "Ma! Ma!"

The cab pulled in front of Dana. She waved him off as she headed down the street.

"I think I saw my mother. Let me call you back," she said to Jeff.

"Okay, but be careful," Jeff told her.

"I will." Dana put her phone in her purse and yelled to the woman again. "Ma! Stop! Wait!" The woman kept going. Dana walked fast in order to catch up with her. She needed her mother to know she was pregnant. She was going to be a grandmother. Maybe if she knew, it would change things. Make her want to go to rehab.

The woman made it to the corner of Nostrand and Fulton, looked around, then ducked into the subway station. "No!" Dana lost sight of her. She took off running, still screaming, "Ma! Is that you? Wait! I have something to tell you."

The subway was so crowded with people she couldn't see the woman. She nudged and pushed her way through the crowd. She felt like a kid in need of her mommy. How she would love to rest her head on her mother's shoulder and listen to her sing a lullaby. Her mother had had a beautiful voice before the drugs destroyed it.

Peeking over the throng of people, Dana saw the woman in the lime-green tank top standing by the turnstile. "Excuse me, excuse me." She pushed and pushed her way through the crowd. She sprinted down the subway steps. Eyes scanning, searching. Dana was moving too fast down the stairs. Her three-inch heel turned on something and she went tumbling to the ground.

She yelled as her knees hit the ground first, then she fell on her back. Holding her belly like she was protecting the crown jewels, Dana let out an *oof* from the impact of hitting the concrete floor.

"Lady, are you all right?" asked a woman with concern etched on her face. She held out a hand to help Dana up.

"I think I had the wind knocked out of me." Dana took the woman's hand and pulled herself back on her feet. "Thank you."

"Be careful out here." The woman left Dana standing there.

Dana looked down. Her left knee was bleeding, her back ached, and the heel of her shoe was cracked, yet she still looked around, trying to see if Vida was there. When she didn't see her, Dana limped her way back onto the street, hailed another cab. Once she was seated in the back seat of the cab, she called Jeff. "Babe, I fell."

"What? Where? What's going on?"

"I was chasing after my mother. She went into the subway, so I followed, but I fell down the steps, and now my back is hurting."

"Okay. I'm leaving work now. I'll meet you at the hospital."

Dana shook her head as if Jeff could see her. "I don't feel like spending hours at the ER. I want to go home. I didn't fall on my stomach, so I'll be all right." She hung up, not wanting to argue with him. She was a little sore, but the baby was okay. However, Dana was not. She needed her mom and was out of sorts about the whole situation.

When she arrived home, Dana ran her bathwater, sprinkling Epsom salt and bubble bath in the water. She doctored her knee, wiping away dried blood, then took a book off her shelf and settled into the hot water for a soak while reading a mystery.

Dana had read three chapters when her water started to cool off. She got out of the tub. Her knee and back felt better, but she still put a bandage on her knee in case the bleeding started again.

Throwing on a pair of pajamas, she checked her messages before climbing into bed. Jeff had called while she was in the tub. *"I called your ob-gyn. She can see you at five o'clock. I'm on my way home. I picked up some soup for you."*

Soup sounded good to her. She hadn't been able to hold much else down lately. The doctor's visit, not so much. Dana touched her stomach; she had a baby to consider. She wouldn't be like her mother, doing things she wanted, whether it was good for her child or not. So as Jeff opened the front door, Dana looked at the clock on the wall. It was three in the afternoon. She had time to eat her soup and then go to the doctor for a checkup.

"What did you bring me?" She looked at the bag in Jeff's hand.

"Clam chowder today."

She smiled. "I love clam chowder." Dana sat down at the dining room table and ate her soup.

Jeff stood next to her, staring, as if he could tell how she was doing by looking at her.

"I'm fine," she said between bites.

"When you finish the soup, you need to get dressed so we can go, and it might be time for you to go down to two-inch heels."

"Never," Dana joked.

The doorbell rang. "Are you expecting someone?" Jeff asked.

"No."

Jeff walked over to the door. "Can I help you?" he asked before opening the door.

"This is the police, sir. We are looking for Dana Jones."

Jeff glanced back at Dana.

She shrugged, but she was nervous as he opened the door. Were they coming to arrest her? Had they discovered her secret? She had come so far from the girl she used to be. She needed a bit of grace. There was no way she was going to give birth to her child in prison.

Dana wanted to run, but she couldn't leave Jeff to deal with her chickens coming home to roost. Dana stood, but her legs felt like tree trunks—planted and rooted. She couldn't move. *This is it . . . This is the day I pay for my sins.*

"Her name is now Dana Williams. I'm her husband. Can we help you?"

The police officer looked past Jeff to where Dana stood in the dining room. "Sir, do you mind if I step in? I really need to speak with your wife."

Jeff pointed toward Dana. "She's right there. Yes, come in."

The officer took his hat off and walked over to Dana. "Ma'am, I am Officer Ronald Stokes. I believe you are related to Vida Jones. She had your business card, and information in our system shows her as your next of kin."

Dana nodded. "She's my mother." Releasing the breath she had been holding, Dana asked, "Did Vida get herself into trouble after I tried to chase her down this afternoon? Whatever she did, I'll cover the cost. Has she been arrested?"

The officer lowered his head, tightly gripping his hat. "I am sorry to inform you that Vida Jones passed away this morning."

Dana squinted. Her head swiveled one way, then went the other.

"We found her in an abandoned building. She was taken to the hospital, but she didn't make it."

Something wasn't adding up for Dana. "Are you sure it was her? I saw my mother this afternoon." She lifted her pajama pants and showed the officer the bandage on her knee. "I got this when I fell in the subway station chasing after her."

"Are you sure you saw your mother? Because this woman was taken to the hospital this morning."

"She's not dead." Dana would not accept this. She saw her mother run into the subway station this afternoon, so how could she have died this morning?

"Would you come to the hospital to identify the body?"

Dana looked from Jeff back to the officer. "I-I—"

Jeff came over to her. "It's okay, hon. We'll go together."

"B-but I have a doctor's appointment." It wasn't her mother. She didn't want to go. Dana turned to Jeff with a plea in her voice. "She's not dead, Jeff. I told you, remember? I saw her today."

Dana closed her eyes and pictured the frail woman in the lime-green shirt again. She looked so much like Vida. But this officer was standing in their home telling them that Vida was dead. Jeff put his arms around her. "It's probably not her, but we need to go see."

Fear clenched Dana's heart. She tightened her hold on Jeff. "I don't want to do this."

"I'm here, Dana. We'll do this together."

He kissed her forehead, the way he always did to calm her. She could do this . . . She could face whatever was to come as long as Jeff was with her.

When they arrived at the hospital, Dana's heart raced. She took a few deep breaths to calm her nerves, then closed her eyes. Her nose twisted at the bitter smell of body odor, antiseptic, and a mix of fragrant soaps and cleaners that lingered in the air.

She held on to Jeff's hand. He guided her into the room the officer said her mother was lying in.

She still thought the officer had gotten it wrong. Her mother wasn't dead. Vida was going to be a grandmother, and Dana couldn't wait to tell her mother about the baby. She prayed the knowledge would cause her to change her ways. Her baby needed a grandmother.

"Is this your mother?"

Dana heard Jeff ask the question. She slowly opened her eyes. They were standing directly in front of the bed. Dana looked at the sunken cheeks, the light skin contrasting with brown lips. Her breath caught, and she stumbled backward.

Tears stung her eyes and drenched her face with a downpour of sorrow. "It's her. Oh God, how can it be her?"

Jeff pulled her into his arms. "I'm so sorry, hon. I'm so, so sorry."

It was her mother, lying in that bed, not moving . . . dead. "Why? Why? Why?" She beat on Jeff's chest as the tears kept coming. Dana could feel herself shaking. This was too much. She stepped back over to the bed. Put her hand on her mother's thin arm.

Her head lowered as her heart cracked into a thousand little pieces. Dana doubted her heart would ever mend. Her chin quivered, and the tears came again. All her hopes, all her dreams about her mother one day getting clean and becoming a responsible parent and grandparent were over. Her mother had been a junkie for most of Dana's life, and now it was over.

The nurse came into the room with paperwork for Dana to sign. She sat down and filled it out. She gave the nurse her information and asked for the bill to be mailed to her. This was the last thing she would be able to do for her mother. Vida had little dignity in life. She was going to make sure all Vida's affairs were in order and she received the best headstone she could find.

While Jeff took the completed forms to the nurse's station, Dana stood by her mom. She placed a hand on her stomach. "You're going to have a grandchild, Ma. I was hoping you would come visit me so I could tell you my good news.

"You have a son-in-law who is a really good man. He's not like the kind of men you used to bring home or the one I fell for back in the day. Jeff loves me, and he's going to take good care of me and the baby, so you rest easy, M-Mom."

Her throat constricted as she said "Mom." The tears came again. Dana lowered her head, suddenly feeling a heavy weight descend on her. "I wish you could have met my new family, that's all."

Jeff came up behind her. He pulled her into his arms and wept with her. Dana felt silly for crying like this. Vida hadn't been much of a mother, but she was the only mother she had . . . the only one she would ever know. Her baby would never get to meet Vida, and she didn't know whether that was good or bad.

Then suddenly she felt a pain in her abdomen. It caused her knees to buckle. She held on to her stomach with one hand and grabbed Jeff's arm with the other. "The baby. Something's wrong with the baby."

CHAPTER 25

Lisa lost the election. Devastated, she went to Bible study the next night and lay on the altar, crying her heart out and calling out to God. "Why is this happening, Lord? I have served You. I have been faithful. I don't deserve this."

"Take heart, daughter. God has not forgotten you," Pastor Jonathan told her as she was leaving service.

"Why does it feel like He has, Pastor? I don't get any of this."

Pastor hugged her, then said, "I'm praying for you. Don't lose hope. Things will turn for your good."

But Lisa didn't see how anything good could come from all the terrible things she was dealing with. What hurt even more was Mike Barnes won the election, like it didn't even matter he publicly revealed her personal information. Lisa figured someone at the precinct must have filled him in on the case she filed. She wanted justice but didn't know how to get it.

So she called the precinct on Thursday morning and demanded to speak with Officer Roberts. She waited on the line for two minutes before he picked up the call.

"Good afternoon, Mrs. Coleman. I was getting ready to call you."

"Oh really?" Lisa said, a bit chippy. "Were you calling to tell me how my information found its way to Mike Barnes? That's what I want to know."

"I know you're upset, but I didn't tell Mike about your case." He then spoke lower, almost in a whisper. "I don't know how he found out about the credit issue, but believe me, I will work tirelessly to figure out who gave him your information."

"How am I even supposed to trust you?" Lisa was so shaken up by how she was blindsided at the debate, she didn't know what to believe or who she could trust anymore.

"I'm not asking you to trust me. I know how this looks, but I have information and I wanted to share it with you."

She didn't trust him. But curiosity made her ask, "What information do you have?"

"The owner of the apartment building finally went to her father's storage unit. She brought the lease agreement to me."

Lisa perked up. "So you know who stole my identity?"

He was hesitant. "I'm not saying that. There was only one name on the lease."

"What's her name?" Lisa quickly asked.

"Do you know Yolanda Pierce?"

Lisa racked her brain. *Yolanda Pierce. Yolanda Pierce.* "Doesn't ring a bell. But I have worked with hundreds of women throughout the years at social services. She might have met me there and somehow got hold of my information."

"I need to find Yolanda Pierce and then get the name of

her roommate. Once I have information on both ladies, I will get back with you."

Lisa was feeling some kind of way about the phone call. Maybe they were getting closer to finding out who stole her identity, or maybe this was another dead end. It was strange to Lisa how her life had been going in the right direction for so long, then things started unraveling, due to no fault of her own.

She sat at her dining room table looking through the classified ads. John could handle the mortgage on his own, but they still needed to eat and pay the electric bill, and the temp jobs wouldn't cut it. So she was planning to polish her résumé this week and apply for some jobs. She prayed a manager would give her a chance, even after the lies Mike Barnes told about her. *Lord, please let someone give me a chance.*

Kennedy would be home soon. She went into the kitchen and began preparing her meal. Spaghetti was on the menu tonight. It was easy and cheap to fix. She put a pot of water on the stove and then searched the cabinet for the spaghetti noodles. There was no spaghetti, only macaroni noodles, and there was no way she was leaving this house to go to the store.

The looks she received at church last night had been painful enough. She was not about to walk through the grocery and see the looks of pity on the faces of some of her neighbors. She pulled the box of macaroni out of the cabinet and decided they would have chili mac tonight.

She browned the hamburger meat, added her favorite Ragú sauce to it, then boiled the macaroni. Simple was all she had the space for in her brain right now.

Lisa heard the front door open and then slam. She peeked

into the living room and saw Kennedy throwing down her book bag and kicking her shoes off like somebody had pulled her ponytail or something. "What's going on? Why are you slamming the door?"

Kennedy turned toward her mother. She balled her fists and yanked her arms in a downward motion. "I'm so mad."

Me too, Lisa wanted to say. But she waved Kennedy forward. "Come in this kitchen and get something to eat, then you can tell me all about it."

Kennedy washed her hands at the sink, then sat down at the kitchen table. "Mama, would you be mad if I punched Bobby Mitchell?"

Bobby Mitchell was a kid who lived two doors down the street. He and Kennedy were in the same grade and therefore had some of their classes together. "Why would you want to punch Bobby? You've always gotten along with him." Lisa put the bowl of chili mac in front of Kennedy along with a glass of apple juice.

Kennedy took a sip of her juice, then said, "Bobby says you deserved to lose the election.Says you owe too many people."

Sharp intake of breath. Lisa stepped backward, putting a hand to her face as if she'd been assaulted.

"You know what I'm going to do?"

Lisa didn't want to engage with this conversation anymore, but she couldn't ignore her daughter, so she said, "What?"

"I'm going to run for office when I get older, and I'm going to make sure I don't owe nobody nothing when I do." Kennedy harrumphed and then started eating her dinner like she'd said what she said and wasn't taking it back.

Lisa was about to tell her daughter she didn't owe

anybody either, but the phone rang, giving her an excuse to end this humiliating conversation. She picked up the phone without checking the caller ID.

"Hello. Can I speak with Lisa Whitaker, please?"

She wanted to correct the woman on the other end of the phone. Her name was Coleman, not Whitaker. But since she didn't know, Lisa wasn't volunteering any extra info. "Who's calling?"

"This is Chase Bank."

Before the woman could get out another word, Lisa yelled into the phone, "Why do y'all keep calling me? I told y'all I don't owe for that credit card. Someone used my identity, and you all let them do it."

"Ma'am, I'm not calling to collect anything from you. Your account has been paid in full. You no longer owe us anything."

"Wh-wh-what did you say?" Lisa was practically hyperventilating. Did the woman say the bill had been paid off?

"The credit card balance has been paid in full."

"Who paid it?" Lisa asked.

"I don't have information on the payee. There was a notation on the file for us to call to inform you once the payment was processed through our system."

"What about my credit file? When will you remove the inaccurate information from there?"

"All information from the credit card should drop off your credit file in seven years."

"*Seven years*?" Lisa shouted. "What is wrong with you people? I didn't apply for your credit card; I didn't use it. This should not be on my credit file."

The customer service rep responded, "Once you're able

to show us proof, we will have it removed from your credit file, but that's all I can tell you for now."

They hung up and Lisa rubbed her temples. She felt like she was about to faint. Her blood pressure must be through the roof. Why was this happening to her, and who paid the bill?

CHAPTER 26

Dana hadn't realized her heart could hurt so much over losing her mother, but it did. The shock of losing Vida and falling on those subway steps had caused complications with her pregnancy. She had been hospitalized for two days, but she was thankful she didn't lose her baby.

Once she was released from the hospital, she and Jeff had a small, private funeral for her mother. She was now left to grieve and mourn.

But Dana didn't want to mourn. She didn't want to think about all she had lost.

When Thanksgiving rolled around, Jeff said, "My mom invited us to dinner."

Dana rolled over, facing the wall. "You go without me."

On Christmas, Dana was in pajamas channel surfing when Jeff came into the room and handed her a box. "Merry Christmas!"

Guilt knifed through her heart like a diver plunging into ice-cold water. She took the box but didn't open it. Tears were in her eyes as she looked up at him. "I'm so sorry, babe. I kept meaning to shop, but I didn't get you anything."

Truth was, even though she hadn't spent many holidays with her mother since she'd grown up, she didn't want to do the holidays without her.

Jeff put a hand on her arm. She felt the warmth and closed her eyes, wanting to lean into it. But the pain in her heart wouldn't let her.

"It's okay, hon. Get dressed so we can spend the day with family."

"Mmm." She scratched her eyebrow. "I can't today. Things are really busy at work. I need to go into the office."

"You're joking, right?"

"No, I'm not." Dana glanced at the clock on the end table. "I'm meeting Sierra at noon."

Sierra didn't have family in New York and didn't go home for Christmas, so she agreed to come into work for an hour or so.

Jeff went to his family's house, and Dana went to work, busying herself with new ways of marketing her hair-care products. She and Sierra discussed a mailer campaign and how they could gain more customers by mailing samples or newsletters to potential customers.

"Where would we get a mailing list with people who would be interested in our products?" Dana asked.

"We can purchase customer mailing lists from companies who sell to African American women."

Dana didn't believe it. "Companies I do business with are allowed to give my information to another company?"

"It happens all the time," Sierra told her.

As far as Dana was concerned, that was a shady way of doing business. She didn't know if she wanted any part of this mailer business. And now she was concerned about all the companies she had done business with. Were they out there selling her information? That would explain why she received so much junk mail.

Things were going well with Hair Fabulous. They were still shipping out products to stores and making money like leaves falling off trees in autumn. So Dana tabled the mailing-list idea. "Let's see if we can find new stores to partner with."

Before leaving, Dana walked through the building. The production line was shut down today, but she stood in the area, looking at the conveyor belt that guided her products along the way. Her staff packaged and mailed the hair-care products here. It was a beautiful thing to see. "This is where the work gets done," she said, imagining her mother was standing next to her, spending Christmas with her.

"We're employing people from the neighborhood, Ma. That's a good thing." A tear drifted down Dana's face as she turned the lights out. "I wish you could have seen it."

After Christmas, Dana kept a grueling schedule, with Jeff complaining all the way. "I don't think you should work such long hours. Think about the baby."

"The baby's fine," she would assure him. But work . . . work was the only thing that eased the pain.

It was almost eight at night in late January and Dana was talking on the phone with Jeff. "Are you on your way home?" he asked.

"I'm locking up now." She did as she said she would and went home before Jeff filed a missing person's report on her.

"Hey, babe. Did you eat?" Jeff asked when she walked into their apartment.

He was always asking if she had eaten, like she was so

out of it she was going to forget to feed herself and the baby growing inside of her. “I’m fine. Just want to soak in the tub and then go to bed.”

“You want me to run your bathwater?”

He was standing in the living room, looking like he’d lost his best friend. She walked past him, headed to the bedroom. “No, Jeff, I don’t need you to run my bathwater. I am capable of doing things for myself.”

“I never said you couldn’t do things for yourself. I’m here for you, but you are shutting me out.” He shook his head. “This is not the way to deal with your grief. We need each other.”

Dana stopped walking. She turned to face him again. Something in the way he said the word *we* touched her heart. “I’m sorry. I know I’m not the easiest person to live with right now. Give me some time, please.”

He nodded. “I’m not going anywhere.”

“I appreciate that.”

She soaked in the tub for thirty minutes and silently cried the entire time. When she came out of the bathroom, she felt her stomach growl. She wanted to sit down and eat with Jeff, but when she saw the look of pity on his face, she decided to go to bed and get some sleep, hoping by morning she would feel better about this life she was living.

But in the morning, as she and Jeff were preparing to leave for work, the doorbell rang. When Jeff opened the door and she saw another police officer standing on the other side, Dana knew with certainty life was not going to get better for her.

“I’m looking for Mrs. Dana Williams,” the officer told Jeff.

Jeff looked back at her. She hoped he couldn’t see how

she was shaking. It was never a good thing to have the police at your door.

Jeff turned back to the officer. "I'm her husband. Can you speak with me?"

The officer shook his head. "This is a criminal investigation. I must speak with your wife directly."

"*Criminal*? Why do you need my wife?"

Dana had been holding her breath, but a whoosh of air escaped her lips as she sat down at the dining room table. She had kept so much from Jeff that he naturally wouldn't think she would have anything to do with something criminal. She waved the officer in. "Can we talk here?" she asked.

"Yes, of course." He stood in front of her. "I'm Officer Roberts, and I'm investigating an identity theft case against Lisa Coleman."

Dana opened her hand in the direction of the chair. "Have a seat."

Officer Roberts sat in the chair next to Dana. Jeff came to the table and sat across from Dana. "I saw something about this on the news a few months back. But why would you think we know anything about it?" Jeff asked.

The officer turned to Jeff. "You can sit here if your wife doesn't mind having this discussion in front of you, but I must ask you to allow me to do my investigation."

Jeff directed his gaze at Dana. "Is it okay with you if I stay?"

Her chest heaved as she sighed. It was time to stop hiding the truth from him. If he decided to leave, then she and the baby would be alone, as she always was. "I want you to stay."

Officer Roberts pulled a notepad and pen from the front pocket of his shirt. He set the notepad on the table and opened it. "Now, can you tell me how you know Lisa Coleman?"

"I didn't say I knew anyone by the name of Lisa Coleman."

He nodded, then tapped his fingers on the table. "Right. You know her by Whitaker. Isn't that right?"

His eyes bored into Dana's, daring her to lie. "Yes, of course I know Lisa Whitaker. We grew up together. Went to the same schools and all."

"So how did you get your hands on Lisa's Social Security information?"

"Excuse me?" Dana said as if she didn't have a clue what he was talking about.

Officer Roberts flipped a page in his notepad. "Let me come at this in a different way. All the accounts Mrs. Coleman said weren't hers when she filed the report for identity theft have since been paid off, and they were paid off by Hair Fabulous." He looked back at her. "That's your company, isn't it?"

Dana rubbed her belly. Six and a half months . . . two and a half to go. "Yes, it is."

"And you were once roommates with Yolanda Pierce, correct?"

"What does Yolanda have to do with anything?" Dana asked.

"The person who lived in that apartment also had a UPS mailing address where they received bills for the items on Lisa Coleman's credit file. We think you owned the mailbox."

Jeff stood. He looked from Dana to Officer Roberts. Shook his head. "We aren't answering any more questions. You will need to speak with our lawyer."

Officer Roberts asked Dana, "Is this how you want to play it?"

Jeff walked to the front door, opened it. "That's the way she wants it. You will not accuse my wife of things she has not done. We contributed to Mrs. Coleman's campaign for goodness' sake."

Officer Roberts stood. He looked down at Dana, smirked as he asked, "Did you like your four-year stay in New York's prison system so much that you wanted to go back?"

Dana didn't respond. Her attention shifted to Jeff as he held the front door open. She saw his eyes grow wide with shock, and she knew she had some explaining to do.

"Did you say *Dana Jones*?" Lisa's mind rolled back to the commercial she'd seen Dana in. The company she owned.

"She's married now, so her name is Dana Williams. Her company paid off those accounts on your credit file," Officer Roberts told her.

"Dana paid the bills for me?" Her business must be doing well. Lisa felt good about purchasing her products. But then she found herself wondering why Dana would pay off those bills without saying anything to her.

"We believe Dana Williams is the person who stole your identity."

Lisa's mind drifted back to first grade when she and Dana first met. Dana was sitting next to Lisa at the cafeteria table. She was crying. Lisa noticed she didn't have a lunch tray in front of her.

"You okay?" Lisa asked.

"I-I lost my lunch t-ticket," Dana said through sobs.

Lisa opened her lunch bag, pulled out a turkey and cheese sandwich. Her mother had cut it in half. She handed Dana half of her sandwich, then gave her half of her apple slices.

Dana wiped the tears from her face. "Thank you."

From that day on, they became best friends. Until Dana got herself hooked up with the stick-up kid. And now, according to Officer Roberts, Dana was responsible for all the horrible things Lisa had been enduring. And after all the years she spent praying for that girl . . . Just went to show, some people never change. Dana went to prison for stealing, and now she had stolen from Lisa as well.

CHAPTER 27

When Dana got out of prison, she was determined to get her life back on track. But even though she put in applications every day, she received only a few callbacks. Once the background check came back and they discovered she was a felon . . . deal breaker. Heartbroken by a society that gladly imprisoned her for wrongdoings but refused to give her a second chance once she was released from prison, Dana was ready to give up.

Her roommate, Yolanda, was working at a hair salon. She suggested Dana go to hair school. But Dana didn't know where the money would come from.

She went into her bedroom, sat on her bed with her back against the wall, brought her knees against her chest, and wrapped her arms around her legs. Rocking back and forth, Dana cried for the little girl who'd once believed she could become somebody in this world. Cried for all the nights the lights were turned off on her and she was forced to go to bed whether she wanted to or not. Cried for the girl who got out of prison thinking she could make a new start.

After hours of crying, Dana took a few napkins off her dresser, wiped her face, and blew her nose. She then noticed the envelope containing her photos sticking out of her purse. The store had been able to develop the film after all, even though it had been four years since the pictures were taken.

She grabbed the envelope. Sitting back on her bed, Dana began to thumb through memories of the people she hung out with on Lewis and Halsey. She smiled as she saw the pictures of Shayla, Jasmine, and Lisa. Those had been her girls a few years back.

But Lisa had been the one shining light in her life. The one person who tried to steer her in the right direction. She missed that girl . . . wondered what Lisa was up to now . . . wondered why she never wrote to her while she was in prison. She was sure Lisa had graduated from college by now.

Lisa had a bright life ahead of her. That girl was lucky. She had good parents. Had been raised right and set up for success while Dana had been left to raise herself. But Dana obviously didn't know what she was doing since she couldn't even get a job.

She continued flipping through her photos, even smiling at the pictures of her and Derrick. She had once tried to capture the beauty in life with her camera, but now the world was like a dark, dark canvas with no love, no light . . . no beauty.

When she reached the last two photos, Dana sat up in bed, absolutely stunned as she gawked at pictures of Lisa's state ID and Social Security card. What in the world? *She didn't take pictures of Lisa's documents. How did they get there?*

Tapping her fingers on her comforter, her mind drifted back to one hot summer day when Mr. Adams unscrewed the fire hydrant and let them jump in the water to cool off. With the commotion from Vida overdosing, no one noticed Jasmine stealing her camera and Lisa's purse. But Dana knew Jasmine had done it. She went to her apartment to get her and Lisa's stuff back.

Dana had returned Lisa's purse to her, but she never imagined Jasmine had thought to take photos of Lisa's personal information—personal information that was needed when applying for a job or a loan.

Her fingers tapped against the comforter again. Dana was sure Lisa wouldn't have a problem getting a job. Her background check wouldn't come back showing a prison record. Her old friend had gotten a scholarship to college, so financial aid for hair school shouldn't be a problem.

Maybe the world wasn't as dark as she thought. Maybe she would have to find beauty in her own way, and once she did, she would make this world glow for her.

"And that's when I knew what I was going to do. I was going to become Lisa Whitaker and get some respect in this world." Dana sat on the sofa next to Jeff. She finally opened up and told him why she decided to steal Lisa's identity. He deserved the truth.

Jeff was pacing the floor as she recounted events from her past. "I don't get it." He rubbed his forehead with the palm of his hand. "I mean, I get things were bad for you, especially since you had been in prison."

He stopped pacing, turned to her with an accusatory finger wagging in her face. "Another thing you didn't tell me about."

"I'm sorry, Jeff. I know I should have told you." She lifted her hands, then let them drop to her sides as her head dipped in shame. "I couldn't."

"I married you, Dana. I'm building a life with you. How could you not tell me about your past?"

She didn't like the way he was looking at her. It reminded her of the way he looked at Jasmine when she asked them for money. Dana's heart constricted as tears rolled down her face. "This is why I couldn't tell you about my past!" she yelled at him. "I knew you would think the worst of me." She got up and stormed out of the living room. Slammed the bedroom door and locked it.

Jeff followed her. He turned the doorknob. "We're not finished talking about this. Be an adult and come back out here."

"No!" she yelled. "I'm not going to work today, and you can sleep on the sofa when you get back home."

Dana meant what she said. She wasn't planning to speak to Jeff for at least a week. But when he didn't come home after work, she got worried and started blowing up his cell phone. He didn't answer. Dana called his parents' home.

Patricia answered. Dana was a little embarrassed, but she hadn't heard from Jeff all day, and it was almost nine o'clock at night. She didn't know if he had left the house and gotten hit by a bus . . . a car . . . a train . . . She didn't know, so she said, "Hey, Patricia, I hate to bother you this late at night, but I haven't heard from Jeff, and—"

"Are you telling me Jeff didn't let you know he was over here?" Patricia tsk-tsked. "Jeffrey wasn't feeling well, so Junior picked up his medicine at the pharmacy and has been sitting with him since he got off work."

"Does he need to go to the hospital, or is he doing better?" Dana didn't think she could take any more bad news. She closed her eyes and said a silent prayer. *Please let him be okay.*

"He's doing better. It's a flu bug. Let me get Junior for you."

Dana didn't realize she was holding her breath until she opened her mouth to say thank you and a whoosh of air escaped.

Jeff came to the phone. "Hey."

He sounded dry, like he thought he was picking up a telemarketer call. "Jeff, it's me. Why are you sounding like that?"

"Did you need something?"

She took the phone away from her ear and looked at it. He had never been so dismissive of her. When she put the phone back to her ear she said, "I was worried. I hadn't heard from you." When he didn't respond, she said, "Come home, Jeff. I need you."

He whispered into the phone, "Are you ready to talk, or do you have the sofa made up for me?"

The way he had looked at her made her feel like nothing. So, she'd told him to sleep on the sofa. It reminded her of the way she felt when she was younger. "I know you're upset, but this isn't easy for me."

"It's not easy for me either. Remember, we promised to tell each other everything. But now it seems like I don't really know you at all."

Her heart hurt so bad she wanted to scream. Dana's life had finally started going in the right direction, and she had Jeff to thank for that. She couldn't face what was to come without him. "No more secrets, Jeff. I promise I'll tell you everything. Come home."

It was almost midnight when Jeff made it home. They sat on the sofa staring at each other, saying nothing for long stretches. Jeff scratched his forehead, then told her, "I guess

I'm having trouble with this. I've told you everything about my past . . . but I didn't even know you had been in prison. I think that's something I should have known."

Deep, heavy sigh. "I should have told you about my past, but I was so terrified, thinking you might not see me the same way."

"You never gave me the chance." Jeff put his hands to his face and rubbed the line of his chin. "I don't know you."

Fighting back tears, Dana's hand went to her chest. "I'm the same person you fell in love with. I haven't changed."

His eyes bored into her. His lips twisted like he wasn't so sure.

She held up her hand. "Okay, I told you about the day I watched the guy I was dating die, but what I didn't tell you was that he was a thief. And one day he decided to rob a pizza parlor. He asked me to be his lookout. Honestly, I didn't want to do it, but I was a stupid eighteen-year-old kid."

"So he died, and you got arrested?" Jeff said.

She nodded. "Exactly what happened. I didn't rob anyone, but the courts didn't care. They knew I was with Derrick, and I paid for it."

"So you're telling me you went to prison for four years for someone else's crime and then when you got out, you decided to steal Lisa's identity?" He shook his head. "I guess I don't understand."

Dana's lips tightened. She felt completely out of her league with this husband of hers who never knew what it was like to be so low you'd do anything to get back up. "I was frantic. I'm sure you've always known where you were going to lay your head at night and how you were going to pay the rent, but I didn't. I got desperate and did a stupid thing."

Jeff put a hand on Dana's arm. "I'm not trying to judge

you. I know your life wasn't any kind of fairy tale growing up, but this is not going away, babe. Your friend was on the news for several days about debts they thought she owed. The reporters will come after you when the truth comes out."

Dana didn't want to cry anymore. To her, it seemed she had been crying about her lot in life since she was a child. But a tear rolled down her face despite her protest. "I paid off everything I put on Lisa's credit. I should have done it when I started making money, but everything has been moving so fast, I let it slip."

Jeff wiped the tear away. "One of the elders at the church I grew up attending is a criminal attorney. I'm going to call him in the morning to see if we can put him on retainer in case we need him."

Dana didn't want to think about attorneys or police. What she wanted to do was stick her head in the sand and pretend like everything was still okay, even if it wasn't.

"Babe, the police aren't going to give up. From the way Officer Roberts was talking, it sounds like he knows you did it. We need to get in front of this."

Dana wasn't the same broke kid who grew up in Bed-Stuy needing someone to share their sandwich with her. She had money now. Life should be better, but it felt like she kept coming up on the losing end. "Give me a couple of days. I need to think about this."

Jeff agreed, but unfortunately for Dana, time had run out.

The next day, while she was in the office conducting a meeting about adding more employees in the manufacturing department, Officer Roberts entered the room.

Dana turned to look at him. "I'm in a meeting. If you have any more questions for me, it will have to wait."

Officer Roberts took out his handcuffs. "This can't wait," he told Dana as he walked over to her. "Stand up, please."

Flashes of iron bars, dirty cots, and deep, deep darkness burst inside her head. Kim came running into the room. "I tried to stop him, Dana. He wouldn't wait."

"What are you doing?" Dana touched her protruding belly, blinked a couple of times as she focused on the handcuffs he was holding.

"I'm not going to ask you to stand up again."

Dana stood, the size of her belly causing her to lean backward a bit. "I don't understand. My husband told you to speak with our attorney." They hadn't actually hired an attorney yet, but that was the last thing they had said to Officer Roberts.

Dana faced the officer, the same way she had stood in front of corrections officers as they patted her down and caused her to feel more animal than human. He turned her around and put the cuffs on her wrists. "Dana Williams, you are being charged with identity theft."

Collective gasps were heard around the table.

"You have the right to remain silent. Anything you say may be used against you in a court of law . . ."

Dana scanned the room. Her employees averted their eyes or raised their eyebrows as they sat around the conference room table watching as she was walked out. She started trembling.

Kim seemed frantic as they passed by her. "This is crazy. You can't come in here and arrest Mrs. Williams."

Correct, Dana thought. She wasn't the same eighteen-year-old, know-nothing girl. She couldn't let the police and the court system do whatever they wanted to her. Not this time. Her eyes met Kim's, and she said, "Call my husband. Tell him to bring our attorney to the precinct."

She wouldn't throw herself on the mercy of the court this time. Dana had learned the hard way that the court system didn't care about the circumstances leading up to her crime. They would judge her only by what she had done in her past. But she wasn't going to go down in flames without a fight. Not this time.

CHAPTER 28

Jeff hired an attorney and bailed her out of jail. "I need you to stay calm," Jeff told her. "I'm going to get you home so you can rest."

After being booked and then put inside a room with iron bars, Dana needed more than rest. She wanted a drink—anything to numb her mind. The baby was still inside her, so she couldn't do anything like that. But every day she grew more stressed until one night she got up from bed to use the bathroom and the floodgates opened. She turned to her husband with fear in her eyes. "I think my water broke."

"What? No way. You're only eight months." He walked around to the side of the bed where she was standing, saw the puddle on the floor, and his mouth gaped. "This can't be happening."

Dana sat back on the bed. "Call my doctor, and get my hospital bag."

Jeff ran around the apartment. He called the doctor, called a cab, then put a few extra items Dana requested in her suitcase. He then helped her off the bed, held on to her arm, and walked her to the front door.

Dana sucked in a breath. "This is going to be good, right? We're ready for this."

"Yes, baby, this is better than good."

"And we're going to be good parents. Our child will not want for anything."

"Nothing," Jeff agreed.

They got in the cab and headed to the hospital. She was a month early, but the baby was coming. She was going to love this child in all the ways she'd never been loved. She was going to be there for her child and never, never let her baby down. She could do this with Jeff by her side. She wouldn't fail her child.

"Push! Push!"

Jeff was in her ear telling her to push, but she was tired and wanted to sleep. But the pain was so severe, she couldn't close her eyes for more than a second before she would feel another jolt. It left her whole body reeling in pain. "I'm trying," she cried.

She'd been in labor for twelve hours. This felt more like torture than what she imagined labor would be like. Why wouldn't her baby come on out? "*Argh!*" she screamed as another pain hit her. Panting several times, she positioned her body so she could give one more push.

"I see the head. Keep pushing," Dr. Lark instructed.

"It hurts," Dana cried out.

Jeff wiped the sweat from her forehead. "I know it hurts, baby, but give us one more big push. Try, okay?" He kissed her forehead.

She blew out hot air and then grunted as she pushed. She was about to pass out—no, not pass out. She was about to die. She wouldn't be here to greet her baby. She was going to die right on this bed.

"Got him," Dr. Lark said as the baby slid out.

Dana flopped, totally drained. She looked at Jeff. "Did he say 'him'?"

The baby started crying as the nurse cleaned him up. Jeff was beaming. "He sure did. We have ourselves a baby boy!"

"Are you serious? Bring him here. I want to see him." In a matter of moments, Dana went from the kind of excruciating pain where she thought she was about to die to being overjoyed at her child was now in the world.

"I'll bring him to you," the nurse said. "Give me a few more minutes to clean him up."

Jeff held her hand. "You did it, honey." He bent down to kiss her. "I love you so much. Thank you."

"I love you too." Her eyes were drooping. Sleep was finally taking over, but she didn't want to sleep now, not before she saw her baby. "I'm falling asleep, Jeff. Wake me when they bring the baby."

"I will, don't you worry."

She yawned. "Are we naming him Jeffrey?"

Jeff shook his head. "Our little boy is a gift from God. I want to name him Judah."

Dana didn't know what the name Judah had to do with God, but she liked the sound of it. As she closed her eyes she said, "Judah."

She didn't know how long she had been sleeping, but Jeff nudged her. "Wake up. Judah wants to see you." He nudged her again. "Dana."

Her eyes fluttered open. Jeff was holding the baby. He was wrapped tight in blankets. Jeff laid him on her chest. She looked down at her newborn baby and saw him as the best part of her—something good she had created. She started crying. "He's beautiful!"

Later in the day Jeff Senior and Patricia came to see the baby. They sat in Dana's hospital room oohing and aahing over Judah.

"He's so precious," Patricia said.

Jeff's dad nodded in agreement. "Our first grandbaby. And they named him Judah. Well, I'll be."

Dana turned to Jeff, who was sitting next to her bed holding her hand. "What is so special about the name Judah?" Her eyebrow lifted. "I don't get it."

Jeff squeezed her hand. "Judah means the praise of the Lord, so it's like we're giving God praise for allowing us to raise our son."

"Oh," was all she said. The thought that God was allowing them to raise Judah sounded like a heavier weight than simply being a parent. Her mother was a parent, but Dana was positive God had nothing to do with the way she was raised.

Dana tried to push her self-doubt to the back of her head and enjoy the moment. She and Jeff had done something amazing. They had brought a child into the world. She wasn't going to be negative today or think about all the negativity in the world. She wanted to be happy and enjoy her new family. They laughed and smiled at the baby. Dana was beginning to feel their excitement.

But later, when she was alone in her room watching the local news, a housekeeper entered her room at the very moment Lisa was being interviewed by a reporter. Lisa told the reporter she wanted to start an organization to help the little guys who had been victims of identity theft. It seemed to her far too many people only got a slap on the wrist after ruining other people's lives.

Then the reporter showed a picture of Dana, who gasped as the reporter said, "Dana Jones Williams is a wealthy woman. She made her money by creating a brand of hair-care products. But the face of Hair Fabulous has now been accused of committing identity theft against Lisa Coleman."

"Oh wow! That's you, isn't it?"

Dana had forgotten housekeeping was still in her room.

Dana picked up the remote and quickly changed the channel. She turned to the woman who was holding a trash bag in one hand and pointing an accusatory finger at her with the other. "Can you please finish up in here so I can get some sleep?"

"That was cold-blooded, what you did to the other lady. She lost the election because we all thought she couldn't pay her bills."

"Get out!" Dana screamed at the woman.

Dana's scream must have scared her. She quickly put the new trash bag in the trash can and rushed out of the room.

One moment Dana was happy to finally be a mother, and the next she felt like her whole world was being destroyed . . . Lisa would never forgive her.

Yes, Lisa had been victimized by Dana's senseless act of identity theft, but didn't people realize Dana had spent a lifetime being victimized by poverty and her mother's drug abuse? Who would cry for her? It wasn't so cut-and-dry as "the rich lady stole from someone." Her back had been against the wall, and she had been trying to survive.

But no one cared . . . No one would ever care about her

pain. Tears ran down Dana's face. She would never escape her past. She would forever be the Dana from Halsey Street and Lewis Avenue—the Dana with a drug-addicted mother and a criminal boyfriend. She would always be the lady who committed identity theft, and she didn't know if she could face another day with the whole world pointing fingers at her.

CHAPTER 29

Good interview." Lisa pumped her fist in the air. "Oh yeah, she'll get her just deserts soon enough."

John was seated next to Lisa in the living room, watching the news. He didn't respond to her, and her mouth turned down in a frown. "What?"

"Nothing."

"Then why are your lips all . . ." She pursed her lips together, mimicking his expression.

He hesitated, then clasped his hands together. "I don't think we should be so gleeful about another person's demise."

"Are you serious?" Lisa rolled her eyes as she got up and walked out of the living room. People in this city needed to know she told the truth when she claimed to be a victim of identity theft. And Dana Williams, the so-called success story, the same woman who received the Businesswoman of the Year award a few months ago, had stolen her identity.

She was glad they arrested Dana and couldn't wait for the trial. She didn't care what John said—she was going to celebrate when they threw Dana back in jail.

Lisa had done the interview to set the record straight about people like Dana, but there was one more person on her list. The next day she went to see Mike Barnes at the city council. She needed to get the anger that was boiling in her off her chest.

"You lied on me and destroyed my reputation."

Sitting behind his big mahogany desk, which looked to be hand carved with beveled edges, Mike rubbed his chin, then spoke in a slow, deliberate manner. "I should have checked my facts before accusing you of being irresponsible. I wasn't thinking about how you might suffer. My mind was only on competing for this seat."

"Was it worth it? You won the election. But now everyone knows you lied."

He corrected her. "I didn't actually lie. Those items were on your credit report. I had no way of knowing someone had stolen your identity."

Lisa doubted he was telling the truth. She still believed he received his info from someone at the precinct. She couldn't prove it, so she didn't mention it, but said instead, "How do you think your lies are going to play out in the next election?" Lisa smirked at him.

"Are you planning to run against me?" he asked.

Lisa glared at him. "You tainted my image in such a way that, even though the truth is finally coming out, there will still be people who believe that what you said about me is true."

Mike opened his desk drawer and took out a notepad. He uncapped his pen. "Okay then, what was one agenda item you really wanted to work with the council on? If you're not going to run for office, I can at least put it on my agenda and try to make it happen."

Lisa gaped at him. Councilman Barnes had asked about her agenda as if it mattered to him. Being on the city council was not the most important thing in life; getting things done for the people in the community was always the end goal.

"When I was a teenager," she began, "I worked at my dad's corner store with a woman who left her children at home alone while she worked. She couldn't afford daycare or any after-school program being offered.

"The youngest child started a fire in her apartment while I was away at college. The kids made it out of the house alive, but Child Protective Services took them from her, and she spent a year dealing with the system in order to get her children back."

Mike put his pen down. "You want me to fight the system? Might be too big a job for the city council."

Lisa agreed with him. "I understand why they took the children. I have a child, and I want her in a safe environment. But that's why one of the initiatives most important to me is creating several after-school programs within the Bed-Stuy area. These programs won't be babysitting zones but learning facilities to set our children up for higher education and scholarships."

"Where would we get the buildings to create these learning facilities, and who would run these programs?"

Lisa's mother had told her how in the sixties, Elsie Richardson had taken abandoned buildings, fixed them up, and turned them into thriving businesses. She wanted to use that model for the learning facilities. "Why not make use of three to four of these abandoned buildings we have in our community?"

She didn't know if she could really trust him, but she had no one else to turn to. "I have already written a plan for how this can work. You'll have to get funding, but then things should fall into place nicely if you follow my business plan."

He stood up, stuck out his hand. "Bring me your business plan, and I'll see what I can do. I promise you."

Lisa shook on it and then left Mike's office feeling like she had done some good for her community. Before going home, she stopped at her church, went to the altar, and prayed that God would give Mike Barnes the wisdom to do the right thing for the community. She also prayed for Dana's soul. When they were younger and she found out Dana had been arrested, she'd prayed for things to turn around for Dana. She had even prayed God would send a man after His heart to Dana.

Obviously, her prayers worked. Dana was now very successful. But something was still wrong, or Dana wouldn't have stolen her identity. "Fix her, Jesus. Help her to come to know You and not to ever desire to be criminal-minded again."

Lisa still wanted Dana to pay for her crime against her, but that had nothing to do with Dana's soul. Her soul belonged to God, and as a Christian, Lisa's responsibility was to pray for all souls.

When she arrived home and checked her answering machine, she had a call from Karen, the manager who took her place in the social services department. She quickly called her back.

"Hey, Karen. How are you doing?"

"I've been good. We all miss you around here," Karen told her.

"Nice of you to say." Lisa had always liked Karen. She was a hard worker, and she cared about the clients they served.

Karen told her, "Of course. I also wanted you to know we

have an opening in our department. I received your résumé from a temp agency, so I assume you're still looking for a job."

Lisa was embarrassed to admit she was currently working at a department store to someone who used to work for her. But she had been stripped of her pride, and all that was left was the truth. "It's been hard trying to get a job when so many people remember the newsclip of me saying I was a victim."

"But you were a victim," Karen interjected, "and I'm glad your name is starting to be cleared. It must be tough knowing an old friend stole your identity . . . someone you trusted."

"I never would have guessed it was her in a thousand years. I'll be thankful when the trial date is set."

"I hope they throw the book at her," Karen said.

"For all the heartache I've experienced since discovering what she did, I hope they do too."

"So what about the job?" Karen asked. "Are you interested?"

"Since when do we keep alcohol in the house?" Jeff walked into their bedroom holding a bottle of vodka in his hands.

Their baby was now a month old. Dana was putting a diaper on him while he cried and cried and cried. Dana had cried too—watching Jeff's family gush over Judah like he was the second coming but not being able to show him off to her mother had been depressing.

"I needed something to take the edge off."

"*Edge off* of what?" Jeff's face set in a frown. "You have a child to take care of."

"Yes, I have a child, but I don't have a mother." She laid

Judah on her bed and started putting his clothes on. "I'm dealing with a lot, Jeff, so please leave me alone."

"The trial starts next month. You can't be drinking . . . not now." He went to the kitchen and poured the contents of the bottle down the drain. When he came back to the room, he said, "And not in front of my son."

Dana handed him the baby. "Not everyone can be as perfect as you." She rolled her eyes at him. "I'm going to work." She walked out and left him with the baby.

"I'm here to see Dana Jones."

Dana was heading toward the break room when she heard someone ask to see her. She turned and peeked around the corner, looking toward the receptionist desk. She heard Kim ask, "Do you have an appointment?"

"Tell her Jasmine is here. She'll see me. I guarantee that." Jasmine grinned, showing rotted teeth.

Jasmine looked like she'd found a laundromat since the last time Dana saw her, but she was thin as a rail and had the same sunken cheeks her mother once had.

"Mrs. Williams has a very busy schedule, so if you don't have an appointment, I don't think you'll be able to see her today," Kim told her.

Jasmine put her hands on the desk and leaned closer to Kim as she demanded, "Call Dana! I swear if you don't pick that phone up, I'm going to go find her myself."

"I'm right here." Dana stepped into the reception area. "How's it going, Jasmine?"

Jasmine turned in Dana's direction. "Well, don't you look like a million bucks."

Dana glanced at her watch. "I have a meeting in ten minutes, but I can speak to you now if you'd like."

"And all professional too." Jasmine cackled, showing off her rotted teeth. "You sure aren't the same girl I grew up with."

Dana wasn't taking the bait. Jasmine had tracked her down for a reason. She was giving her exactly five minutes, for old times' sake. "Follow me." Dana turned and started walking back toward her office.

Jasmine said, "Look at you . . . Look at the big rock on your finger."

Dana smiled. "Married, and I have a baby."

Dana took the seat behind her desk and directed Jasmine to close the door as she entered the room. Jasmine closed the door and then stood in front of Dana's desk, looking around her office like she was staking the place out. "I can't believe this. When I heard you were the owner of Hair Fabulous, I almost passed out."

"I've worked hard to build my business," Dana told her while silently wondering how to approach the subject of Jasmine's obvious drug problem. The girl was fidgety and scratching her left arm like fleas were attacking her.

Pointing toward Jasmine's itchy arm, Dana said, "My mother struggled with her demons until she overdosed. I don't want you to go the same way."

Waving that off, Jasmine said, "I'm good. You don't have to worry about me."

"Have you considered rehab?"

Jasmine shook her head as she sat down in the chair in front of Dana's desk. She leaned forward and spoke in a low voice while looking behind her like she was trying to make sure no one else heard. "I was sorry to hear about your recent troubles. From what I was told, the prosecutor is trying to figure out how you got hold of Lisa's identification."

Jasmine turning up right before her trial began was no coincidence. The girl wanted something. Dana was silent, waiting to see where this was going.

Jasmine made a cross sign in front of her chest. "He won't find out from me, you can be sure."

Dana's case was high profile in the New York area. Her attorney was expensive and very good at getting his clients cleared of all charges or at least getting them reduced sentences. So the assistant DA, Mark Stevenson, who was said to be a bulldog, was trying her case. Dana was a little nervous, but Jeff trusted their attorney.

Now she had another problem. Even though she wanted to play dumb, like she didn't know what Jasmine was getting at, Jasmine was the only person who knew exactly how she received Lisa's identification. "Thanks, Jasmine. I appreciate it."

"I mean, just because I took pictures of Lisa's state ID and her Social Security card and left them in your camera doesn't mean anything to me."

Jasmine stood and lifted her arms as she turned this way and that. "But since you have come up in the world like this, and I had a hand in helping you, don't you think I deserve more than the forty dollars you gave me?"

Dana stood, glanced at her watch again. "I have a meeting to get to."

"And your trial starts next month. I doubt you want your baby visiting you in prison."

Dana's hand went to her chest. "How dare you. I am not who I used to be. My child will not visit me in prison." Dana went to her office door, then turned back to Jasmine. "And you need to be thanking me for not ratting you out back in the day. You could have been in prison with me."

"From the way you sound, I need to be thanking everyone who was on the block that night. None of them ratted me out either."

"That's because New Yorkers mind their business." Dana threw up her hands and then opened the door wide. "I would say it was nice seeing you, but it wasn't."

Jasmine walked through the door. She handed Dana a piece of paper, then said, "I'll be staying at my mom's place this week, waiting on your call."

"Bye, Jasmine." Dana pursed her lips.

"Be reasonable, Dana. I can be like your best friend again—or I can be your worst enemy."

"You were never a friend to me. I learned that lesson the hard way, so please stay away from me." Dana watched Jasmine walk to the front of the building, then she went into the conference room to conduct her next meeting. She looked calm, but deep inside she was nervous.

CHAPTER 30

"All rise," the bailiff said as the judge entered the courtroom and was seated behind the bench.

Dana stood, trying to calm her nerves. She glanced around the courtroom, checking to see if Lisa was in the gallery. She was seated in the second row behind the prosecutor. Dana wanted to rush over to her and apologize for all she had done, but the way Lisa's eyes narrowed on her, she didn't think her old friend would want to hear anything she had to say.

Turning back toward the front of the court, she glanced at the seven women and five men who would decide her fate. Her attorney had suggested she purchase clothes from Walmart so the jury wasn't constantly reminded of her wealth. Today Dana wore a white top with blue and yellow stripes and a pair of navy blue dress pants. Even her navy blue pumps were a discount special from Walmart.

They were instructed to take their seats, then the judge said, "Good morning, ladies and gentlemen. I'm calling the case of the State of New York against Dana Jones Williams into order." Judge Monroe looked from the prosecutor's table to the defendant's table. "Are you ready to present your opening statements?"

The prosecutor said, "Ready for the people, Your Honor."

Dana's attorney said, "Ready for the defense, Your Honor."

The jury was sworn in, then the assistant district attorney stood and presented his opening statement. He smiled at the jury, gave them an I-know-something-you-need-to-know look, and then began. "Good morning, Your Honor and members of the jury. My name is Mark Stevenson, and it is my honor to represent the great state of New York as the assistant district attorney."

He then pointed at Dana and said, "The defendant has been charged with the crime of identity theft. In fact, she stole the identity of a woman who wanted to do nothing but good for this community, a woman who has lost job opportunities and so much more since the wealthy and successful"—he stretched out his arm toward Dana again—"Dana Jones Williams decided to take advantage of someone who once called her a friend."

Dana felt like sinking under the table as the assistant DA pointed an accusatory finger in her direction. Her hands wrapped around the cold arms of her chair as she tried to fight the impulse to hide.

Her attorney leaned close to her and whispered, "Sit up straight." He then stood and faced the jury to give his opening statement.

"Your Honor and ladies and gentlemen of the jury, the thing I need you all to remember is, under the law, Dana Jones Williams is presumed innocent until my esteemed colleague can prove otherwise. During this trial, you will hear no real evidence against my client. The prosecutor only has hearsay and happenstance to go on. As the trial progresses, you will get to know Dana and the hardships she has endured and overcome. You will see that my client has redeemed herself a thousand times over from any follies of her youth, and then you will see clearly that Dana Jones Williams is not guilty."

Jeff was seated directly behind her in the courtroom. He leaned forward, took her hand in his, and squeezed it. Dana gave him a weak smile. He squeezed her hand again, giving her the courage to believe she could get through this.

But then the prosecution called its first witness. Yolanda Pierce, her ex-roommate, took the stand. The clerk swore her in. Dana thought the prosecutor was going to try to imply Yolanda was in on the identity theft. She hated they were dragging Yolanda into this when she had nothing to do with it. Dana hadn't seen her ex-roommate in years.

The prosecutor asked Yolanda, "How did you come to know Mrs. Williams?"

Yolanda had her arms folded across her chest. She rolled her eyes at the prosecutor and said, "We met in prison. But you already know that or you wouldn't have asked the question."

"Let the record state Ms. Yolanda Pierce is a hostile witness and is here only because she was subpoenaed," Stevenson said before turning back to her. "Now, exactly how soon after Mrs. Williams was released from prison did the two of you become roommates?"

With another roll of her eyes, Yolanda answered, "About three days."

Stevenson looked as if he was about to walk back to the prosecutor's table but stopped and turned back to Yolanda with, "One final question. Were you in prison for a misdemeanor or a felony?"

"A felony. And I did my time and haven't had any trouble since."

Next on the witness stand was Dana's ex-probation officer. Dana didn't understand what a roommate from five years ago or a probation officer had to do with her identity theft case, especially since she was no longer on probation.

After the witness was sworn in, Stevenson made things a bit clearer for Dana. He pointed in her direction and then asked the probation officer, "Do you recognize the defendant?"

He nodded. "She was on probation for two years after being released from prison. I served as her probation officer."

Stevenson tapped a finger to his chin while walking back and forth in front of the witness stand. "Let me make sure I understand the rules. When a felon is on probation, are they allowed to associate with other felons?"

"That is prohibited," the probation officer said.

"So if you had known the defendant moved in with a known felon three days"—he held up three fingers to the jury—"after being released from prison, what would you have done?"

"I most likely would have put her back in prison and let her serve the remaining two years of her sentence."

As Stevenson walked back to his seat, he said, loud enough for the jury to hear, "Maybe if she had served all of her time, she wouldn't have victimized Mrs. Coleman."

Dana's attorney jumped to his feet. "Objection, Your Honor. The prosecutor is dramatizing for the jury."

The judge said, "Sustained. The prosecutor will address questions to the witnesses."

Dana bit her lip, glanced at Jeff. He smiled at her and put a hand on her shoulder. He was her knight in shining armor. The one true thing she could count on. She rubbed the side of her face against the back of Jeff's hand.

She tapped her foot underneath the table and squirmed in her seat each time her attorney questioned a witness after the prosecutor. All her attorney asked was what kind of person did they believe Dana to be. Both witnesses stated they thought she was nice and respectful. Yolanda had added rehabilitated. But when Dana glanced at the jury, she didn't think they bought that comment.

Then the prosecution called his star witness. Jasmine took the stand. She swore to tell the whole truth and nothing but the truth and started lying so quick Dana nearly fell out of her chair.

Dana felt sorry for her former friend. Wished she could do something to help her.

After the prosecutor established how Jasmine knew Dana, he asked if she knew how Dana came to possess Lisa's personal identification information.

Jasmine lowered her head as if what she was about to say bothered her immensely. "I'm ashamed to say it," Jasmine began, "but Dana and I used to steal from people all the time."

Dana jumped out of her seat. "That's a lie! I wasn't like you. I didn't go around stealing anything I could get my hands on."

The judge banged the gavel, then set his eyes on Dana's attorney. "Keep your client in line. I'm not going to warn her again."

"Yes, Your Honor." Her attorney stood, took hold of Dana's arm, and helped her back into her seat.

"But she's lying," Dana told him.

"I'll get her on cross," her attorney said. "But please don't pop up again, no matter what she says."

That proved to be a hard task for Dana as Jasmine went

on to say, "Dana and I planned to rob Lisa the day she hung out on our block. I took Dana's camera along with Lisa's purse. Dana and I split the money and then I took pictures of Lisa's identification in case we could use it later. But Dana got arrested doing another job with her boyfriend before we could develop the film.

"I never knew Dana went ahead with our plan. She didn't tell me anything, and I was completely rehabilitated by the time Dana got out of prison." After those words, Jasmine started scratching her arm.

Dana wanted to laugh out loud. "*Completely rehabilitated*," her foot. She couldn't wait for her attorney to cross-examine her lying so-called friend. But the judge called for a recess. Dana was thankful for a breather. She needed to take the edge off. Hopefully she could sneak in a drink during the break.

She and Jeff pushed and shoved their way through the throng of reporters. Jeff took her to the cafeteria inside the court so they'd have some privacy. "This is a circus." Dana put her elbows on the table, scowling. "I need something to eat."

"You stay seated. I'll go grab you a sandwich."

"Okay, thank you." Dana rubbed her forehead with her hand as her mind rewinded through today's events. The jury seemed to think it was wrong of her to stay with Yolanda after being released from prison. But none of them had her life. They didn't know how it felt to have no place to go and to have a mother who was unstable.

Wishing for the thousandth time she could relive all the yesterdays that had brought her to this moment, Dana took a flask out of her purse and took a quick sip while watching Jeff stand in line for their food.

"Is it true? Did you and Jasmine really conspire to steal from me? The same day you attended church with me and pretended to be my friend?" Steam was blowing out of Lisa's nose as she stood in front of Dana. Her husband took her elbow and tried to move her away, but Lisa shrugged away from him.

Dana stood. "I didn't do what Jasmine said. I promise you. It wasn't like that."

Crossing her arms over her chest, Lisa demanded, "Then how was it? Please do tell, because I'm confused."

Tears formed in Dana's eyes. She was so sorry for what she had done. Lisa didn't deserve it, but Dana had been desperate—and desperate people sometimes did things they later regretted. She opened her mouth to try to explain. "I-I . . ."

Jeff rushed over to her and pulled her away from Lisa. He whispered in her ear, "You're on trial right now. You can't talk to her. Let your lawyer handle this case."

"So you're going to walk away? Do your dirt, mess up other people's lives, and then go on about your business, huh?"

Dana turned back to Lisa as they continued to walk in the opposite direction. She mouthed, "*I'm so sorry.*"

Lisa shouted, "I guess I should say congratulations on your marriage! Oh, and congratulations on being Businesswoman of the Year while my life has fallen apart."

Jeff kept moving her forward, but Dana didn't want to do the smart thing. She owed Lisa something and needed to give it. "Jeff, please, I need to talk to her, make her understand what happened."

Jeff shook his head. "She's angry. She'll run straight to the prosecutor with whatever you tell her. We have our baby to think about. Let's go back to court." He had a bag in his hand, and he showed it to her. "You can eat this sandwich outside the courtroom."

Jeff was right. She needed to eat something and keep her mouth shut, but her heart hurt with the knowledge that things would never be the same between her and Lisa.

A reporter came up to her as she chewed her sandwich. She stuck a small recorder in Dana's face. "I saw the interaction between you and Lisa Coleman. Would you like to tell us why you said you were sorry?"

Dana looked around. She was caught. Why had she mouthed those words? Those words had been in her heart. But she couldn't tell this reporter.

Jeff stepped to her side. "She's eating. Please leave us alone."

The reporter walked away. But each day of the trial seemed to get worse and worse with reporter intrusion. Dana was thankful her son was still too young to understand the neighbors' whispers.

CHAPTER 31

Since Lisa was working for the county again, she couldn't attend every day of the trial. The first day had been plenty for her anyway. It aggravated Lisa to see Dana looking so vulnerable and repentant. Was it an act designed to keep her out of prison?

Lisa would soon find out. After five days of the trial, the jury deliberated for one day before Dana struck some type of deal with the DA. Lisa was going back to court today. The judge wanted to hear from her before sentencing. Lisa took a bottle of pain pills out of her desk and popped one in her mouth before leaving work.

She massaged her forehead while waiting for John to meet her in front of the courthouse. She was thankful John took off from work. The pain pill hadn't kicked in by the time he arrived. He took her hand, and they went inside the courthouse. Dana was seated next to her attorney.

The judge asked Lisa to take her place on the witness stand. She didn't understand why. It wasn't as if she was being cross-examined. Lisa was supposed to speak only on what identity theft had cost her.

Lisa sat down. She glanced over to where Dana was seated. She was wearing a black jacket and pants. She had a short, layered cut, and even though Lisa hated to admit it, the hairstyle looked good with the oval shape of Dana's face. She averted her eyes.

The judge said, "How are you doing today, Mrs. Coleman?"

"I've been better," Lisa said as she glanced in the direction where John was sitting. She found comfort in his eyes.

"The prosecutor told me you'd like to give a statement before we move to sentencing."

Lisa nodded. "I would." Then she turned to where the cameras and reporters were, not wanting to look at Dana. "I discovered my identity had been stolen when my husband called and told me the bank denied our home loan.

"My dad wants to move down south. He has so many aches and pains now, and our cold winters are too much for him. He and I wanted to keep our brownstone in the family, but since my husband and I weren't able to get the loan, we couldn't give my father the money needed to buy himself a condo in Florida. He is now stuck here."

Lisa wiped a tear away as she added, "My daughter now has bullies at her school telling her I'm a deadbeat and we don't pay our bills. And I lost out on a prestigious job opportunity with Liberty Advocates after my background check came in."

She then turned to Dana. "So you see, it wasn't just my life you destroyed. Other members of my family are also dealing with the fallout from your theft." Her eyes bored into Dana's. "I thought you were better than this. I even prayed for you when you were sent to prison for something your boyfriend did, but you haven't changed."

Lisa turned back to the judge. "Your Honor, I want you to know that I forgive Dana for what she did, and I will accept whatever sentence you impose as penalty for her actions."

Lisa took a seat next to John. He reached over and held on to her hand. She was feeling good about the way she declared her forgiveness for what Dana had done to her. As a Christian she was supposed to forgive. But forgiving didn't mean forgetting.

The judge told Dana to stand. He then gave her a chance to address the court. Dana turned toward Lisa. "I wanted to take this moment to apologize to you. I was a stupid young kid, and I was desperate. But that doesn't excuse what I did, because you were always a friend to me. I wish I could take it back." Dana's head dropped. "I'm so sorry for the heartache I caused you." She then turned back to the judge and said, "Thank you for allowing me to speak."

The judge nodded. "I have read the letters the court received on your behalf, and I've taken note of the fact you've already paid all the bills that were added to Mrs. Coleman's credit report, so the court is prepared to accept the deal you made with the DA's office."

Lisa squeezed John's hand as the judge continued. "You are hereby sentenced to two years' probation and one hundred sixty hours of community service. The community service will start immediately."

"Community service!" Before Lisa knew it, she had jumped out of her seat. "The prosecutor told me she was going to get jail time."

The judge banged the gavel. "Sit down, Mrs. Coleman."

John grabbed hold of Lisa's arm and pulled her back into her seat. Lisa looked at him as if she wasn't computing what happened.

"She should be in prison," she insisted.

The judge banged the gavel again. "Enough. Another word, and I'll hold you in contempt of court."

Lisa was absolutely shell-shocked by this turn of events. Yes, she'd told the judge she would accept his ruling, but that was when she thought Dana would get at least a year behind bars for her crime.

What kind of punishment was community service? It felt to Lisa as if she had been violated again. Once from the identity theft and then again from the judicial system, showing leniency to Dana. Her wealth and her custom-suit-wearing attorney meant more than what she'd done.

Dana exhaled as the judge accepted the community service deal. The chair didn't feel as cold as she gripped it to stand. Warmth spread through her body as she realized her son would not be visiting her in jail. She would not have to be degraded by the daily treatment prisoners received. Breathing a sigh of relief, she and Jeff walked out of the courthouse. Walked away from Lisa and her anger.

Dana hoped some way, somehow, she could mend things with Lisa. But with the way Lisa showed out in the courtroom, Dana doubted her old friend wanted to hear "I'm sorry" again. So she signed up for her community service, hoping she'd be able to get her life back on track when she finished.

Dana knew Lisa believed community service was equivalent to getting the easy way out. But while Dana was doing community service, her business had gone off the rails due to the constant news coverage. The-rich-lady-involved-in-the-identity-theft-of-someone-who-used-to-be-a-friend wasn't playing well with her customers.

Hair Fabulous had lost their biggest customer. The grocery store chain stopped doing business with them. Pulled all the unsold products off its shelves and sent them back with a request for payment.

Dana now owed millions of dollars and was a pariah in her hometown. Jeff had taken over operations at Hair Fabulous for her. If he hadn't stepped in while she was doing community service, Dana imagined she would have lost everything. But Jeff came home the night after the grocery store chain had sent their shipment back and declared, "I have an idea."

Dana took several deep breaths before asking, "What's your idea?"

"I'm going to hire a street team and make sure each person has a vendor's license, then we are going to rent space outside of locations in Chinatown, Harlem, and Brooklyn."

"So you want to sell our products on the street?" She scrunched her nose. The baby started crying. She lifted him out of the bassinet and rocked him. "With how much my company was on the news during the trial, I doubt many people in New York are going to be interested in supporting us."

"That's the beauty of setting up a vendor table on the sidewalk. New York City is the 'Big Apple.' Everybody wants to visit this town, so we won't be trying to sell only to New Yorkers but to the millions of tourists who pass through each year."

"I don't know. This sounds like we're going to be stuck

paying a bunch of vendors without making the type of sales we need to clear out all the returned products."

Jeff took her hand in his. "Hon, do you trust me?"

"Of course I trust you."

"Then it's settled." He rubbed the baby's head. "You finish up your community service and take care of our little one, and I will make sure your business survives. I got you, baby."

"And I got your baby." Dana patted Judah's bottom and leaned in to kiss her husband. "Thanks for loving me."

"That will never change. I'm yours forever."

CHAPTER 32

What do you mean, the mayor won't speak to me?" Lisa's neck rolled from side to side as she held the phone to her ear. "I'm a tax-paying citizen. I have a right to speak with our mayor."

The secretary on the other end patiently said, "I have let you speak to the mayor twice already, and I have relayed all your messages. The mayor cannot help you with this matter. The judge has already ruled on your case."

Lisa was seated in the break room at her job with the county. She had been back to work for a few months, but things were so different from when she managed the group. Lisa kept her thoughts to herself. She had bigger fish to fry anyway.

With each of her breaks, she was on the phone or writing letters to express her discontent with the judge who handled Dana's trial. There had to be some way she could convince the judge he had made a mistake and needed to lock Dana up for her crimes.

Later in the evening when she went home and checked the mail, there was a letter for her from the office of Judge Stanley Monroe. She opened the letter and frowned at what she saw. By the time she entered the house, steam was blowing from her nostrils. "You won't believe this," she said to John as she handed him the cease-and-desist letter.

"Looks like Judge Monroe wants you to stop calling him." John handed the letter back and opened the fridge. He took out the container with salad in it and put some into a bowl.

Lisa stared at him like she didn't know who he was. She waved the cease-and-desist order in the air. "You act like this isn't a big deal. He failed to do his job, and now he's denying me the right to speak to him about it."

John poured ranch dressing on his salad. He put the dressing on the counter and then sighed. "Don't you think it's time to move on from this?"

Once again, Lisa felt like she didn't know who this man standing in front of her was. "*Move on*? How can I move on when I still haven't received justice?"

"Remember what your dad said the other night? 'God knows how to deal with our enemies better than we do, so why don't we leave the vengeance to Him'?"

Wildly shaking her head, Lisa told him, "I don't want to hear it. Daddy isn't the one who lost a dream job, nor has he been humiliated in this town the way I have been."

"But he has a point." John put a fork in his salad bowl. "I mean, open your eyes.God has been good to us."

Rolling her eyes heavenward, Lisa pressed her lips together, then huffed. "I know you and Daddy want me to say, 'God is good all the time and all the time God is good,' but I don't feel that way right now . . . nothing that happened to me was good."

"You're joking, right?"

"No, I'm not." She wasn't backing down. Her life was not how she planned it, so it wasn't good.

"Look around, Lisa." John waved a hand. "We couldn't get the bank loan to buy this house, but we still have it. We have food in our refrigerator, our daughter is happy and healthy, and even though you didn't get your dream job, your old job allowed you to come back."

"I'm no longer the manager of the department, and I now work for my former employee." She stomped a foot. "I hate my job."

John shook his head. He picked up his salad bowl and headed out of the kitchen, but then he apparently had another thought. He turned around and said, "What happened to you wasn't right, but you need to pray about how you've decided to respond to this situation. I don't think you're doing the right thing."

The phone rang as he walked out of the kitchen. Lisa wanted to tell John a few things she didn't like about him, but John hadn't done her wrong. He was her husband, and she loved him, even though she vehemently disagreed with him.

She answered the telephone and was surprised. It was the reporter from the local news station. She had contacted him a week ago when she felt like she wasn't being heard.

"Thank you so much for returning my call."

"Of course," the reporter said. "I'm intrigued. Your case has been closed, so I'm not sure how I can help you."

"I want to let people know how identity theft can ruin lives. People are out here stealing identities and getting off scot-free. That's not right."

"Would you be willing to do a live interview? I'd love for our viewers to understand how Dana Williams stole your identity before she became the Businesswoman of the Year."

John thought she needed to let go and let God. Would she have gotten this interview if she hadn't pursued it herself?

"When I knew her, she was Dana Jones, and yes, I'd love to tell you all about how I befriended her in elementary school. I even shared my lunch with her on numerous occasions, then she turned around and stabbed me in the back."

PART 3

Let all bitterness, and wrath, and anger, and clamour, and evil speaking, be put away from you, with all malice: And be ye kind one to another, tenderhearted, forgiving one another, even as God for Christ's sake hath forgiven you.

EPHESIANS 4:31–32

JOURNAL ENTRY

They tell me I'm dying, as if life hasn't already been hard enough. Now I must contend with the fact that it will soon be over. But as I look back over my life, I can clearly see that God has been good to me. I was too foolish to see what was right in front of me, and I let life slip away like a whisper. Oh, how I wish I could get those quiet moments back—the times when I was alone and refused to acknowledge God's goodness in my life and only saw the pain.

CHAPTER 33

TEN YEARS LATER
MAY 17, 2011

It was her birthday. She should be happy. But as Dana made her way down the winding stairs of her four-thousand-square-foot penthouse apartment with a bottle of Cîroc vodka in her hand, she was anything but.

She opened her stainless-steel refrigerator, took the cranberry juice out, and set it on the counter next to her half-empty vodka bottle. Taking a glass out of the cabinet, she put ice cubes in it, poured a few drops of cranberry juice in the glass, then filled it with vodka and swirled the glass before taking several long sips.

She exhaled as the fiery liquid made its way through her system. The doorbell rang. Dana rubbed her forehead. Someone was always bothering her at the most inopportune moments. She took another sip of her drink as she walked through the dining room and the spacious living room.

Dana lost her footing as she entered the grand foyer and stepped on her silk robe. It was two in the afternoon, and she hadn't bothered to get dressed. She did have on a pair of heels though, which felt a bit slippery against the marble floors they had recently been waxed.

The doorbell rang again. "I'm coming."

Dana took another long sip of her drink, set the glass on the foyer table, then took her heels off. Still holding the heels in her hand, she stumbled toward the door; twisted the knob to open it, once, twice. "It won't open." Dana slurred her words.

"It's locked, Dana. Unlock the door and let us in," Sheri said from the other side of the door.

Dana laughed like that was the funniest thing she'd ever heard. She unlocked the door and threw it wide open. "Sis!" She hugged Sheri with the hand that wasn't holding her heels. "It's so good to see you."

"You talk like you didn't expect me."

Dana stumbled backward. She scratched her head, then Ebony stepped in front of Sheri. "What are you doing with Ebony?"

She and Jeff now had two children. Judah was ten, and Ebony was five. "Ebony . . . Ebony . . . Ebony." In her drunken state, she repeated her daughter's name over and over. Dana had always thought the name was beautiful. She had a perfect little ebony princess. Dana loved her kids. Thought she would shower them with love and goodness. But it hadn't worked out the way she planned.

"You asked me to pick her up when I picked Cory up."

Cory was Sheri's five-year-old son. She'd married seven years ago, right after she opened her third hair salon. Cory was the same age as Ebony, and they attended the same elementary school.

"I did? Where's Judah?" Dana squinted as if she was thinking hard on the matter.

"Jeff is picking him up." Sheri rolled her eyes. "I smell the Cîroc. Do you really think you should be d-r-i-n-k-i-n-g this early in the day?"

"What's Mommy drinking?" Ebony asked as she and Cory ran into the house.

Sheri's eyes shifted from Ebony to Dana. "I forgot how much of a smarty-pants she is. Can't spell around her."

Dana tried to snap her fingers, but the action caused her to move sideways, then stumble backward. "Of course she's smart. Both my kids are smart."

"They are," Sheri agreed, then turned toward the door as if she was about to leave, but had a second thought and turned back to Dana. "Can I make you some coffee?"

"I don't want coffee. I only drink coffee in the morning."

"You need some now. I thought Jeff was taking you out for your birthday."

Dana put her hand to her mouth, eyes popping out. "Oops, I forgot."

Sheri took her purse strap off her shoulder and hung it on the coatrack. She grabbed Dana's hand and took her to the kitchen.

"Be careful," Dana said. "This floor is slippery."

"The floor isn't slippery. You're drunk." Sheri sat Dana on a stool at the kitchen island. She then picked up the bottle of Cîroc. "Did you drink all of this today?"

"Sheri, don't be so judgmental. I get enough of that from your saint of a brother."

Pouring the last of the vodka in the sink, Sheri told her, "My brother loves you. You need to be thanking God He sent you a man like Jeff." Sheri opened the cabinet next to the refrigerator and pulled out a can of Folgers.

"Your brother thanks God enough for the both of us."

When things got hard for them, Jeff didn't turn to vodka as she had. He turned to God. So her husband spent his days being the savior of Hair Fabulous and then spent two to three days a week in church praying for her wretched soul.

"Did you see the paper this morning? Saint Jeff looks like the savior of the world while I'm still the thief who stole Brooklyn."

"I read the article in the newspaper this morning. I thought it was good."

"Good for Jeff, but not for me. It's been ten years since my trial. Why do these reporters have to mention it in any news coverage the business gets?"

Sheri shrugged. "Most women would be happy to have a husband who gave up his own business to ensure your dreams didn't die after you fell apart." Sheri filled the coffee filter, then started the coffee maker.

"I am happy. Don't you see me smiling?" Dana lifted her head and showed off her fake smile.

She appreciated what Jeff did for her. But she wished he wasn't so much better at running the company than she was. Jeff had been the one who hired all those street vendors and had them sell their products to tourists passing by, even while the residents in Brooklyn blackballed them.

Jeff had been the one to start their mailer campaign after she had vetoed the idea with Sierra, their marketing manager. He came home one day and told her he liked the idea and thought they should go for it. Dana had thought they would lose everything, but Jeff saved the day.The business prospered and the mailers brought in new customers.

Shaking her head, Sheri turned back to Dana. "I don't

understand you. God has blessed you with so much, but you're miserable."

Pointing a shaky finger in Sheri's direction, Dana said, "That's right. You'll never understand my misery. You still have your parents and you don't have people calling you a thief and spitting at you like you're an animal or something."

Sheri raised a hand. "Stop it, Dana. Nobody spit at you. From what I was told, he spit on the window at Hair Fabulous, and all those things happened years ago."

Dana's voice caught as a tear rolled down her face. "It felt like he was spitting at me. Like he was saying I'm nothing." The incident happened five years ago, but to Dana it was like yesterday. Her mind wouldn't let it go.

"Two teaspoons of sugar, right?"

This wasn't the first time Sheri had fixed her coffee. She used to come over and make her coffee about an hour before Jeff arrived home, but her help played out last year when the coffee wasn't sobering her up enough to fool her husband. "Yes, two teaspoons, please."

Sheri stirred the sugar into the coffee, poured in a little bit of French vanilla coffee creamer, and then set the mug in front of her. "You are my sister, and I love you. From the moment you walked into my hair salon, I could tell there was something special about you. I don't know why you can't see what we all see."

"Oh you don't, huh? Well, why don't you ask the people in Bed-Stuy. They think I'm trash, and I grew up over there, so they know all about my mother."

"Not everyone in Bed-Stuy thinks you're trash."

"How would you know?" Dana sipped her coffee.

"I live in Bed-Stuy, and I don't think you're trash. My neighbors buy your hair products, so they don't think you're trash either."

Dana twirled a finger in the air. “Big whoop. Three people. Go ask the rest of the people who Lisa poisoned against me.”

Sheri shook her head.

Dana grabbed her head. “My head is aching.”

“Did you eat anything today?” Sheri held up the empty bottle. “Or was this your breakfast and lunch?”

Dropping her head on the kitchen island, Dana moaned. “You’re always so mean to me.”

“*Argh!* You get on my nerves with this pity party you throw every day. Do me a favor—don’t invite me to the next party, okay?” Sheri rolled her eyes. She opened the fridge and took out some lunch meat, slapped a few pieces of the ham between two pieces of bread, and shoved it in front of Dana. “Eat.”

“I can’t. Jeff is taking me out tonight, and I don’t want to spoil my appetite.”

Sheri sat down in the seat next to Dana. She had sympathy in her eyes as she let Dana lay her head on her shoulder. “I know you don’t like leaving your house, but you can’t turn to the bottle because your husband wants to take you out to celebrate your birthday.”

“I don’t like being recognized,” she admitted and then sipped more coffee.

“Why didn’t you tell Jeff you want to order in tonight? You could have saved yourself a lot of heartache, and maybe you wouldn’t have me scared to leave Ebony alone with you right now.”

Dana started crying. “You don’t trust me with my own child. How do you think that makes me feel?”

“Stop crying, Dana. Drink your coffee.”

Wiping her face, Dana picked up her coffee mug again.

She drank all the coffee and even calmed her nerves a bit. Then she turned to Sheri. "I'm forty-four years old today. I'm a long way from the kid who didn't know where she was going to lay her head from one month to the next. But I can't stop feeling like"—she waved her arms around, indicating the penthouse and everything in it—"this is all an illusion. And at any minute, I could be back on Lewis Avenue holding an eviction notice and wondering where I'm going to live."

"I wish I had known you when you were younger. It sounds like you really needed a friend."

"I had friends. Lisa was my best friend when we were younger, before I started hanging with the wrong crowd. And then I did her wrong, and I don't think she will ever forgive me."

"But can you forgive yourself?" Sheri asked her.

Dana didn't know if she could forgive herself or if she was worthy of forgiveness, which was the reason she found herself stumbling through her penthouse a few days later. Jeff was at work, the nanny had called in sick, and the kids were at home with her.

"Mommy, Mommy, what's wrong with you?" Ebony asked as Dana came into the kitchen carrying another bottle of Cîroc.

Dana patted Ebony on the top of her head. "Nothing's wrong, baby. Eat your sandwich."

Judah was only ten years old, but he knew how to make a bowl of cereal or a sandwich when he was hungry, the same way she used to do when her mother had an all-night bender and Dana had to scrounge around the kitchen for something to eat.

Opening the fridge, Dana pulled out the cranberry juice. She set it on the kitchen island, then grabbed a glass out of the cabinet. As she was mixing her drink, she glanced over at Judah. He was sitting next to his sister on the opposite side of the island.

Judah had his father's almond complexion. He was already five feet five, so she was no longer looking down when she talked to him but face-to-face. And she didn't like what she saw when she looked at her son. With eyes shaped like hers, he shot daggers of hate in her direction. That expression looked so much like hers when she was a child, looking at the waste that had become her mother. The condemnation was too much. She couldn't stand under the accusations she saw in Judah's eyes.

She had promised she would be a better mother than Vida had been to her, but she had let the censure of the world dictate her self-worth.

Originally, she needed a drink to get over her mother's death. After the trial, she needed a drink to get out of bed each morning. She had not been the mother Judah or Ebony deserved, and she was sorry for that—sorry she needed the drink in her hand to cope with all her shortcomings.

She lifted the glass to her mouth and gulped it down. With her liquid courage making its way through her system, she stared back at Judah. Smirked. "What?"

"Nothing," he said tightly.

Was he calling her a nothing? Dana wondered as she headed back upstairs to the safety of her bedroom. She was going to look for a nanny who could work more than four days a week. The three days she was left alone with her children was too much for her.

Heading up the stairs, she turned to look at her children, still seated at the kitchen island. Guilt tortured her, but she couldn't figure out what to do about it. Didn't they know she was doing the best she could? At that moment, Dana thought of her mother. She thought of the pain she sometimes saw in Vida's eyes.

As she continued walking up the stairs with misery for company, she stepped on her silk robe and felt her foot slip. She tried to grab hold of the banister, but she missed and went tumbling backward. Her head bounced off several steps until she was in the fetal position at the bottom of the stairs. Pain like she'd felt only during childbirth assaulted her body.

Ebony ran over to her. "Mommy, Mommy . . . are you all right? Say something. What do we do?"

Then she heard Judah say, "I'm calling Daddy."

Dana tried to focus, tried to tell her kids not to worry, but as she looked up, everything seemed to blur until she turned her head to the left and saw as clear as day a long ladder stretching from earth all the way to the heavens. Strange. How could a ladder be so long?

But then she saw angels going up and down the ladder as if being sent to earth for an assignment and then returning to heaven when it was done. She had a thought . . . *What if one of those angels is looking for me?* Lisa had told her she'd been praying for her. And Jeff prayed for her during Friday morning prayer.

Maybe God was sending an angel to her. She reached out a hand toward the ladder and pulled one of the angels toward her bosom.

The angel protested. "*You must let me go, Dana.*"

"I can't. I need you."

"*You cannot wrestle with God*," the angel told her.

"I don't want to wrestle with anyone. I need you to take the pain away." She let go. The angel flew away, and then everything went dark.

CHAPTER 34

Lisa sat at her desk, wondering why she hadn't followed through with calling out sick today. She hadn't been feeling well all week. Lisa thought the fluttering of her heart each morning as she got ready for work was a sign that she seriously needed to contemplate early retirement. If it weren't for the fact she and John were still paying off the mortgage on the brownstone, then she might consider it. They were finally able to get a mortgage on the house nine years ago. Her father moved to Florida and visited them in the summer months.

She also couldn't retire now. Kennedy was graduating from college tomorrow and then heading to law school. Her beautiful and smart daughter received a full ride for undergrad, but they would have to pay half of the cost for grad school. To be honest, she never would have even thought of retirement if life had turned out differently for her.

There was a knock on her cubicle—boy, did she miss her office. Now coworkers walked right up, and there was no door to separate her to give her a moment to prepare for the visit. Nothing.

"Hey, Lisa. Your two o'clock is still waiting."

Lisa glanced at the clock on her desk. It was 2:35 p.m. She jumped out of her seat. "I forgot to get her folder. Let me go get her."

Her coworker handed her the folder. "I grabbed it for you on my way over here. I'll let her wait a little while longer if you want a moment to review the file."

Lisa opened the file but didn't look at the information it contained. "Send her to me, please."

Within a minute or so, a woman stood in front of Lisa's cubicle. She was about to knock, but Lisa said, "Have a seat." She pointed to the chair in front of her desk as she opened the file.

The woman sat down, and Lisa asked without looking up from the file, "What brings you here today?"

"Evidently I need to reapply for assistance. I didn't receive my food stamps this month."

If Lisa had a nickel for all the attitude she had to put up with every time one of her clients didn't receive a check or had their food assistance cut off, she'd already have enough to retire with. "Did you turn in your pay stubs from your job as requested?"

"I never received a request for my pay stubs," she said as she switched positions in her seat and folded her arms across her chest.

Lisa glanced through the file. She didn't see the request, but it must have gone out. That was the normal process. She held out a hand. "Give me your pay stubs for the past two months, and I will input the information in our system."

The woman opened her purse. "I only have a month worth of pay stubs with me."

Lisa sighed deeply, visibly annoyed. She opened her desk and pulled out an envelope. "Mail the other pay stubs to me within ten business days or I will close out your account and you'll have to take out a new application for assistance."

"What? But that's bull. I didn't know you needed two months' worth of pay stubs."

"Now you do," Lisa told her. "Get me the other pay stubs, and I will reactivate your account." Lisa stood. "I have another appointment waiting."

The woman handed Lisa the pay stubs she had with her and left her cubicle. Lisa rolled her eyes as she looked at the file. She would have to keep this one until the other pay stubs were sent in. She threw it on a pile of file folders on the floor behind her desk and went to get her next appointment.

When she got back to her cubicle, she saw she had missed a call from her doctor. She had been late getting her annual checkup, but she had been having so many headaches lately she made an appointment. Her doctor was probably calling with the results, but she didn't have time to deal with that now. She needed to get done with her workday. She and John were getting on a plane to North Carolina and attending Kennedy's college graduation.

Kennedy had been attending North Carolina A&T State University. Kennedy was passionate about attending an historically Black college and university, so even though Lisa missed her daughter terribly, she let Kennedy have her dream.

After seeing her last appointment, Lisa left work and caught a cab to the airport. John was meeting her there with their bags. She hadn't seen Kennedy in three months. She couldn't wait to lay eyes on her baby—her twenty-one-year-old baby who would soon be a college graduate.

John met her at the check-in desk inside the airport. They checked their luggage and then rushed to their gate.

"Babe, I can hardly believe this day has come. Can you

believe it? Kennedy is all grown up." Her husband had aged well—not a wrinkle on his face, but a sprinkle of snow was growing on the top and especially in his sideburns.

"And she looks more like you every day. I don't even see a trace of me in her."

"You're kidding, right?" John took his phone out and pulled up a picture of Kennedy. "Is that not your nose?"

"She should be grateful." Lisa poked John's oversized nose with her index finger. She smiled. Kennedy did indeed have her small, rounded nose.

They got on the plane and flew to Greensboro, North Carolina. John rented a car and took her out to dinner. He'd heard about Stephanie's, a soul food restaurant, and couldn't wait to get there. Lisa had to admit the food was good. She was trying to keep up with everything John was telling her, but her head was pounding so bad all she wanted to do was go to their hotel room and lie down.

"You tired?" he asked as they split a peach cobbler.

Lisa sighed. "It's been a day."

John and Lisa spent the night at the Marriott in the downtown area. The next morning, they drove to the Greensboro Coliseum. They sat in the audience with the rest of the attendees, watching their loved ones walk across the stage to receive their diploma.

When Kennedy walked across the stage to collect her diploma, John stood, and Lisa was about to stand when it felt like a switch went off in her head and she couldn't move. Something deep inside told her she should be screaming for help, but she couldn't get her mouth to work.

As John stood clapping, he turned to Lisa. He was smiling. Truly happy. Then the expression on his face changed from happy to horrified. "Lisa, Lisa." He dropped down beside her. Took his handkerchief out of the pocket of his suit and wiped her mouth. "You're drooling . . . Your face is drooping."

She didn't respond . . . couldn't respond.

He stood back up. "Help! Help! My wife is having a stroke." He pulled out his cell phone.

Somewhere in the distance, like words being carried on a cloud, she heard the word *stroke*, and then everything went dark.

CHAPTER 35

"You almost killed yourself—you know that, don't you?" Jeff asked Dana as he stood beside her hospital bed.

Dana's head was bandaged. She had cracked it in the fall. Only Judah's quick thinking to call for help saved her from bleeding out at the bottom of those stairs.

"I know. And I'm so sorry for what I did. I'm such a loser."

"You're far from a loser, but as long as you keep turning to a bottle for comfort, you'll never know how amazing you truly are."

"I wouldn't drink so much if you were at home more." She said those words even though she knew they weren't true, but right now she needed to blame someone other than herself.

"I have to work, Dana. I've been trying to keep your business afloat until you can take over."

"It doesn't seem like it's my business anymore. You've taken it from me."

"Not true, and you know it. I haven't even been able to work my own business while putting my all into saving what you created."

"And when you're not at work, you're at church. You and the kids don't want to spend time with me. I'm not important to you anymore."

Jeff grabbed her by the shoulders and forced her to look him in the face. "Now you listen to me and listen good . . . I'm so tired of this. The kids and I go to church because we love the Lord and want to be in His presence. And we pray for you and want you to be there with us. But you'd rather drown your sorrows in a bottle of vodka."

Squirming, she cried out, "Let me go, Jeff. You're hurting me."

Jeff released her and backed away from the bed. Pain was etched across his face as he told her, "I knew you had a lot of baggage to deal with when I married you. I thought I could love you through it." He shook his head. "But my love isn't enough for you, and I can't let you destroy our children with your sickness."

Tears sprang to Dana's eyes. "What are you saying?"

"I-I want to separate."

"Jeff!" She shot up in bed, then grabbed her head as pain ricocheted through her like a bullet. She fell back against her pillow.

"Once you're out of the hospital, I'm going to take the kids and move. I wouldn't do this if kids weren't involved. But I can't let you do to them what your mother did to you." He turned and walked toward the door and opened it, then before leaving he said, "I'm sorry, Dana. I really do love you. Probably always will."

He left her alone with her thoughts and her sorrow. Dana cried for hours thinking about the things she had let slip away. She had been with Jeff for more than a decade.

They had two children and a successful business. The only kind of men she'd known before Jeff were the kind who were takers. The guy who got her mom hooked on drugs had taken everything from them. Then she went and fell for Derrick, another taker, but one masquerading as a giver. Derrick had cost her freedom and had stolen her belief in herself.

But Jeff wasn't a taker. He had given her so much. She didn't get why he now thought his love wasn't enough for her. Dana had always thought Jeff's love was everything, but if that was truly the case, then why had she turned to vodka? Why was she drinking around her children?

There was a knock on the door. It opened. Sheri peeked her head in. "Hey. You want company?"

Dana touched the bandages on her head. "Depends. If you're going to make me feel worse than I already do, then I'd rather be alone."

Entering the room and sitting down in the chair next to Dana's bed, Sheri said, "You've been beating on yourself for years. I thought you might need a friend."

"Some friend." Dana huffed. "If you hadn't introduced me to your brother, I wouldn't be laying here with a broken heart right now."

"You also wouldn't be a multimillionaire, so I think I've been a good friend and sister to you."

Dana acquiesced. "You've been better to me than I deserve, for sure."

Sheri scooted closer to Dana's bed and put a hand on her shoulder. "Maybe that's the problem. You don't think you deserve kindness."

"I've done a lot of things wrong, Sheri. Why do you think my husband is leaving me?" When Sheri didn't look surprised by this revelation, Dana rolled her eyes and hit the bed with her fist. "He told you, didn't he?"

"Jeff loves you, Dana. He really does. But he's worried about how your drinking is affecting the kids."

Dana's lips tightened. A tear slid down her cheek. "I swore I would be a better mother than Vida was. I never wanted my children to be ashamed of me or to suffer like I did.

"But I couldn't handle the pressure of so many people knowing the things I did in my past and then thinking I don't deserve what I have."

Sheri sighed.

Dana held up a hand. "I know you think I'm throwing another pity party, but I'm not. This is the truth of how I feel. I can't get past what I did."

"I wasn't sighing because I think you're throwing another pity party. I'm only wondering if you've ever asked God for forgiveness for your sins."

"*Sins*?" Seemed like such a harsh word to describe what she had done. "I mean, I was in the wrong place at the wrong time, following behind the wrong guy, when I got arrested, and I know I did wrong when I stole Lisa's identity, but I didn't kill anybody."

"But you did sin," Sheri declared forcefully. Then in a gentler tone she added, "Look, I understand how hard it is for people to admit they have sinned, especially in the day we're living in where people think they can do anything and everything, but God's Word is true, and it will always remain no matter what laws this world comes up with to say sins are not really sins."

"So you're saying that I am a sinner?"

Sheri nodded. "But you're not alone. All have sinned and

fallen short of God's glory. But when we sin against God, we must go to Him and ask for forgiveness. I truly believe once you receive God's forgiveness, you will finally be able to forgive yourself for the things you've done."

When Sheri got up to leave, she said, "I'm praying for you, Dana."

Sheri was praying for her. Jeff was praying for her. Even Lisa had prayed for her. It made her head hurt trying to figure out what she was supposed to do with all those prayers. Dana tried to ignore that small voice telling her to pray for herself. What would she even say? She didn't know how to pray.

She tried to get some sleep, but her mind took her back to the ladder that was so long it went all the way to heaven. She had been lying on her floor in a pool of blood, but she still remembered seeing those angels and asking one of them to take the pain away.

She'd first heard about a ladder to heaven while attending Lisa's church when she was eighteen. The pastor preached a message that had scared her. He'd titled it "Your Struggle Is About to Change Your Whole Life."

Back then her struggle had been being a Black girl living in poverty with an addicted mother, and her struggle had indeed changed her whole life. It had dictated the mistakes she made—the mistakes Sheri called *sins*.

Maybe she was a sinner and needed to ask for forgiveness. But would God listen to her? Would God hear her cry? Or had He already given up on her as Jeff had? Then she wondered if Lisa could ever forgive her. Her eyes began to droop, and she finally fell asleep with forgiveness on her mind.

Dana had been in the hospital three days. She was surprised Jeff had not brought the kids to see her. But maybe he didn't want them to see her bandaged and bruised. When the doctor came to see her and removed the bandages, she looked in the mirror and saw her face was still a little swollen, but at least she wasn't bandaged up.

Later that night she called Jeff. As soon as he picked up the phone, she said, "I got my bandages off today."

"I'm glad to hear it. How is your head feeling?"

He sounded truly happy for her, not at all the way he sounded yesterday. "It's getting better, but I'm still a little sore."

"When are they going to release you?" he asked.

"Dr. Thomas says I can go home tomorrow. Will you come pick me up?" She was so nervous, her hands were sweaty. When he didn't answer right away, she added, "I want to see the kids."

"I don't think that's wise right now."

"Why not?" She couldn't believe what she was hearing. "Jeff, it's me. I'm your wife. I gave birth to Judah and Ebony. You can't keep them away from me."

"I'm sorry, Dana, but Ebony has been having nightmares." He hesitated a moment, then said, "Unless you stop drinking, I don't think it's a good idea for you to be around them."

"Jeff!"

"I'll have Sheri pick you up from the hospital tomorrow. I'll be in church with the kids. We'll stay at my parents' house until I can find a suitable place for us."

"So I'm supposed to be in our big house all by myself? What if I need help?"

"I've already hired a nurse to take care of you for a few

weeks. But I want to make this very clear to you: I threw out all your liquor bottles, and I don't want to be there when you get more."

Dana was so mad she could scream. "What makes you think I'm going to get more? How do you know? Do you think I'm happy my kid had to call an ambulance for me? I don't want to be like this, but I need help."

"Yes, you do need help, but I'm obviously not the one to help you."

"Why do you keep saying that? We love each other. We belong together. You and me against the world, right?" She was sobbing into the phone, ready to beg him for another chance.

But Jeff said, "You need Alcoholics Anonymous or rehab. But even more than AA, you need Jesus. He's the One who brought me comfort after you turned to the bottle."

"I'm not an alcoholic. I can stop drinking if I want."

"You will never stop drinking unless it's what you want. Tell me, Dana, do you want a drink right now?"

How did he know? Yes, she wanted a drink. She even felt like she needed a drink. Her head had been bothering her all day and Dana thought a drink might take the edge off. "No, I don't want a drink."

"I know you, probably better than anyone else. And right now you are lying to yourself."

"Daddy, I'm scared. Can I sleep in here?"

Dana heard Ebony's voice. Her daughter hadn't asked to sleep with them in over a year. It broke her heart to know she had caused her baby to fear. Tears, tears, tears flowed down her face.

"I'll call you back," Jeff said before hanging up.

She hung up the phone as pain gripped her heart. Dana

wrapped her arms around herself and brought her knees up to her chest until she was in the fetal position. She was shaking, but it wasn't from the pain she felt in her heart. She wanted a drink. Wanted to numb the pain.

"Dear God, help me. I still want a drink."

CHAPTER 36

Lisa was in a North Carolina hospital, far from her beloved Brooklyn. She wanted to go home, but she couldn't get anyone to understand what she was saying. John and Kennedy were hugging each other and crying.

"I'm not dead. Stop crying."

Lisa knew what she was saying, but it came out garbled. John came over to her bed. He wiped the tears from his face. "Good morning, hon. How are you feeling?"

She wanted to answer him, but she didn't like the garble coming out of her mouth. Lisa pointed to her lips.

"You had a stroke, honey. It affected your speech. But once we get you home, you'll be able to work with a speech therapist."

Stroke? How could she have had a stroke? She was only forty-four years old. People didn't have strokes in their forties, did they?

"Mama, I don't want you to worry about anything. You're alive, and that's what matters most." Kennedy's face was wet with tears. "I'm going to get you some paper so you can write down what you want to say. I'll be right back."

Lisa watched Kennedy walk out of the room. She wished she could get out of this bed and hug her. This was supposed to be Kennedy's big weekend. But instead of celebrating her college graduation, Kennedy was stuck in the hospital with her mother.

John sat down next to her bed and put her hand into his. "I called your dad. He's flying out here in the morning."

In the morning? How long was she going to be in the hospital? When would they let her go home? She had a thousand questions she wanted to ask, but she knew John wouldn't understand her, so she lay there looking at the ceiling, feeling sorry for herself.

Kennedy came back into the room with a notepad and pencil. She handed them to Lisa. At first, when Lisa tried to grip the pencil with one hand and hold on to the notepad with the other, she noticed her left arm seemed weak and felt heavy to her. She laid the notepad on her lap. Things were so jumbled in her head she couldn't form a complete sentence, so she wrote: WHAT HAPPENED?

She hated the look of pity she saw on John's face as he told her, "You had a stroke."

HOW? She wrote the word on her notepad.

John told her, "We were at Kennedy's graduation when your mouth drooped and you became unresponsive."

WHERE? She pointed around the room with questioning eyes.

"Oh," he said as he looked around. "We're still in Greensboro. We can't go home until they release you from the hospital."

Lisa had never imagined she would be laid up in a hospital in her forties, especially one in North Carolina. She didn't feel right being here and wanted to go home. What happened to her? WHY DID I STROKE?

John sighed. Lowered his head.

Kennedy put a hand on her father's shoulder as she said, "The doctor said your blood pressure was 200 over 140. He said you're lucky you didn't die."

Her daughter's words scared her. How could she die when she never really got a chance to live out any of her plans? She lifted her eyes heavenward and silently prayed, *God, I need You. Please don't let me down.*

Dana had been discharged, but she didn't want to go home. She was afraid of what she would do if she was alone. Closing her eyes, she saw her mother. They were sitting in the living room in their apartment on Lewis Avenue. Vida hugged her and said, "*I'm sorry.*"

Back then Vida couldn't stop destroying their lives, so Dana didn't believe her mother was sorry for her actionss. The shoe was on the other foot now, which made Dana wish she had given her mother a little more slack.

She felt her mother's struggles all the way through her bones as she realized what her drinking had done, but she didn't know how to stop herself from doing the very thing that was destroying the family she and Jeff had built.

"Is anybody home?" Sheri asked as she knocked once, then opened the door.

"You're late," Dana said as her sister-in-law entered the room.

Sheri stopped walking, wrapped her arms around her chest, and leaned back. "Somebody got up on the wrong side of the hospital bed this morning."

"Don't mess with me. I'm not feeling good."

Sheri unwrapped her arms and walked over to Dana, who

was in one of the chairs in front of her bed. Sheri sat down in the chair next to Dana. She put the back of her hand against Dana's forehead. "You need me to get the doctor in here?"

Dana held up a hand. "I'm not that kind of sick. Let's just go."

Sheri opened her mouth to say something, thought better of it, then leaned over and hugged Dana. "I love you, girl. Don't you know how much you're loved?"

Dana hugged her back. "I love your big-head self too."

Sheri touched her head. "Oh, so now I'm big-headed. All right. I'ma let that one slide."

The nurse came in with the wheelchair. She smiled at Dana and asked, "Are you ready?"

Dana nodded. She walked over to the wheelchair and sat down.

Sheri stood. "Let's blow this joint." Sheri walked in front of the wheelchair, and the nurse pushed Dana as they headed to the main entrance.

"I don't even have the keys to get into my house," Dana told Sheri.

"Jeff gave me your purse and your keys."

"So sweet of him." Dana rolled her eyes. Her husband should have picked her up from the hospital rather than sending his sister as if she was nothing to him. They were everything to each other—at least they had been before Jeff started going back to church. "Is my wonderful husband at church?"

"Be nice. Jeff worked really hard to get the house cleaned up for you before he and the kids left."

The nurse rolled her through the double doors of the main entrance. Dana got out of the wheelchair, thanked the nurse, then told Sheri, "I don't want to go to the house."

Sheri had used her key fob to unlock the car door. "Then where do you want to go . . . and don't say the liquor store, or I'm telling you now, Dana, I will knock some sense into your head."

Dana opened the passenger-side door of Sheri's white BMW and sat down. When Sheri got in, Dana turned to her. Tears rolled down her face. Yes, God help her, she did want a drink. But she wanted—no, needed—something even more than a drink in her hand. "Take me to my family."

"They're at church. I can't take you over there so you can act a fool and embarrass Jeff and the kids."

Dana put a hand on Sheri's shoulder. "I don't want to embarrass them. But I don't want to go home either. I'm afraid of what I will do if I'm alone. I need my family. They're all I have in this world, Sheri. Please take me to them."

Sheri started crying. She sniffed, wiped her face, and then hugged Dana again. "You have so much, but as I look in your eyes, I can see that nothing you have means more to you than Jeff and those kids."

Dana blinked back tears. Jeff, Judah, and Ebony meant the world to her. She needed to figure a way to keep her family together. "I'll catch a cab if you don't want to take me."

"No! No!" Sheri took a tissue from her console and blew her nose. "You don't have to do that. I'm going to take you to them, but please, Dana, get some help. Don't throw away everything that the Lord has blessed you with."

Hearing Sheri say that the Lord had blessed her gave Dana pause. All these years she had thought that God was against her. He had to be, or why else did she have such a terrible childhood?

But then Dana's thoughts turned to Lisa again. Why had Lisa invited her to church that Sunday? Could she have been on assignment from God? Was God trying to get her attention all these years?

When they arrived at the church, Dana had every intention of going down each aisle until she spotted her family. She was going to beg Jeff to take her back. She couldn't make it in this world without him. But as she and Sheri walked into the sanctuary, the choir was singing a song by Kirk Franklin, "Help Me Believe."

The words stuck to Dana's very soul. It was how she had been feeling. She wanted to believe in God. Jeff believed. Her kids believed. Sheri believed. Lisa believed. Why couldn't she?

Then the pastor stood behind the podium and said, "Aren't you tired, son? Aren't you tired, daughter? Don't you want to be free of the guilt? Come to the altar and let Jesus show you how to truly be free."

The choir started singing, "*Help me believe*," again.

The pastor's words and the song hit like lightning to a hundred-year-old tree, and all her defenses came tumbling down. This was how she had been feeling for so long. She needed to be free from all the shame and blame that had been dumped on her throughout her life, but no one had ever showed her how to release the hold guilt had on her.

As tears flowed down her face, Sheri whispered in her ear, "If you want to go to the altar, I'll walk with you."

So much was bubbling inside her that Dana didn't know how to express herself. She nodded and then put a hand to her mouth as sobs escaped. Suddenly, realization hit her. "I need God. I can't get better without Him." She started walking down the aisle.

The choir kept singing, kept drawing her nearer and nearer to the cross. Kept encouraging her to give it all to God.

Halfway to the altar, Dana lifted her hands. Still sobbing, she declared, "I want to believe!"

Sheri was beside her. She was crying as hard as Dana was. When Dana reached the altar, she looked up. The cross was in front of her. She got down on her knees and pleaded with God to take the desire for alcohol away from her . . . to give her another chance with her family . . . to take the shame and guilt away so she could hold her head up again. "Can You help me, Lord? I want to believe You can. Please help me!"

Dana's nose was running. A puddle of tears formed on the floor before her as she opened her eyes and saw Sheri, Jeff, Judah, and Ebony holding on to her and crying too. God was doing surgery on her. Removing her old, bruised, battered, and dark heart and replacing it with a new heart. One that pumped with the blood of the risen Savior—her Savior, Jesus Christ.

And finally, she was free.

CHAPTER 37

Lisa spent two weeks in the hospital before she was allowed to travel back home to Brooklyn. At her first doctor's appointment since arriving home, Dr. Lawrence informed her he had called in a prescription for blood pressure medication after her last appointment. "My nurse left a message on your cell phone, but I'm not sure if you ever received it."

Lisa didn't remember getting a message, but she searched through the messages on her cell phone later and found it. The call had come on the same day she left for Kennedy's college graduation. She had been in such a hurry she hadn't listened to her messages that day.

Dr. Lawrence also told her that if they couldn't keep her blood pressure stable, she would very likely have another stroke, and he doubted she would survive it. She wanted to tell him to stop speaking those negative words over her life, but he wouldn't understand her, so she lowered her head and prayed.

Lisa had been doing a lot of praying lately. Within the last few years, as her life seemed to fall apart, Lisa had stopped praying . . . she didn't see the use. But with each prayer she prayed while in the hospital, the Lord seemed to be playing back moments in her life that clearly proclaimed the many ways God had showed up for her; but since things didn't go as she planned, Lisa had ignored God's goodness. She'd chosen bitterness and unforgiveness, and now she was reaping the harvest of all she had sown.

"How are you doing this morning?" Riley Storm, her physical therapist, asked as he entered her room.

Lisa had a physical therapist for her weakened left arm and leg. She also saw a speech therapist. She was now a month into her therapy and making progress. She wrote on a notepad, DOING FINE. Then she tried to sound the word *fine* out. "F-f-ine." Some words came easier than others, but Lisa was encouraged, so she wasn't giving up.

"Okay, let's get you out of this bed and walking around the house."

Lisa's bed was now in the dining room. John had drywall put up to separate the living room from the dining room. Drywall and a door also separated the kitchen from the dining room, which was now their bedroom. She hated that they had changed the footprint of the house but couldn't imagine going up and down those stairs at this point in her recovery.

John had helped her shower this morning before he left for work. Kennedy was home with them to help Lisa during the day. She appreciated John and Kennedy's help.She truly needed it. John had to rent out the lower-level apartment to help with some of her hospital bills so her father had to go back to Florida.

She wanted him here with her. It was funny how that worked. When she was younger she couldn't wait to go to college and get out from under her father's thumb; now she cried every time they ended the Skype call.

"I'm ready," she said as she threw the covers off. Her voice . . . she hated it. She had always been a good communicator. Now she opened her mouth and things came out jumbled.

"Good job, Mrs. Coleman. I understood 'I'm' and I could hear the *r* in the next word you said. You are making great progress with your speech therapist."

Lisa couldn't help herself. She beamed at the compliment. Therapy was hard, but living without the use of her voice and with a weakened left side was worse, so she got out of bed with the use of a walker and was engaged for the entire hour of her session.

When her physical therapy session was finished, Lisa got back in bed and took her Bible off her nightstand. Before the stroke, Lisa could count on one hand the number of times she picked up her Bible to read while at home in the last ten years. She was always too busy doing this or that. And besides, she had read the Bible from front to back twice in her lifetime.

Those were the things she had once told herself about why she wasn't reading her Bible anymore. But life had a way of slowing things down . . . and then in the quiet moments, when everything but God had been stripped away, somehow there was time.

Lisa was discovering new joy in the Scriptures. The passage bringing her comfort now was Psalm 37:25: "*I have been young, and now am old; yet I have not seen the righteous forsaken, nor his seed begging bread.*"

This scripture meant everything to Lisa. Her daughter had to put law school on hold after Lisa's stroke. They didn't have the money to send her to school. But Lisa was holding on to the promises of God, particularly the one in this scripture: the righteous wouldn't be forsaken and their seed would not have to beg for their needs.

Oh, she knew her bitter and unforgiving heart was not righteous and her high blood pressure had been brought on by stress and bitterness, but this was a new day. So she asked the Lord, her Savior, whom she had loved for most of her life, to forgive her.

As she asked the Lord to forgive her for hardening her heart, she realized it was time to release Dana and move on from the hurts of her past. So she asked the Lord, "Please help me to forgive her. I know I should have done this a long time ago. But I need Your help. I don't want to be bitter any longer."

Kennedy came into her room with a bowl of soup. After the stroke, Lisa had issues with swallowing, another thing she had to relearn. Thankfully, she was doing better. But she was still on pureed food or soup.

"I've got tomato soup today, Mom. I know how much you like it."

Lisa sat up and clapped, but in her head, she was saying, *Yummy.* She really did like tomato soup. Would have loved to have some crackers with it, but she would get there. Lisa picked up her notepad and wrote, THANK YOU. She then flipped the pad around so Kennedy could see it.

"You're welcome." Kennedy set the fold-up table in front of Lisa, then helped her mom sit up and slowly swing her legs off the bed so she was in an upright position while eating her soup.

"Mmm," Lisa said as she took a spoonful of the soup.

"Oh, Mom, I almost forgot. I ordered a journal for you. Something you can use to write your thoughts." She ran out of the room and then came back with a beautiful journal.

It had three dancing women on the cover with the caption "Too Blessed to Be Stressed."

Lisa smiled at the phrase. Life would be much simpler if she could let issues roll away like the arch of a dancer's back. Like there was nothing in this world that could make her lose her composure—she knew where her blessings came from. How she wished she'd had this epiphany when she was younger.

Lisa picked up her notepad. It still had the words *thank you* on it. She showed it to her daughter again, then continued eating her soup.

Later in the evening when John came home, Lisa used her walker to go into the dining room to eat dinner with him and Kennedy. Her days were a lot simpler, but they were filled with love, and she was thankful.

John did most of the talking. Lisa listened and nodded in understanding and smiled at his attempts at jokes. Lisa wondered how long it had been since she let John get two words in before she went in about all the grievances she had during her day. She was ashamed of the way she had treated her husband.

"I must be talking your ear off," John said when they were almost finished with their meal.

John and Kennedy were having taco salad while Lisa ate another bowl of soup. She held up a hand, then wrote on her notepad, I LOVE LISTENING TO YOU TALK.

John blushed as he read her comment. "You don't have to say that."

Lisa went back to her notepad. IT'S TRUE. I WISH

I HAD LISTENED TO YOU MORE. PLEASE KEEP TALKING. Lisa felt as if she was finally getting to know her husband, even though they had been married more than twenty years.

Kennedy stood. "I feel like I'm in the middle of a personal conversation, so I'm going to leave you two alone."

"Realizing your parents are people, too, huh?" John joked with Kennedy.

"Yeah, and I don't need to know any more, thank you."

John and Lisa laughed as Kennedy rushed out of the dining room. Then John said, "I really think she was bored. I mean, how much can she take? She is stuck in this house with two old fogies."

WE'RE NOT OLD, Lisa wrote on her notepad and then showed it to John.

He shook his head. "No, we're not old. I don't even know why I said that. Kennedy should be honored to sit with us."

Then John's eyes bored into hers, and Lisa felt the heat between them.

"But to be honest, I like being with you. Maybe I can talk Kennedy into cleaning up the kitchen and then we can go to our room and watch a movie."

The way he was looking at her, like he was hungry for her, Lisa knew he had more on his mind than a movie. It had been a while, and with her new reality, she wasn't sure if she was comfortable with what he wanted. Nonetheless, she needed his closeness, so she let him take her to their room.

Days seemed to turn into months as Lisa continued to rehab her mind, body, and soul. She was practicing her words more and was feeling more strength in her arm. Her left leg continued to be weak, even after six months of rehab.

Lisa was still reading her Bible and finding new scriptures to soften her heart. Like Romans 8:28: "*And we know that all things work together for good to them that love God, to them who are the called according to his purpose.*"

Lisa grabbed hold of this scripture, believing God would somehow find a way to use everything that had occurred in her life for His glory. God was good, and she was amazed at how she had fallen in love with her Savior and her husband all over again.

She had also been writing in her journal, which mostly included her reflections on the things that had brought her to this moment in her life. It started off with angry notes of how she felt everything started going wrong in her life.

She spent a year writing her thoughts and feeling all the feels. Then a funny thing happened as she spent more time with God and her family: Lisa became honest with herself. She admitted that at one point in her life she regretted the prayers she'd prayed for Dana. God had obviously answered her prayers, and she didn't think Dana deserved it.

But then one day she picked up her journal and wrote . . .

May 1, 2013

I have spent over a decade of my life being bitter about things I could not change. I now realize when all is said and done, God blesses whomever He chooses. It is not my job to complain about the blessings of the Lord. It is my job to pray and to forgive. And today, I am finally ready to be the person God has always wanted me to be. Today, I forgive Dana for everything, and I pray God does something to bless Dana's life and forever change her.

That was the last page in her journal. When Lisa closed the book, God had changed her forever, and all she could do was weep. She felt like Mary Magdalene, but instead of bringing Jesus her alabaster box, Lisa was laying her journal at His feet and allowing Him to cleanse her of all the unforgiveness and bitterness that had tried to swallow her whole. "I thank You, Jesus, for rescuing my soul."

CHAPTER 38

MAY 5, 2013

Dana had spent the last two years detoxing and praising God for His goodness. She had even become a praise dancer at her church. Now she understood why Jeff wanted to name their son Judah . . . praise was everything.

Today the choir was singing "Second Chance" by Hezekiah Walker. Dana had requested this song for her praise dance. She was almost two years sober and was grateful for the second chance God had given her.

As she kicked out her leg, leaned back, and twirled in unison with the other two dancers, tears streamed down her face.

She had truly been given a second chance, and she would spend the rest of her life giving God praise for taking the shame of her past and casting it into the sea of forgiveness. She was no longer listening to the voices of the world saying her previous mistakes meant she was of no use for the rest of her life.

As she two-stepped across the floor with the other praise dancers, Dana stepped into her newness—her destiny. God was in control, and she was allowing Him to lead her. As the song ended and the praise dancers left the sanctuary, they were now on the side of the church where the pastor's office was and the room they used to change their clothes. The other two dancers went into the room, but Dana was so amped up she needed a moment.

With hands lifted in praise, Dana walked the length of the hallway. She wasn't done giving praise to God for the second chance He had given her. Dana went up and down the hallway shouting, "Hallelujah! Hallelujah!"

She was so thankful God had brought Jeff into her life. She found herself wondering why God had decided to do something so amazing for her even before she gave her life to Him. That in itself deserved a hallelujah, so she shouted again.

"You 'bout to make me praise Him too," a man said.

Dana didn't recognize the voice. She whirled around and came face-to-face with State Senator Mike Barnes. She still remembered how smug he looked the day of the debate when he exposed Lisa for not paying her bills. Dana was sure he now knew she was the one responsible for those bills.

"Senator Barnes, I didn't know you attended Brooklyn Tabernacle."

"To be honest with you, I stay so busy I have missed more church services than I have attended lately. But no, I do not attend your church. I came to see you today."

He walked a little closer to her. If she had run into him two years ago, she would have lowered her head in shame, wondering what he thought of her, but she was a new creation in Christ, and she was not about to let anyone else shame her because of her past.

Standing straight, head lifted, she asked, "What can I do for you?"

"Actually, I was hoping you and I could do something for Lisa Coleman." He pointed toward the fellowship hall. "Do you mind if we sit down and talk for a minute?"

She folded her arms over her chest. This man was not going to make her feel guilty. Her sins were covered under the blood, and that's where they would stay. "I completed my community service years ago, Senator, so I'm not sure what else you need from me."

Then he asked, "Did you know Lisa had a stroke two years ago?"

Dana's arms immediately unfolded and fell to her sides. She lifted her right hand and touched her heart. "No, I didn't. Oh my goodness. I'm so sorry to hear this."

"From what I was told, she almost died." He pointed to a table with four chairs in the fellowship hall. "Can we sit?"

"Yes, yes, of course." His news shook Dana. She never would have put Lisa's name in the same sentence as *stroke.* How could this have happened? She wanted to ask questions but didn't feel like she had the right. She sat down and waited for Barnes to fill her in.

He took the seat across from her and said, "I'm not going to beat around the bush. I'm here because I owe Lisa for the way I slandered her name during my first run for city council."

"And I owe her for stealing her identity and causing her to lose out on so many things she planned for her life. Is that what you're saying?"

Barnes shook his head. "I'm not saying you owe her anything. Like you said, you've already done your community service. But I paid close attention to your trial. And from what I grasped, you and Lisa were once friends."

Dana smiled as a distant memory played in her head. "Best friends."

He nodded. "After I was elected to the city council, Lisa came to see me. I felt so bad about how I had slandered her, so I offered to put one of her agenda items on my list. I really did try to get it accomplished during my first year, but when I saw the money wasn't there for the proposal, I gave up. I'm trying to forgive myself for what I did, and I'm hoping you will help me."

"I'm guessing you're coming to me for the money, right?"

Barnes laid his brown leather satchel on the table. He opened it, pulled out a binder, and handed it to Dana. "This is the proposal Lisa put together. She had some really good ideas. I need the funding to open the center. If it's a success, I believe we could open these after-school programs in communities all over Brooklyn."

Dana took the proposal along with Barnes' business card. "Let me look over this information, and I'll get back with you."

Later, while she and Jeff were lounging in the family room and the kids were in their rooms, Dana handed him the proposal. "Senator Barnes came to see me at church today. He said Lisa Coleman had a stroke."

"That's awful. I'll make sure to include her in my prayers."

"Thank you. From what Barnes told me, Lisa almost died." Saying those words caused her eyes to moisten. Lisa had once shared her sandwich with her when she was hungry.

Had invited her to church when she was lost . . . Dana couldn't turn away now that her old friend was in need.

Jeff scanned through the proposal. "Why did Senator Barnes give this proposal to you?"

"He's looking for funding. Years ago, he promised Lisa he would add her agenda to his list, but he never got around to it. Now he feels guilty."

Jeff's lips tightened. "He wasn't trying to pull a guilt trip on you, was he?"

She put a hand on her husband's thigh. "No. He thought I might want to help make Lisa's vision come to life."

He handed the proposal back to her. "And . . . do you?"

It took Dana a moment to respond, but when she did, she said, "I think I want to go visit an old friend."

Lisa was no longer using her walker. She was now able to walk around her house using a cane. Kennedy had a job interview today, so Lisa went into the kitchen and fixed herself some turkey bacon and eggs.

It felt good to be able to cook a meal for herself. She turned on her praise music and then sat down at the kitchen table. She picked up the knife she had laid on the table with her left hand, then put her right hand over her left and sliced a grapefruit. Her left hand was getting better, so she kept working it.

Lisa bowed her head and prayed over her food. She also slid in, "And, Lord, can You please help Kennedy? She has been so good to come back home and help me during my time of need. Please, Lord, Kennedy deserves to be in law school rather than applying for a clerk position at a law firm." She looked to heaven. "I'm not going to worry about what I can't do anything about. I'm going to leave it in Your hands."

Lisa ate her breakfast. She even washed her plate and then went back to her room to watch television. Honestly, outside of reading her Bible, the days were quite boring. Lisa was beginning to think about her next act. There had to be something useful she could do in this world.

Lately, she'd been praying not only for Kennedy but also for herself, asking God for direction. She was only forty-six years old, so unless they were giving out TV-critic jobs, she would need to find something to do.

Halfway through *House Hunters*, Lisa started nodding off. Lying around was making her tired. She took a nap, then got up and went to the bathroom. After using the bathroom and washing her hands, Lisa looked at her reflection in the mirror. Right after the stroke, the left side of her lip had drooped. She was thankful her speech had returned and the left side of her face had regained its structure.

Her cane clicked and clacked on the tile of the bathroom floor as she made her way back to the bedroom. But then the doorbell rang. Lisa lifted an eyebrow. She wasn't expecting anyone but her father, and he wasn't due to arrive in town until next week.

Slowly, she turned toward the door, making sure she had a firm grip on her cane. She then began walking toward the front of the house. "One moment, I'm coming!"

Lisa smiled at the sound of her voice. She talked a bit slower these days, but her words were no longer garbled. She praised God every day for blessing her. Lisa was even thankful for the cane she was now using to walk toward the door. She had graduated from her walker.

But as she stood in front of the door and looked out the glass inserts, she almost lost her balance. The stroke had not affected her vision, but Lisa still wondered if she was seeing things.

This was definitely a blast from the past, but then Lisa looked to heaven and asked, "What are You up to?" She was intrigued.

CHAPTER 39

The limo driver turned from Lewis Avenue onto Halsey Street.

Dana looked around the old neighborhood. Things had changed. The corner store Lisa's father used to own was gone; a restaurant was now in its place. She had also noticed the game room she used to play in as a teen was closed. The building had been boarded up.

The In Loving Memory mural was still on the wall at the corner of Halsey and Lewis. Dana hadn't thought much about this mural through the years, but her heart ached to see it now. "Stop the car," she told the limo driver.

Her driver pulled over, parked the car, then got out and opened Dana's door. As Dana walked over to the mural, she spotted faces from the old neighborhood. Her mother's face was on the mural. Mrs. Brenda, Lisa's mother, was there. Dana also saw Derrick. Her mind drifted back to all the havoc one wrong choice of getting in that car with Derrick had brought to her life.

Her chin quivered. So much history was on this wall. So many of the faces painted on the mural had been a part of her early years, whether for good or for bad. As Dana continued to scan the mural, her hand went to her mouth.

Her eyes watered as she saw Jasmine's face. That girl had gone all the way wrong. But Dana wondered: If a program like the one Lisa had proposed had been available when they were growing up, would things have been different for them?

As she turned away from the wall, she didn't feel like getting back into the limo. She pointed toward Lisa's house. "I'm going to the house over there," she told her driver, then headed up the street. Lisa's house was on the opposite side of the street, so Dana crossed over. As she walked toward her old friend's house, she wasn't surprised Lisa had stayed in the family home. A lot of families passed down their brownstones from one family member to the next.

But what did surprise Dana were all the white faces she saw on this side of Brooklyn. When she was growing up, this side of town had mostly African American residents. She also noticed renovations were underway on a few of the brownstones. Workers were throwing old carpet out of one house. She saw another group of workers bringing the railing from the staircase of a brownstone out on the lawn. Things were definitely changing in her old neighborhood.

Butterflies flew around in Dana's stomach as she climbed the stairs and rang the doorbell. She stood and waited, tried not to look through the window insert as she heard the *tap*, *tap*, *tap* of something on the hardwood floor.

When the tapping stopped, Dana could feel someone staring at her from the other side of the door. She was looking toward the house on the right while standing on the stoop. She did not want to face forward. She was concerned about the way she might be received. If they decided not to open the door, at least she wouldn't have the disapproving glare branded into her mind.

But the door opened. Lisa looked past Dana, toward the limo parked in front of her house. "Really, Dana? You brought a limo to Bed-Stuy?"

"You know how hard it is to get a cab in this town," Dana joked as Lisa opened the door wide.

"Come in."

Dana stepped inside and followed Lisa to the living room. She was amazed at how much the interior had changed while still giving the feel of the brownstones of old. The banister on the stairs leading to the third level used to be a mahogany brown; now it was black. The walls had once been white but were now a light gray. A wall now separated the living room from the dining room. So you had to walk all the way down the hall to get to the kitchen. The furnishings flirted with the off-white and gray tones. Dana remembered a brown and white sofa in this living room back in the day, and the sofa used to have a plastic covering.

Dana hated seeing Lisa with a cane, but she tried not to make a big deal of it by staring at it. When they sat down, she pointed toward the outside. "What's the deal with all the white people I see in the hood?"

"Gentrification," Lisa said. Then they both laughed.

Dana said, "It's happening all over."

"The neighborhood has been changing for a few years now. Some of the neighbors are getting million-dollar offers on their properties, so I really can't blame them for selling."

Dana didn't want to pry, but she had to know. "Are you planning to sell?" For some reason, this house being in someone else's hands didn't sit well with her.

"I don't want to." Lisa sighed. "But after spending the money we saved for Kennedy to go to law school on my medical expenses, we might have to."

Dana frowned. "I'm sorry to hear that. Senator Barnes told me you've been ill. So I stopped by." Then she admitted, "I honestly didn't know if you would open the door once you saw it was me, but I'm so glad you did."

Lisa laughed, then admitted, "If you had come a year ago, I probably would have opened the door so I could slam it in your face. But God has been healing me physically and spiritually."

Smiling, Dana told her, "You'll probably be surprised to hear this, but I have finally allowed the Lord to guide my life as well. My husband, my children, and I, we all attend church regularly now. But it's not about going to church for us; it's about the relationship we are building with Christ."

Lisa's eyes filled with tears. She reached over and hugged Dana. "I can't believe you are sitting here telling me this." Lisa then looked to heaven and said, "Thank You, Lord." She turned back to Dana and told her, "Years ago, right after you were arrested, I felt so bad for you, so I started praying for the Lord to not only save your soul but to bring a good man into your life. I didn't ever want you to fall prey to the Derricks of this world again."

Tears cascaded down Dana's face. She looked up. God was so amazing to her. To think, even with all the years of struggle she had endured, God was always there guiding her home because someone bothered to pray for her. She looked back at Lisa and asked, "Can I tell you something?"

"Of course. Anything."

Dana gulped back the shame of her past and said, "I meant what I said to you in court. I am truly sorry for everything I did to you. And I'm here with a proposal I hope might take a bit of the sting of my betrayal away."

Lisa put a hand on Dana's shoulder. "Listen to me, old

friend. God has already taken the sting away. I have forgiven you."

Dana lost her composure then. She sobbed as if those words out of Lisa's mouth meant everything to her. "Th-thank y-you for f-forgiving me." Dana finally pulled herself back together, wiped her face. She then took a tissue out of her handbag and blew her nose.

There was another item in her handbag. It was Lisa's proposal for after-school facilities to help the youth in the community with homework, study skills, and SAT exams and be a hangout spot where the children received positive reinforcement and encouragement to further their education.

Dana handed the proposal to Lisa. "Senator Barnes wants to bring your vision to life, and he asked me to partner with him to create the first facility."

Lisa looked down at the proposal. "I wrote this thing about thirteen years ago. I thought Senator Barnes had only humored me by taking it from me. Nothing ever came of it."

"He told me he couldn't get the funding, so he shelved it. But he thinks if we can open one facility, then it might lead to funding for other sites." Dana stuck her hand out. "What do you say, Lisa? Are you up to working with me to bring your vision to life?"

Lisa's eyes widened. "Are you serious? You really want to do this . . . with me?"

"I wouldn't be here if I didn't. But I need to know if your heart is still in this project."

"Oh my God. Yes! Yes, it is." Lisa ignored Dana's outstretched hand and hugged her. "I can't believe this."

"Believe it, Lisa. This is an excellent idea. If we had a program like this when we were younger, maybe so many of us wouldn't have gone down the wrong path."

When they finished discussing the program, Dana stood to leave. She turned back as if remembering something. "Which law school is your daughter planning to attend?"

Lisa got a sorrowful look on her face. "Kennedy put off attending law school after I had my stroke. But since things have been better for me, she's out looking for a job at a law office, hoping she can pay her way through law school that way."

"So she hasn't applied to any colleges yet?"

"Oh yes, she's doing both. Kennedy applied at New York Law School and Columbia Law School. She's waiting to hear from one of them to find out if there is a scholarship available."

"And if she doesn't get the scholarship?" Dana asked.

Lisa frowned. "Then I might have to sell this house. It would break my heart, but Kennedy's dreams are the most important thing to John and me right now."

"I hope things work out for Kennedy. I'd hate if you had to sell this house." Dana's voice broke, and tears came to her eyes. "Your prayers turned my life around. If you hadn't been here when I needed you, I don't know where I would be. I'll forever be grateful to you."

CHAPTER 40

Oh my goodness, this food is delicious."

"I told you. Jeff and I have been here a few times. We love it," Dana told Lisa.

They were doing brunch at a restaurant called Martha on DeKalb Avenue. It was an American with Pan-Asian influences style of restaurant with milk bottles hanging overhead serving as lamps. Lisa liked the cozy wood-and-tile interior and eclectic decor. It felt friendly. "John and I had talked about doing dinner, but then I got sick."

Dana put her fork down. A frown crept across her face. "I hate I wasn't here for you during those months."

Lisa waved that off. "You're here now, and I'm thankful. She dug back into her cast-iron cooked pancakes topped with créme fraîche and apple compote. The cakes were soft and delicious. "Mmm. How's your food?"

Dana was having the fried chicken, crispy Brussels sprouts doused with fish sauce, peanuts, and pickled jalapeños. She also had the duck-fat biscuits with sweet butter and fruit compote.

"It's amazing. The chicken has a sweet and nutty flavor." Dana's fork jutted back and forth toward her plate. "But these Brussels sprouts are my jam."

"Are they good?"

"I wouldn't tell you lies. Take one."

Lisa wasn't a Brussels sprouts kind of woman, but those things were looking good on Dana's plate, so she took one and bit into it. Her eyes widened in surprise. "Is this what I've been missing all the years I refused to eat these things?"

"Don't get inspired and try to cook them at home. I can tell you from personal experience, they won't be the same."

Lisa laughed, but then her eyebrow lifted. "You cook? I pictured you with maids and cooks in that fancy penthouse you told me about."

"You'd be surprised. We live a normal life." Dana took a bite of her Brussels sprouts and then added, "Now, I do pay a cleaning service for bimonthly cleanings."

"Who doesn't," Lisa said with a giggle. "Must be nice over there on easy street."

Leaning back in her seat, Dana said, "To tell you the truth, it hasn't been easy. Losing my mother was one of the worst things I've ever experienced. I started drinking after she died and didn't quit until the Lord rescued me."

This moment taught Lisa something. For years she regretted praying for Dana. She thought her old friend had everything while she was constantly losing the things she wanted most in life. But now she knew Dana had suffered also.

"I wish I had prayed for you more." Shaking her head, Lisa admitted, "I was so selfish."

"Nope. You're not going to do that. It's all water under the bridge. I don't want to think about yesterday. I want to enjoy this good meal with a good friend—if I can still consider you a friend."

Lisa nodded. “I missed your friendship.”

They finished eating, then got back to the reason they were hanging out. Dana wiped her mouth with her napkin. “Okay, we toured three buildings this morning. Did you like any of them?”

Lisa took out her notebook. “I really liked the one close to downtown, but there were too many thugs hanging around on the block. I don’t want to bring kids into a dangerous environment.”

Dana agreed. “They might not be able to concentrate on learning if they’re worried about their safety.”

Lisa’s cell phone rang. It was Kennedy. She answered and started smiling as Kennedy screamed, “I got the job! I am now a paralegal for Fitch and Hoffs.”

“Oh my goodness. Congratulations, hon. I’m so proud of you. I knew one of those law firms would hire you.”

“I wasn’t sure, but I’m so excited, Mom. I really am.”

“I’m glad. Let’s celebrate when I get home. I’m still out with Ms. Dana right now.”

“Tell her I said hello.”

They hung up. Lisa told Dana, “Kennedy said hello.”

“Did I hear you say a law firm hired her?”

Lisa put her napkin on her plate. “Yes, ma’am. She’s going to do paralegal work for Fitch and Hoffs.”

“I’m happy for her.”

Later, Lisa walked a bit slower with her cane than Dana when they left the restaurant. But honestly, Lisa was happy to be able to get out of the house, so she didn’t mind the tiredness leaning heavy on her shoulders. They got in the back of the cab and headed back to Halsey Street.

“How old are your kids?” Lisa asked.

Dana took out her phone and showed pictures of her

children. "Judah is twelve, and Ebony is seven. And they're the most precious kids in the whole wide world."

"Of course they are. I think the same thing about Kennedy." Lisa leaned back in her seat. She enjoyed being with Dana. It felt as if their friendship had never ended . . . conversation with her was easy.

The cabdriver turned on Halsey and continued driving up the street. Lisa looked out the window, and all of a sudden she knew. "Wait! Stop the car! Pull over, please."

Dana glanced around. "But we're not at your house yet."

"Right here, ma'am?"

"Yes. Pull over right here."

When he stopped the car, Lisa opened the door and got out at the corner of Lewis and Halsey. She lifted her cane and pointed at the boarded-up building. Dana came up behind her. "This is it. This is where the first learning center should be."

"The old game room?" Dana scrunched her nose. "Don't you remember all the guys who used to hang out on the side of the building?"

"Yeah, but they don't hang here anymore. This neighborhood is more laid back these days. At first I hated the new feel of our old hood, but now I'm thinking this is the perfect place to start." Actually, the game room was a small storefront connected to the building. But Lisa wanted the entire building for the learning center.

Looking up at the building, Dana nodded. "Basically, we'll be taking a troublesome place and turning it into something good for the kids in this community. I like it."

"Me too. Now we need to find out who owns this building."

"Let me work on that," Dana told her. "You start getting

your plans in order." Smiling she added, "We're about to build our first learning center."

They shook on it, then looked at each other as if the handshake wasn't enough, and they hugged.

Dana took her cell phone out of her purse. "Wait. I've got to capture this with a photo." The two women stood in front of the old game room where Dana got into mischief as a teen—the game room Lisa had always tried to steer clear of. Now they were getting ready to make something out of the place.

"I see you're still obsessed with taking pictures," Lisa said as Dana snapped a selfie.

"Gotta capture the moments. Never know when you might need something to remind you how beautiful life can be."

Lisa liked the sound of that. "Send the photo to me. I want to remember this moment also." Then she turned and looked at the boarded-up building. "This place is hideous, isn't it?"

Dana cocked her head to the left, looking at the building. A smile crept across her face. "Open your eyes to the possibilities. It's hideous now, but a few hammers, nails, paint . . . and once those kids start walking through these doors and becoming all God created them to be . . . we'll see the beauty then."

CHAPTER 41

Lisa now had a new mission in life. A reason to get up and get out of bed in the morning. Kennedy and John were as excited as she was.

John purchased a scooter for her, which they kept locked at the bottom of the steps. After feeling as if she had been sealed away in the house for years, suddenly Lisa had wheels, even if it was only a scooter she drove down the street to check on the construction for the learning center.

When John arrived home from work, his eyes were beaming with excitement. "It looks like they've done some more to the learning center. Come on. Let's walk down there and see."

"I thought you didn't like going down there every day. You told me to give it a rest, so I've stayed away all week."

"There wasn't much progress last month when you kept going down there every single day."

"I couldn't help it. It's so exciting to see my vision come to life like this."

John smiled at her. "I love seeing you like this, so forget what I said before. I'll walk down there with you three times a day if you want."

They went outside. Lisa laid her cane in the bed of her

scooter, unlocked it, and got on. She and John then headed toward the learning center.

It had been four months since Dana purchased the building, and the construction started a month after that. Lisa parked her scooter by the front entrance of the center and retrieved her cane. She and John then went inside the building.

To the left was the space where they would have their version of a game room so kids could enjoy themselves once they finished studying or doing homework. The cafeteria was on the right side of the building, along with Lisa's office. The elevator was next to Lisa's office. It went to the second and third floors. The second floor would have study pods where kids with the same classes could study together. The third floor was for test prep. Each floor would have computers for research or test-taking.

"The place is really coming along. Your office is ready for the furniture to be moved in," John told her as they walked around.

"All the furniture and computers are coming next week," Dana said as she entered the building.

Lisa and John turned to greet her. Lisa walked over to Dana and gave her a hug. "I didn't know you were coming down here today."

"I had to," Dana said with mischief dancing in her eyes. "The sign came today, and I wanted to be here when they put it on the building."

"Oh wow! I thought Senator Barnes was still deciding on the official name." Lisa looked from John to Dana. "When did he make a decision?"

"About a month ago," Dana said nonchalantly. "I must have forgotten to tell you." Then Dana pointed toward John. "But I did let John know the sign was going up today."

Lisa turned to her husband. "You knew?" She scrunched her nose. Of course he knew. That's why he rushed her out of the house, pretending he was so excited about looking at drywall.

Lisa was about to step outside, but Dana stopped her. "We have to wait until they get it affixed to the building. You don't want to get in the way and have the sign fall on your head."

Lisa nodded. "All right. I'll wait."

John took her hand and squeezed it, then Kennedy came running into the building. "Sorry I'm late. I almost missed it."

"How did you know about the sign?" Lisa asked.

Kennedy pointed at John. "Dad called me."

"So who's going to tell me the name of this new learning center I'm supposed to be running?" Lisa put her right hand on her hip and stared at all of them. The crane that was in front of the building pulled back after hoisting the sign to the top.

"Why don't we go outside and see?" Dana said.

Lisa was beginning to feel some kind of way about this situation. If she was supposed to run the center, she would have thought they'd want her input on the name. How many other decisions would be made without her knowledge?

She didn't want to be ungrateful. Dana had put up a lot of money to bring her vision to life. But this was *her* vision, and she needed to be heard. Nonetheless, she decided to see the name they picked before expressing her displeasure. She, John, Kennedy, and Dana all turned around and looked up at the same time.

Lisa Whitaker Coleman Learning Center were the words printed on the sign. Lisa turned around, looking from John to Kennedy and then to Dana. She didn't know what to say. That they would name the center after her meant so much.

Lisa lowered her head as tears sprang to her eyes.

"Mom, don't cry. This is good. I was ten years old when you worked on the proposal for this center. You've always had so much passion for this neighborhood. It is fitting for this center to be named after you."

Turning to Dana, Lisa could barely get the words out through her tears, but somehow she managed to say, "My father will be so happy that you put *Whitaker* on the sign."

There were men on the landing where the sign was. After they affixed the sign, they then adjusted the lights being placed above it. Lisa shook her head. "We don't need those lights. It's not like we're going to be open at night."

But Dana smiled as she looked above. "They are perfect." She turned to Lisa and said, "To me, you have always been the light on Halsey Street, and now everyone will be able to see it as clear as day."

Lisa touched her hand to her heart, gulped.

She couldn't believe Dana felt this way about her after all these years. "You being able to say such a thing after how horribly I treated you completely blows my mind."

"I did you wrong," Dana said. "You had a right to hate me."

But Lisa wagged a finger. "I didn't have a right to hate you. I chose vengeance rather than trusting that God was able to turn things around for my good. My husband and my father tried to warn me about what I was doing, but I wouldn't listen."

John put a hand on Lisa's shoulder. "Hon, you don't have to rehash all of this. It's okay."

Patting John's hand, Lisa kept her eyes glued on Dana's.

"You thanked me for forgiving you. But today, I want to thank you for caring about me, even after I was so horrible to you." She got choked up, tears flowing down her face. "Thank you for helping me bring my vision to life."

"Ahh." Dana wrapped her arms around Lisa. "It's an awesome vision. I can't wait to see the kids' faces when they come to this place."

Lisa wiped her face. "You and me both." She stared at the building and then pointed at a door on the first floor. "I can't believe this is the same game room my father warned me to stay away from."

"For good reason," Dana said. "I still remember the hoodlums who used to hang around here." Then Dana smiled as she looked back at the building. "Imagine, this building is going to provide a new mindset for kids. And help them to choose education over the streets. This is God's work."

"God's work indeed," Lisa agreed.

Lisa then got back on her scooter and headed home with John and Kennedy. John and Lisa sat down in the family room to relax before dinner. Lisa rubbed her husband's back, then leaned over and kissed him. "Thank you for keeping the secret. It truly blew my mind when I saw the sign."

"I wanted to tell you so many times," he admitted. "But I couldn't deny you the thrill of the moment."

John was leaning in for another kiss when they heard Kennedy scream.

"I can't believe it! I can't believe it!" Kennedy kept screaming as she ran into the family room with an envelope in her hand. "Check it out," she said as she handed it to John.

John's eyebrows lifted. "Columbia University, huh?"

"Columbia!" Lisa sat up straight. "Is this your letter from Columbia Law School?"

Kennedy jumped up and down in front of them. "Yes! I've been accepted."

Lisa reached for her cane, then stood and hugged her daughter. "I'm so happy for you, honey." Immediately, concern about how they would pay for law school tried to creep in and steal the joy of the moment, but Lisa pushed it back. She would not allow doubt and worry to take anything away from Kennedy's accomplishment.

Kennedy said, "Thank God for my job at the law firm. I'm not sure how I will fit my classes in, but at least they will pay 40 percent of my tuition once I've been employed there for a full year."

John held the letter up. He pointed at the third paragraph. "Did you read this letter?"

"No, I got so excited after seeing I was accepted that I ran in here to show you."

Lisa took the letter from John as he said, "You are the recipient of a full scholarship by an anonymous donor." John stood up and lifted his hands in praise. "You don't owe them a penny!"

Overwhelmed, Lisa sat on the sofa. All she could say was, "God is so good."

CHAPTER 42

2018

Dana had made some changes to the way Hair Fabulous went to market. Actually, the times had forced them to make changes. The mailer campaign no longer brought in business as it had before so many people turned to social media as if it was their lifeblood.

Sierra had her iPad in front of her as she said, "The Facebook ad is doing well, and we have garnered some serious attention with the hashtags we use on Twitter."

With a roll of her eyes, Dana said, "I still don't get the hashtag stuff or the people who use Facebook like it's a drug."

"Drug or not, our ads are bringing in tons of orders."

"Score another one for you, Sierra." One of the best decisions Dana made was when she hired Sierra to run the marketing department. They didn't always agree about the best way to market Hair Fabulous products, but Dana was usually standing on the side of wrong when it came to marketing.

"Hashtags are a way of categorizing our content—nothing more. It helps us reach the people who are interested in our products," Kim said.

Dana turned to Kim, who was seated to her right. Kim had started with the company as a receptionist. She was now the director of the production department.

"I get that," Dana told her. "I don't like Twitter, but I do like posting pictures of my family on Facebook."

They ended the meeting, and Dana went to the break room to grab a drink of water. On her way, she was almost run over by Ebony as she, Jeff, and Judah entered the building.

"Slow down, child."

"I'm sorry, Mommy. Daddy said we're going to see Mrs. Coleman's learning center today, and I wanted to come get you before you got stuck in a meeting."

"Don't believe her. She hit me and took off running," Judah said.

Dana put a hand on Ebony's shoulder as Jeff leaned in for a kiss. Ebony was twelve years old and full of energy. Judah had turned seventeen. He was neck and neck with his dad.

"How was your day?" she asked Jeff after the kiss.

Jeff sucked his teeth. "I lost at golf again. I'm beginning to think I need a new hobby."

"Babe, you started playing about six months ago. Maybe you need more practice." Since handing Hair Fabulous back to her, Jeff was taking time to figure out his next move in the business world, and that was all right with her.

"I don't know if I'm suited for a life of leisure, but I'm enjoying hanging out with the fellows from time to time."

She nuzzled up to his ear and whispered, "Are you having second thoughts about being a kept man?"

Jeff looked as if he was thinking it over, then laughed. "No way. I earned my keep."

"You sure did, babe." She laughed with him, then they drove over to the brand-new Lisa Whitaker Coleman

Learning Center. The first learning center on Halsey Street had taken off like a rocket, so they opened the second learning center on Bedford Avenue.

The kids jumped out of the car moments after Jeff parked behind the building. "Now, if they were actually registered for this after-school program, do you think they would be running into the learning center like that?"

Dana watched Judah swing the door open. "I'd like to think so. Lisa has created a learning environment that children love. I wish someone had thought of it when I was a kid."

Jeff and Dana went into the learning center. It was a smaller location than the first, but it still had study pods, test-prep areas, and a game room. Jeff and Dana hugged Lisa. "It's looking good in here," Dana told her.

"I'm loving it," Lisa said. "We didn't have enough space for a cafeteria, but the small break room with snacks is adequate."

Jeff pointed to the game room. "I think I spotted the reason my kids couldn't wait to get in here."

Lisa laughed. "They hugged me and then begged to go to the game room. I didn't have the heart to deny them."

"Well, I'm going to make sure they play one game and then come out of there. My stomach is starting to growl. I need food." Jeff headed to the game room.

"He'll be stuck in there, and I'll have to pull all three of them out," Dana told Lisa.

"Same with John. He goes into the game room at both locations—tells me he's supervising the kids."

"If Senator Barnes would get the funding approved, we'd be able to afford more staff for you; you need help looking after all the kids."

“We have thirty-five kids enrolled at this location.”

Dana put a hand on Lisa’s shoulder. “And almost fifty at the Halsey Street location. I don’t know how you sleep. This is a lot.”

“It’s a labor of love,” Lisa told her. “But Senator Barnes does need to come on with the funding. I would love to hire more employees and not have to work as many hours.”

“I’ll schedule a meeting with him,” Dana told her.

“Better you than me.” Lisa rolled her eyes.

Glancing around, Dana observed the kids as they sat at the study tables with laptops or books open or discussing a subject with a study partner. “You’re doing so much with these kids, and you need more funding than I can give.”

Lisa pointed upward. “God will provide.”

“So true,” Dana agreed. They hugged. John and Kennedy stepped into the center. Dana glanced at her watch. “How much longer until you close up?”

“We close at seven, but Terri can handle the last hour without me.”

Dana pulled her children and her husband out of the game room, then the two families went to DeStefano’s Steakhouse. They had a cozy family atmosphere, and the steaks were cooked to perfection.

The two families sat down. They laughed, joked, and had a good time enjoying the company of friends who had become more like family.

When it was time for dessert, Kennedy came over to Dana. She tapped her on the shoulder. “Can I speak with you?”

Dana put her napkin on the table. “Of course.” She got up and followed Kennedy outside.

As they stood next to the building, Kennedy grinned at her.

Dana looked to her left, then the right. "What are you grinning about?"

"I finally discovered your secret."

She lifted her eyebrows. "What secret?"

Kennedy nudged Dana's shoulder playfully. "You don't have to pretend with me. It all made sense when that woman in the financial aid office at Columbia Law School spilled the beans."

Dana's hand went to her head. The checks she'd sent to Columbia University were written from her personal account.

"Don't be mad. I just wanted you to know how much I appreciate what you did for me."

"She shouldn't have blabbed to you about your donor. I must admit, I'm a bit taken aback by this."

Kennedy hugged her. "Please don't get the lady in financial aid fired for divulging information about my secret donor. I'm happy that she told me."

Dana waved a hand in the air. "You didn't tell your mother?"

"No. I just found out today."

"I'll make you a deal. If you keep my secret quiet, then I won't make a fuss with your school." Dana stuck her hand out, and they shook on it.

"I won't say a word, even though I'd like nothing more than to shout to the world what a wonderful person you are."

Dana was overjoyed at Kennedy's words, but what she said next blew her away.

"I wish my mother had a sister. I've always wanted an aunt who is as amazing as you are."

Dana's eyes watered. She wiped the mist away as she told Kennedy, "I was an only child also, but your mother has always been a sister to me, so I would be honored if you considered me your aunt."

"Wait . . . wait . . . wait." Lisa walked over to them. "If she gets to call you Auntie, then I want Judah and Ebony to call me Auntie too."

Dana swung around. "How long have you been out here?"

Lisa said, "I just came out. Y'all didn't tell us which dessert you want, and I didn't want you two to miss out."

Dana put an arm around Lisa as they walked back into the restaurant. "I do want dessert. Thanks for coming to get us. And of course Judah and Ebony can call you Auntie."

"What else would they call you," Kennedy said, "since you and Auntie Dana are like sisters?"

Lisa stopped walking. She cocked her head to the left as she looked at Dana, then she pulled her into her arms. "I'm so grateful to have you back in my life."

"Ditto," Dana said with a wry smile, then she winked at Kennedy, trusting that her secret was safe with her.

CHAPTER 43

Seven years had passed since they opened the first Lisa Whitaker Coleman Learning Center. The first and second centers had served more than three hundred kids. They were now fully funded by the government and donations. Dana and Lisa sat on the board of directors for the learning centers, and they were opening the third location in Brooklyn today.

Dana was getting ready for the reception when Judah came into her bedroom. "Can I get the car keys?" he asked.

Her handsome son was now nineteen and had received his driver's license, but Dana wasn't ready to hand over the keys so fast. "You can drive me to the reception, but that's it."

"That's not right. I'm in college. You and Dad are always telling me how responsible I am."

"Ohhh, he's bringing out the responsible card. What is our son trying to get out of you?" Jeff asked as he entered the bedroom.

Dana's eyes brightened as she looked at her husband. Jeff had turned fifty-six this year. His hair was now a salt-and-pepper mix, and it had thinned a bit on the top. But if it was possible, the man was handsomer now than the day she met him. She was a blessed woman indeed. "Your son asked me for the keys to the car."

"Boy, go sit down somewhere. That driver's license done went to your head."

Judah shook his head as he left their room. "Y'all not right."

Dana high-fived Jeff. "Thanks for having my back. Having teenagers ain't for punks."

Jeff agreed. "I don't know what we're going to do when Ebony starts asking for the keys."

"Help us, Jesus," Dana said, and they both laughed.

She then headed to the bathroom. "Let me put my dress on before we're late. Oh, and don't forget about dinner tonight."

"How could I forget? We're still going to Clover Hill, right?"

"You know it." Dana and Jeff loved this intimate, thirty-seat restaurant in Brooklyn Heights. They delivered French-inspired dishes in a seven-course tasting menu that was full of flavor and seafood. She couldn't wait for Lisa to experience this place.

With her hand on the bathroom door, she threw back over her shoulder, "Oh, and your son is driving us to the reception."

"Oh Lord. Let me get on my knees and start praying now."

Jeff kept a giggle in her spirit. Dana closed the bathroom door and jumped in the shower, laughing while Jeff prayed.

Lisa hadn't been feeling well all week. John had taken her to the emergency room two days ago, but she was released once the tests didn't show anything alarming to the ER doctor. The reception for the new learning center was in a few hours. John would be home from work in about two hours, so she went to the lower level of their brownstone and knocked on the door.

Her daddy answered. "I thought you were getting ready for this big to-do tonight."

"I will in a few. I wanted to spend a little time with my daddy since I've been so busy." Her dad was visiting for the summer, but he still lived in Florida.

"Well, come on in. I'm going to enjoy this visit. After this new learning center opens, you're going to be so busy, I probably won't see you much this summer."

"Oh, I'll make time. I like being around my daddy." Lisa sat down in the living room and her father sat across from her.

"I'm glad to hear it. When you were younger, I always felt like you would rather be anywhere else but with your old man."

Lisa laughed at the truth of the statement. "When I was a teen, I couldn't wait to go off to college to get away from you. You were so demanding, and I never thought I would live up to your expectations."

David lowered his head. "I'm sorry I was so hard on you."

Lisa lifted a hand, waved away his remark. "You weren't too hard on me, Daddy. I was a kid, and I thought I knew better than you back then, but I am so thankful I had you and Mom in my life. I may not have listened when I was younger, but your words spoke volumes to me when I needed them most. And I want you to know how special you've been in my life."

"I love you, Lisa. And I'm so proud of you."

"Thank you, Daddy." She hugged him and then said, "These learning centers have been the defining moment of my life, but I never would have been concerned about the neighborhood if you hadn't taken me to hear Representative Shirley Chisholm and if Elsie Richardson hadn't spoken at our church when I was younger. I'm so grateful for the foundation you and Mom set before me."

Her father was crying. "I have a confession."

She wiped the tears from his face, then kissed his cheek. "Don't cry. Tell me what's on your mind."

"I did wrong by Dana."

Lisa raised an eyebrow, then scratched her head. "You haven't done anything to Dana." Then Lisa remembered something. "Are you talking about the time you wouldn't let Dana and her mother rent this apartment?"

"No. You were headed off to college. We needed to rent the basement apartment out to someone who could pay rent. There was no way I was going to let you down financially."

Lisa had nothing else. She couldn't imagine anything her father could have done to Dana.

"She called the house collect a few times after she got arrested. She also wrote you letters, but I thought she was a bad influence, so I never told you, but now I'm thinking Dana might have needed you at that time in her life more than I understood."

Lisa thought about it for a moment, then said, "I think God has a way of landing His children on the right road, no matter how many detours we take." She then went back to the main part of the house. She felt like lying down. A nap sounded like the perfect thing.

She was so tired lately. She set the alarm on her phone so she would get up in enough time to get dressed for the reception, then shut her eyes and drifted off to sleep. The moment her head hit the pillow, she was dreaming . . .

"Lisa, girl, get up and out of bed right now. I don't care if it is summertime, you're not going to lay around this house all day."

Lisa heard her father call out to her, but her eyelids felt glued together. She rubbed the sleep from her eyes and then glanced over at the clock on her nightstand. It was 7:52 a.m. on a Saturday . . . a morning she had planned to sleep in, but her daddy was screaming for her.

"We need to get down to the store so we can pass out the hot dogs and hamburgers to our customers in the neighborhood," Daddy hollered up to her. "It's good business to give back to the community on a day like this."

Lisa popped up and flung the covers off. She opened the curtain and looked out the window. She saw the sanitation street-sweeper truck as it slowly drove down the street.

A truck with DJ equipment was parked across the street. Two guys got out and started taking the gear out of the bed of the truck.

How had she forgotten? There was going to be a block party on Halsey Street today.

She rushed downstairs and went to the store to help her dad, but when Dana ran into the store, she took her break.

"Double Dutch time," Dana said.

"Let's do it!" Lisa and Dana found a group of kids and took turns double-Dutching with them while the DJ blasted his music and the neighbors grilled hot dogs and hamburgers in their front yards. She and Dana were going into the ninth grade. High school was going to be so much fun with her best friend.

Dana grabbed Lisa's hand, moving her away from the double Dutch. "Let's go to the game room."

But Lisa started backing away. "You know my dad doesn't want me in that game room."

Dana pointed at the game room. She said, "But it's named after you."

Suddenly Dana disappeared, the block party disappeared. Lisa was left standing there, looking at the building with her name on it. Thousands of kids were going in and out of the building. They seemed older, more mature, more knowledgeable as they left the building. Many of them walked over to her and said, "Thank you."

Lisa was at peace. Everything in her life was not the way she planned it, but she had learned to trust God and move in His time. As she lay in bed, seeing the fulfillment of her vision, she felt herself drifting away.

Come to Me, daughter, for you are My beloved.

Lisa could hear John asking her to wake up, but at the same time she heard the voice of the Lord pulling her ever closer to Him. She loved John, loved their life together, and she didn't want to leave him, but she couldn't stop herself from drifting ever closer to the One who had so thoroughly captured her heart.

She realized her days had in fact been numbered, and this was the day she was supposed to meet her Maker . . . her Beloved, so Lisa kept drifting until it felt as if she was floating on a cloud.

"Mom, telephone. It's Mr. Coleman."

Dana was sitting on the sofa putting her heels on. They needed to be at the new learning center early. She was helping with a surprise they had planned for Lisa. She finished putting her shoes on, then took the phone from Judah. "Don't tell me you spoiled the surprise."

Dana had been grinning, thinking about how much her friend was going to enjoy this night, when the grin was completely wiped off her face. She felt like she was hearing sounds, but the sounds weren't making sense. Tears flowed down her face, and she started screaming.

Jeff rushed into the room. He took the phone out of her hand. "Who is this?" he said into the phone.

Jeff's eyes grew wide, then he said, "I'm so sorry to hear this, John. Thank you so much for calling us."

He hung up the phone and pulled Dana into his arms, but she pushed him away. "No! No! This is not happening. Lisa is in her fifties. This can't be truuuue." She sobbed, and the word *true* seemed to drag as she said it.

"Oh, babe." Jeff sniffed. Wiped his face. "I'm sorry, Dana. John said she passed in her sleep."

Dana's hand went to her head. She swung this way and that. "Why?"

Ebony ran into the room. She wrapped her arms around Dana. "Don't be sad, Mama. I don't want you to be sad."

Dana hugged her child as she looked around at the family God had blessed her with. Life was full of important moments. If she hadn't been paying attention, she would have missed those moments that led to the life she had been blessed with.

Like the moment she met Jeff; and the moment when he wanted to ask her out, but he'd been scared she would think he was after her money. If she hadn't made sure he asked her out, she would have missed out on all the love, and the life, they built.

And like the moment when she sat at the lunch table

crying as her belly ached from hunger. If she had been too embarrassed to accept the half sandwich Lisa offered her, she would have missed out on the chance to have the best friend anyone ever could have had. She looked to heaven, and with tears streaming down her face, she whispered, "I'll see you later, girl. Save a seat for me."

CHAPTER 44

Lisa's face was now on the In Loving Memory mural, but it wasn't only her face. A full-body portrait of Lisa was on the mural. The portrait showed her in a white gown with angel wings, and she appeared to be floating up to heaven right before their very eyes.

The portrait of Lisa was right under the bright light that was attached to the wall above the mural. The light had never shone brighter as it captured the image of Lisa with those angel wings.

Today was Lisa's memorial. It was being held at Praise Ministries, but Dana had to come to Halsey Street to look at the mural before going to the church. She smiled at so many faces she had known and loved. Smiled at the memories of days gone by and the wishes and dreams of a troubled child.

God had turned things around in her life, and thanks to Lisa, the learning centers would continue to turn things around for underprivileged youth in the area. Sadness filled Dana's eyes as she looked back at the painting of Lisa. "I'm sorry you won't be here to see how many people your life's work will benefit."

Dana got back in her car and drove to Praise Ministries. It was a good thing Lisa's church could hold two thousand people. The church was standing room only. Dana was amazed at all the people who came out to pay their respects. But Lisa had been an amazing woman with a heart for the people, so this was a fitting send-off.

Dana and Jeff sat with John, Kennedy, and Mr. Whitaker on a pew in the front of the church as one of the choir members sang "Walk Around Heaven" by Beau Williams; then Pastor Jonathan tried his best to eulogize Lisa without shedding a tear, but his heart won the battle, and before he finished he broke down and cried.

After all was said and done, it was Kennedy's turn at the podium. She would have the last say. Dana grinned like a proud auntie as Kennedy took hold of the microphone.

She cleared her throat. "First and foremost, I want to thank each and every one of you who came out today to pay tribute to my mother. She was a wonderful woman, and no one knew that more than my family.

"I love her so much, and it's so hard to say goodbye." Tears rolled down Kennedy's face. She wiped them away. "I said I wasn't going to stand up here and cry before all of you. Lord knows, I've done enough crying since she's been gone.

"Many of you knew my mother as the kind woman who helped to keep hundreds of kids out of trouble while they studied and then went on to receive scholarships to college, and she was exactly the person you remember. But I want to talk to you about another side of my mother.

"You see, many years ago something terrible was done to her. It ruined her plans and caused my mother to become bitter and unforgiving. My father and grandfather tried to get her to forgive, but she wouldn't hear of it. Instead she let the things that happened to her destroy her from the inside out.

I truly believe my mother's high blood pressure was caused by stress and bitterness.

"But I thank God the story didn't end there. After she had her stroke, Mom found time to read her Bible again, and she found her way back to forgiveness. And you know what? The years my mother lived after her stroke"—Kennedy turned toward Dana—"after she forgave you, were some of her best years.

"And I want to thank you for reaching back and remembering what you still owed an old friend. But I must tell you"—Kennedy wiped the tears from her eyes—"your debt is paid in full. Please don't ever think you owe us anything, and please don't be a stranger. I'm going to need my auntie in my life."

Dana stood. She walked up to the podium and pulled Kennedy into her arms. Whispering in her ear, she said, "You just try to get rid of me." Dana would be there for Kennedy, and she would serve her role as an auntie as best she could. Her actions were no longer to pay a debt, but because she had loved Lisa like a sister.

God had forgiven her; Lisa had forgiven her. Now all Dana wanted to do was to be here for the people she loved as long as God allowed. She looked to heaven and said, "I still wish you were here."

After the service, as she and Jeff walked out of the church, she breathed in the humid summer air, looked around at the people going here and there. She took out her cell phone and snapped a picture. Dana needed to capture this moment and remember how good it felt to be alive and to be free from guilt and shame. It was a beautiful thing.

A Note from the Author

I loved everything about writing this story and I hope you enjoy reading it just as much. First off, although I have traveled to New York on numerous occasions and have great love for the city, I never lived there. And never thought I would write a book about the area . . . until I married my husband.

My husband, David, was born in New York and came of age in the eighties in the Bedford-Stuyvesant (Bed-Stuy) Brooklyn neighborhood. He and I spent hours talking about this family-oriented place with a community unlike any other, where everybody knew who you were. And lifelong friends were made.

As I researched the area, I discovered that Representative Shirley Chisholm and Elsie Richardson worked to revitalize the Bed-Stuy area in the sixties and many Blacks were able to buy homes and own businesses due to the work these women did. Even though this book begins in 1985, I couldn't write a Bed-Stuy story without giving a bit of honor to those two phenomenal women. I pray I did them justice with the mention of their names and the cameo appearance.

Back to why I decided to write this story . . . My husband began showing me pictures of the back-in-the-day Bed-Stuy . . . the Bed-Stuy he came of age in. He showed me pictures of Brownstones, kids shooting hoops in the park, kids spraying water from the fire hydrant on hot summer days, family and friends gathering outside during a block party.

Then he showed me a picture of the In Loving Memory Mural with the faces of people who died in the neighborhood. And a story came to life in my writer's mind.

In the book, I show this mural from the eighties all the way until 2019. Although this mural is a very real thing that loomed large at the corner of Lewis and Halsey in the eighties, it was painted over as gentrification took over the neighborhood. I will be sharing the photo of this mural on my Facebook page, so stay tuned.

If you came of age in the eighties as my husband and I did, you are well aware of the devastation that crack cocaine did to neighborhoods. It was not specific to the Bed-Stuy community. And this book is not meant to imply such a thing. As a matter of fact, I wrote about the destruction of this drug in my first series, the Rain series that was set in Ohio. But God is good and many of us made it out of those days and live to tell about it. In this book, I'm telling the story of a community that has lost its way . . . but one of my characters wants to revitalize it again, just as Elsie Richardson had done.

The premise of the story came from a sermon Pastor Walter L. Bowers Jr. Esq., preached titled "Your Struggle Is About to Change Your Whole World." I sat in church that Sunday, mesmerized by the sermon because I knew I had found the premise to build Dana and Lisa's story around. Struggle . . . and what we do in the midst of it. So thank you, Pastor Bowers, I am so happy to be a member of your church, the Chosen City Church.

I do hope you enjoy Dana and Lisa's story. It is a coming-of-age saga that spans almost four decades. This book speaks volumes about the danger of letting life's challenges make you bitter rather than holding on to God's unchanging hand and becoming better. My prayer is that you take the lessons these characters teach and forever strive to forgive and live free from bitterness.

God's got a blessing for you, my friend. And I'm praying that you receive it.

Blessings,
Vanessa Miller

Discussion Questions

1. This book begins in 1985 when the two main characters are eighteen years old. Do you remember your teen years? If you were given the chance to change one thing from your teen years, what would it be? (If it's too personal, just pray about it.)
2. Dana hated her mother's choice in men, but found herself with a boyfriend who was a thief and caused her to spend four years in prison. Why do you think people sometimes run toward the very thing they know is not good for them?
3. When Dana attended church with Lisa, the pastor preached a message titled, "Your Struggle Is About to Change Your Whole World." Dana's struggle was poverty and lack of self-worth. Lisa's struggle was unforgiveness. Their struggles did indeed change their world, but was there anything Lisa or Dana could have done to eliminate some of the things they struggled with?
4. Lisa seems to have it all together. She's from a two-parent home, college educated, married with a child, and she loves God. It is not until she faces adversity that we see her struggle to forgive and

how that struggle affects her in devastating ways. In your opinion, is there ever a just reason to hold unforgiveness?

5. When Dana first meets Jeff, she looks at him through the lens of past relationships. If she had kept her guard up, she could have missed out on a good man. But how easy is it to let your guard down once you've been hurt? And how much do we miss out on by holding people at arm's length?
6. Even though Dana and Lisa grew up in the same community, they had very different experiences. And they were both a product of their upbringing. What did you think of these two characters? Did you feel for Dana even though she betrayed her friend? Did you understand Lisa, even after she became bitter? Or did you not get one or the other at all?
7. One of the themes in *The Light on Halsey Street* is "What You Owe Me." Have you ever done something to someone . . . knew you owed them, but couldn't figure out how to repay the debt you owed? What did that feel like?
8. When Lisa discovers she has been betrayed by a friend, it seemed that was a bridge too far and she could not forgive such an act. How do you think you would respond after a hurtful betrayal?
9. At one point in the book, John told Lisa, "What happened to you wasn't right, but you need to pray about how you've decided to respond to this situation." So, now I ask you, what length will you go to get vengeance on someone who betrayed you? Can you let it go, or will it fester forever until it kills you?

10. Dana tried to capture beauty in her world with her camera, but kept running into the ugliness of life. It was not until she gave her life to the Lord that she was able to finally see good in herself and in the world. What about you . . . are you looking for beauty in all the wrong places? You'll never know just how much beauty is within you until you allow God to cleanse you from within.
11. Dana's pursuit of her mother's love was heartbreaking. I felt so bad for Dana after she thought she saw her mother, only to discover that she had died and things would never get better between them. What did you think of Dana and Vida's relationship? Did your heart break for Dana as mine did?

About the Author

Photo by David Pierce

Vanessa Miller is a bestselling author, with several books appearing on *ESSENCE* Magazine's Bestseller List. She has also been a Black Expressions Book Club alternate pick and #1 on the BCNN/BCBC Bestseller List. Most of Vanessa's published novels depict characters who are lost and in need of redemption. The books have received countless favorable reviews: "Heartwarming, drama-packed and tender in just the right places" (*Romantic Times* book review) and "Recommended for readers of redemption stories" (*Library Journal*).

Visit her online at vanessamiller.com
Twitter: @Vanessamiller01
Instagram: @authorvanessamiller
Facebook: @Vanessamillerauthor